TG F

TG REID

AGENCY 'O'

Glass Work Press

COPYRIGHT

AGENCY 'O'

Published Worldwide by Glass Work Press.
This edition published in 2024.

Editors: Gordon Robertson, Emmy Ellis
Cover design: designforwriters.com
Typesetting: Emmy Ellis

Glass Work Press

"In all chaos there is a cosmos, in all disorder a secret order."

Carl Jung

*"That was total f***ing chaos, lads."*

Ally McLeod, Scotland Football Manager, 1977-78

Content Note: This book contains swearing and Glaswegians

PROLOGUE

When Paul reached the end of the page, he stopped, stretched, and glanced over at the clock above the issue desk. Six thirty-three. The library was now all but deserted. He'd been typing for over four hours without coming up for air. A librarian at the desk smiled. Over the last three months, he'd become a regular fixture, tapping away furiously at one of the workstations, often from doors open to closing time. They all knew him by name, but between them they called him 'that writer'.

He scrolled back to the beginning to double-check the edits he'd made to the script on the previous pass. With a slow, deep intake of air, he dived in again.

SCRIPT EDIT 27 - DRAFT 3 - REVISION NOTES

AGENCY 'O'

A screenplay by

~~Paul Grant and Richard Gann~~

Tor Fleck

3rd Draft

FADE IN:

EXT. NEW YORK SKYLINE - NIGHT

We weave at speed, eagle-like, above and between illuminated skyscrapers until we reach, and circle, a huge steel-and-glass building. We close in on the vast, top-floor penthouse, and an UPRIGHT FIGURE seated behind a desk.

INT. PENTHOUSE - NIGHT

The penthouse is open-plan, futuristic, and minimalist, with awe-inspiring views over Manhattan.

The figure behind the desk is MARTIN JAMESON, middle-aged and immaculately dressed, his hair heavily oiled. A CEO. He stares straight ahead, devoid of emotion. The desk is stainless steel, impressively large, and completely bare.

From somewhere, a buzzer SOUNDS. Jameson ignores it. He places his palm on the surface of the desk.

A scanner flashes and runs across Jameson's print. Almost immediately, a screen emerges from the surface, followed by an illuminated virtual keyboard.

Jameson types quickly and lightly. Then he stops. Changes speed. Scrolls slowly through virtual pages with his finger, reading carefully, until ...

... the word **CLASSIFIED** appears in bold, red letters.

Jameson enters an encrypted password. The logo ***'Agency O'*** slides elegantly into the centre of the screen. Jameson narrows his brows. Sweat is visible on his forehead.

In slow motion, a droplet of sweat runs down Jameson's forehead. It splatters loudly - SPLASH! - on the smooth, pristine, gleaming surface of the desk.

Jameson flicks through more pages and stops at a signature.

Martin Jameson

Jameson's hand hovers over the keyboard

... he stares at the screen, and then

... HITS the delete key.

The word **TERMINATED** fills the screen.

Jameson closes down the file, and the screen drops silently back into the desk.

Jameson straightens himself up again. Slicks back his hair. Presses a previously-unseen intercom button.

JAMESON

You can send him in now, Sarah.

SARAH (O.S.)

Yes, sir.

A KNOCK at the door.

JAMESON

Come in!

A well-groomed executive - DUNCAN BALLATINE, late 30s - enters, his sharp suit as immaculate as his hair. He has a dark-tan suitcase in his right hand. He approaches the desk and stops in front of it. Jameson offers up a weak smile.

JAMESON (CONT'D)

Everything's done. I'm ready now. Are you?

Ballatine lifts his briefcase up onto the desk and unclips the clasps. The lid pops open, and he reaches inside with both hands, lifting out a bulging handkerchief. Carefully, he unwraps it to reveal ...

... a revolver.

Ballatine covers the handle of the gun with the handkerchief, picks it up, closes an eye, and points the barrel at Jameson.

JAMESON (CONT'D)

Careful.

Ballatine smiles. He hands the gun to Jameson, removes the handkerchief, folds it neatly, and slides it into the breast pocket of his suit, straightening the small exposed silken triangle perfectly.

JAMESON (CONT'D)
Goodbye, Duncan. And good luck.

BALLATINE
Goodbye, Mr Jameson. It was a pleasure working for you.

Ballatine steps away from the desk.

Jameson leans back, sticks the gun under his chin, and FIRES. His body jerks backwards, a wide spray of blood covering the window behind him.

A quick flash of alarm crosses Ballatine's face, replaced just as quickly by a serene calm.

SHOUTING from outside the room. Loud, urgent BANGING on the door. Ballatine glances over his shoulder. The alarm - pretend this time - returns.

BALLATINE (CONT'D)

Noooo!

The door flies open. A gaggle of COLLEAGUES crowd the doorway, aghast at the carnage facing them.

Ballatine doesn't move. A MALE COLLEAGUE rushes past him - almost knocks him out of the way - in an effort to save Jameson. But he's too late. Way too late.

Back in the doorway, SARAH MCCONNELL, Jameson's twenty-something secretary, clutches her throat.

SARAH

Oh my God ... oh my God ... oh my God ... oh my God ...

Ballatine doesn't hear any of this. His mind is racing, and his expression, previously frozen, is thawing. In fact ... is that the hint of a smile?

Paul paused and scrolled back to the front of the script. The title page stared back, the score through his and Richard's name screaming out at him.

Agency 'O'

A screenplay by

~~**Paul Grant and Richard Gann**~~

Tor Fleck

Draft 3

'Three months,' Paul mumbled. 'More like seven fucking lifetimes of living, rancorous shite.' He sneered at the screen. *I could end this nightmare right now.* His finger hovered over the Delete key. One … two … three … *What are you waiting for? Do it.* His heart raced. One … two … He tried to force his finger down onto the key, but his writer brain wouldn't allow it. *End it now, moron. End it!* His hand wavered, but then, defeated, he dropped it to his side, as it had so many times before. His shoulders slouched and his chest sagged. *Enough. I'm done. No more. Fuck the threats and the fear and the intimidation. This malevolent little bastard has pushed us both to the brink and beyond.* It was the end of the road, and it was time to take on whatever retaliation they could muster.

Moving the cursor, Paul quickly put a line through *Draft 3* and typed *FINAL DRAFT.* It felt good. It felt right. One way or another, with or without Richard's help, he was going to put a stop to it all. He was going to drop the bomb and blow their whole fucking world sky-high. He saved the update and turned to the next scene. But he was too wired, and his brain wouldn't play ball. His thoughts flashed backwards and forwards through the recent days and weeks, sprinting past all the threats and relentless intimidation they'd both endured, until finally his mind touched down at ground zero, when it all began, on that innocuous morning after the night before, when Richard, nursing a hangover from hell, laid out his big, fat, stupid idea.

1

Glasgow, 2nd July, 1:42 p.m.

Rap-a-tap-tap!

Paul slid himself further under the duvet. *Leave it. Richard can answer it.*

Rap-a-tap-tap!

Go away. Just–

RAP-A-TAP-TAP! RAP-A-TAP-TAP!

'Fu-u-u-ck!' Paul hauled himself reluctantly from the warmth of his pit. His head was pounding. Christ, how much did he have last night? The floor was a virtual assault course of discarded clothes, dirty plates, half-empty pizza boxes, sucked-clean beer bottles, and ream after ream of scrunched-up paper, the failed writer's signature dish. As he picked his way through it to the door, he wrapped a tattered floral dressing gown around his waist and winced. God, his head ...

'Good afternoon, Mr Grant, I hope I–'

A faded housecoat and teetering beehive, circa 1962, stood opposite him in the open doorway, its mouth agape, as though frozen by the chilled draught floating in from the stairs.

'Mrs McGilvray,' oozed Paul, with more than a touch of sarcasm. 'What can I do for you?'

Mrs McGilvray aimed a wavering finger at Paul's dressing gown and grimaced, her lips tighter than a puckered sphincter on a decaying corpse.

Paul glanced down. His dressing gown had fallen open, exposing his underpants and a not inconsiderable bulge. Was she asking to see more, or less? 'I do beg your pardon,' he said, covering himself up and double-tying the cord. 'Not before lunch, eh?' He grinned.

'It's a quarter to two.'

Ouch. Tough crowd.

'I'm sorry to have to speak to you again, Mr Grant.'

That makes two of us.

'But it's about the smell.'

'The smell?'

'I spoke to your flatmate–'

'Richard?'

'– last week. And the week before that.'

Paul let his face feign ignorance. For weeks now, Mrs McGilvray had been complaining about the reek emanating from their flat: a rank, vomit-inducing odour born of personal and household neglect, namely: overflowing bins, dirty washing, bacteria-loaded dishes, festering sink water, and a fridge slowly incubating the Black Death.

'I explained to him–'

'His name's Richard.'

'I explained to Richard–'

'Or Dick. I'd say he's definitely more of a Dick.'

'– that the smell is clearly coming from your flat, and unless you do something about it, I will be forced–'

A speck of spittle landed on Paul's cheek. He let it sit there, burrowing into his skin, too afraid to wipe it off.

'– to report it to Environmental Health. And the landlord. We're on good terms with Mrs Foyle, as you know, and I'm sure she won't put up with it either.'

Paul closed his eyes and slowly opened them again. He remembered Richard putting something in the gin last night. What was it? Blackcurrant? 'I'm terribly sorry, Mrs McGilvray.' He smiled. 'Richard didn't mention anything to me about a smell.'

Mrs McGilvray was having none of it. 'We have been very patient with both of you,' she lied. 'But the whole close, frankly, is now at breaking point.'

Paul bobbed his head up and down, as though suddenly remembering something important. 'It'll be the plumbing. We've had some problems lately. Mrs Foyle's promised to send her man round sometime this week.' Pure lies, all of it. He just needed to buy some time. Exactly how much was down to the wet-lipped harridan in front of him.

'Two days,' Mrs McGilvray barked and marched back across the landing to her flat, the dramatic slamming of her door reverberating down the stairs like a Rank Organisation gong.

In the kitchen, Paul filled the kettle and ransacked the cupboards for coffee. None. He slumped down at the table, his hangover roared in his skull. Six years …

Six years since he'd left university, and this was as low as he'd ever been. He remembered being ready to conquer the world, spurred on by his tutor's encouraging parting words: "Your stories are not bad, Grant. With diligence, dedication, and time, you might become a good writer, maybe even a great one." It was the 'not bad' that had lit the fire beneath him, setting him off in pursuit of the seemingly impossible dream of literary glory, a romanticised view of the struggling artist that he fostered with bohemian delight, and then, as rejection and failure wore him steadily down, with clawing, soul-crushing despair.

His flatmate, Richard, on the other hand, had no delusions of greatness. After all, he'd chosen acting, a choice he once articulately described as 'the lazy fucker's drug of choice'. Unlike Paul, he could never be mistaken for a slave to ambition. In fact, he'd often quote his own father when describing himself: "You know what you are, son? You're a lanky strip of useless shite." Miraculously, he'd scraped by with a third in Drama. Given the fact he managed only two auditions* after graduating, he may as well have gotten his diploma online.

*Audition 1. Manhandled out of the theatre by two over-enthusiastic security guards after being 'inappropriately offensive' with the female director.

Richard later claimed that the director's misuse of an oxymoron had pushed him over the edge.

*Audition 2. Got drunk and threw up on stage in the middle of his scene from *Waiting for Godot*. He tried to explain it was method, that Beckett would have approved, but the producers didn't listen. Nor did security.

Since then, Richard had avoided any and all contact with actors, the theatre, or anything even remotely resembling 'the arts'.

And yet, despite all that, and despite the catastrophic mess they were both making of their lives, Paul and Richard remained the best of friends. They had a bond that went back a long way, covering a lot of rocky ground and troubled times. When Richard lost his younger brother to cancer, it was Paul who'd stood firm while others fled the carnage Richard inflicted on himself and the world. And though he'd never told him, Richard was eternally indebted to his friend for saving his life. So now, losers together, they clung on to one another as they tumbled further and deeper into personal sinkholes they seemed incapable of avoiding.

'Morning.'

It was more of a yawn than a word. Richard flopped down next to Paul. He was wearing boxers of indeterminate colour and an undersized t-shirt with 'Fuck me I'm desperate' scribbled across the front. Classy.

'Afternoon.'

'What time is it?' Another yawn.

'Ten to two.'

Richard rubbed at his eyes. 'What was I drinking last night?'

'Scotland dry.'

'Great night, though. Where did we end up?'

Paul stared at his friend. 'For fuck's sake. You don't remember?'

'What?'

'When I hailed a taxi, you tried to shag the exhaust pipe.'

Richard grinned. 'Was I wearing protection?'

Paul was in no mood for humour. 'The taxi driver tried to thump you, then he drove off. We had to walk home from Cambuslang. We spent the last of the week's money. It's all gone. There's nothing left.'

'Oh well ... fuck it!' Richard flung his arms up dismissively. 'Is there any coffee?'

Paul, who'd managed not to lose his shit up to this point, now shat out an arse-load of anger. 'No! You finished it last night! You ate it! You fucking clown.'

'What?'

'You heard me. Handfuls of it. Horrific.' Paul shivered.

'That's why I was awake for hours!' guffawed Richard, instantly regretting it. 'Oh, fuck,' he said, rubbing his temples. He pressed his eyes shut. 'Who was that at the door?'

'Guess.'

Richard's eyes sprang back open.

'Oh, for fuck's sake, not Norma Bates again? What did she want this time?'

'Apparently, we are a health hazard.'

'Ha!' Richard found the very idea hilarious. 'Not me. I'm OCD with personal hygiene.' He pushed his hand deep into his boxers and scratched.

'Oh please, don't do that, begged Paul. 'Anyway, she threatened to contact the landlord.'

Richard pulled his hand back out and sniffed. 'Don't worry. I'll charm her with my wit and matinee-idol good looks.'

Paul shook his head. 'You know you're an arsehole, don't you?'

Richard curtseyed with all the finesse of a one-legged goose. 'I aim to please.'

Paul dug out the two least disgusting mugs he could find and filled them to the brim with hot, steaming, freshly bought coffee.

'Oh, you absolute star.' Richard grinned and heaped six teaspoons of sugar into his mug and stirring vigorously.

Paul grimaced. 'Why don't you have diabetes?'

'What can I say, I'm a human fly.'

Paul slapped a loaf and a packet of butter onto the table.

Richard helped himself to three slices. 'While you were at the shops,' he said, spreading an inch-thick slab of coronary heart disease across a doorstep of Paul's newly purchased Mother's Pride, 'I remembered the brilliant idea I had last night.'

'Fuck's sake.' Paul sighed. 'Not another of your *brilliant ideas*. Give me a bloody break. Please.'

'No, no, no,' Richard protested. 'This is *the* one.'

Paul sipped his coffee. Maybe if he didn't feed the fire this time, the flame would just putter out and ...

'It's so obvious!' Richard enthused.

... or not.

'I genuinely can't believe we haven't thought of it before. God ... we are so thick.'

Paul knew he was beaten. He was fighting not a losing battle, but a losing war. 'Okay,' he said grudgingly, 'spit it out. I know you're going to tell me anyway, no matter how much I protest, so we might as well get it over and done with.' With a theatrical flourish, he threw out an arm. 'The idea, please. If you will.'

Over the years there had been endless half-arsed business schemes and scams* to try and make them money. All, without exception, fluttered on the fringes of fraud and were doomed to fail even before they left Richard's head.

*Scam 1: Bendy Wendy, the world's first online sex doll rental scheme

*Scam 2: Blue Sky Thinking, an eBay shop using The Cloud to sell ... actual clouds

*Scam 3: Socks Appeal, based on the mistaken belief that there's a global demand for celebrities' used socks

Richard leaned forward, revelling in the unexpected attention. 'It's so obvious.'

'You've said that.'

'And the perfect solution to our cash-flow problem.' The words came spluttering out through a mouthful of buttery dough.

'But, I'm guessing, illegal.' It wasn't that Paul was a natural sceptic, but his default position with Richard tended to waver between disbelief and fuck right off.

'No, that's the beauty of it,' Richard argued. 'It's totally legit.'

'Yeah, right.' As in, fuck right off.

'No, listen,' said Richard. 'We write a drop-dead brilliant block-fucking-buster screenplay, and then we sell the rights for gazillions of dollars to some big-shot studio exec.' His head bobbed up and down with excitement.

Paul imagined taking a chainsaw to his friend's neck.

'That's it?' Paul asked. 'That's your 'stayed up all night' idea?'

'There's more.'

'Go on.' Paul could barely contain his excitement.

'We call the movie *Agency O*. Good title, eh?'

Paul raised a single eyebrow. *No*.

Richard persevered. 'So, here's the pitch. Young slacker guy, maybe an actor with low prospects.' Wink. 'Answers an ad for an assistant's post for some fat-cat billionaire and his fat-cat conglomerate. Doesn't think he'll have a fat cat in hell's chance of making the shortlist, but to his amazement he gets the call from the recruitment agency, called–'

'Let me guess,' said Paul. 'Agency O?'

'The very same. But the thing is, this agency, they're a bit ... eh … weird.'

'How'd you mean?'

'I dunno. I haven't worked that out yet. Maybe the guy has to go through some strange psychometric shit. Tests, and other mind-fucking bullshit, you know? Anyway, he fucks up his interview, like he always does, but … he lands the job. So far so good?'

Paul waved him on like the world's most depressed bus driver.

'Aha! You're getting into it. I can tell.'

'Finish the bloody story.'

Richard grinned. He had his audience hooked. 'So,' he continued, 'he goes to work for this rich dude, who seems to like him. Pretty soon, he gets promoted and makes his way up the oily pole, until he's living the high life: fast cars, drugs, chicks–'

'Where's this going?'

'Slow down, mister. We're getting there.'

A rolling of the eyes from Paul.

Richard lowered his voice to a conspiratorial mezzo-soprano. 'One day, a couple of years down the line, the big cheese calls him into his office and tells him something that blows his mind sky-fucking-high.'

'What?'

'You're definitely hooked.'

'I'm just trying to speed things along. What did he tell him? And don't do that voice. It's creepy.'

Richard reverted to his normal voice. 'Okay, so the head honcho tells the Young Turk that he's going to hand over the reins of the company to him – the whole shebang, lock stock.'

Paul leaned back. 'Oh, come on. Why would he do that when he's just his assistant? That doesn't make any sense.'

'Let's just say he trusts him to do the right thing.'

'And what's that?'

'Kill him.'

'What?'

'Or "assist" in his suicide.'

Paul shook his head. 'This is stupid.'

'That's the twist,' said Richard. 'Five years before, Agency O had hired this guy to be the PA of the previous CEO. He was made an offer he couldn't refuse, and before he knew it, he was living the life in big-buck town.'

'Can you stop with the clichés? Please? You're making me feel sick.'

'But then … boom! It's payback time, and our man is the CEO's replacement stooge.'

'I don't get it.'

'Don't you see? Agency O recruit receptive personalities like those bozos to do their bidding.'

'But why would this boss let himself be killed? You said he was a billionaire. He can do whatever he likes. Why would he give that up?'

Richard hadn't considered that. 'Okay,' he said. I'll need your help on that. You're the one with the smarty, scribbly brains. I'm just the thick actor. It's all about Agency O and what they're up to.'

'And what *are* they up to?'

'Agency O is a secret organisation whose primary goal is to initiate chaos around the world,' explained Richard. He took another slurp of coffee. 'Business, governments, infrastructure, media, whatever. Their aim is to plant seeds of disorder in every corner of society.'

'Why?'

'Why'd you think? To gain control and power over our lives.' Richard warmed to his theme. 'When chaos and uncertainty reigns, fear prevails. And when they've cranked this fear up to eleven, they intervene. Suddenly, they're benevolent champions of all things good. But their motives ... their motives are pitch-black and downright evil.'

Paul burst out laughing. 'Where do you get this shit from?'

Richard was unfazed. 'Billionaire suicides.'

'What?'

'I was reading about it the other day. They're all the rage, apparently.'

'Are they really?'

'There was a guy recently, some CEO of a multinational transport conglomerate ... threw himself in front of one of his own trains. Then the journalist investigating it got murdered. It's the stuff of conspiracy thrillers.' Richard downed the rest of his coffee and lowered his mug, smacking his lips in appreciation. 'Ahhh ...'

'Okay, so first of all,' reasoned Paul, 'you're expecting me to write a thriller. I don't write thrillers.

I hate thrillers. I would rather have colonic irrigation than write a thriller.'

'It's not a thriller, it's a screenplay of a thriller.'

Paul cut back in. 'Second … I have never written a screenplay. I wouldn't know where to start.'

Richard sighed.

'And third, if that journo got himself killed, do we really want to fuck around with that kind of fire?'

'Oh, come on, Paul.' Richard grunted. 'Stop building walls. You're a writer. Any writer worth his salt would jump at the creative challenge.'

Paul considered this. Was he worth his salt? What was salt worth? Why the fuck were they talking about salt? 'Okay,' he said, 'I'll humour you. For now. Let's pretend I'm interested.'

'Aha! I knew it!'

'I said "pretend". You know? Like an actor?' Paul stared at Richard as though he was a child. 'Do you have any idea how difficult it is to sell a screenplay?'

'Of course I do,' replied Richard. Plus, I know exactly how to sell it.'

'Oh fuck, we're still not done.' Paul drained the last of his coffee, wishing the grounds at the bottom were miniature cyanide capsules.

Richard was pumped. 'We make short films of key scenes and put them up on social media. We get hits – major hits – and before you know it, we have a cult following. And then we pitch it to the money monsters. You write it, and I act it. Dream team!' He thumped the table.

Paul put down his mug. 'I'm going for a shower.'

'Come on, Paul. We can do this.'

Paul was almost out the door.

Richard couldn't let him leave. Not yet. 'I tell you what!' He stopped Paul in his tracks. 'If you give this a go, I'll get a job!'

Paul stopped and turned round. Now Richard *was* taking the piss.

'I'll be the breadwinner,' said Richard, 'and you can be the stay-at-home scribe.'

There was something in Richard's voice that Paul couldn't quite dismiss. Something … genuine. 'This really means a lot to you, doesn't it?'

'I feel it in my kidneys. Come on, Paul. It's all I've got.'

Paul couldn't believe he was about to say what he was about to say. 'Okay. If I do this …'

'I love you!' Richard shrieked, leaping to his feet and running at Paul with open arms.

'I said *if* I do this …' Paul felt uncomfortable with another man's arms around him. Having to remove a human head from his armpit didn't exactly thrill him either. '… I'll need more.'

'Don't you worry about that,' said Richard. 'The wheels are spinning. I'll have nailed it by the time you've scrubbed your arse. And you never know,' he added with a smile of pure, undiluted hope, 'you might even enjoy it.'

Paul held his friend's gaze. 'If you renege on this – on any of this – the deal's off.'

Richard crossed his heart. 'I betroth thine trust to the gods, Obi Wan.' He grinned. 'And of course, you do realise that, as the breadwinner, I will have full conjugal rights.'

Paul had had enough of bad actors and bullshit for one day. His response to both was not only concise but elegant and universal.

'Fuck. Right. Off.'

In the days that followed, and to Paul's disbelief, Richard upheld his part of the deal: he landed himself a job. It may only have been three days a week at the local bookshop, but to say Paul was gobsmacked was an understatement; more so when Richard survived the first day without getting himself sacked.

Richard's out-of-character commitment to their pact meant Paul felt obliged to respond in kind. And so, with grudging reluctance, he borrowed a couple of books on scriptwriting from the local library and wrote. The first few days were slow-going and had him considering how best – and how gently – to let Richard down. But as he persevered, he seemed to find a new kind of rhythm to his writing. Soon words and ideas poured out of him, and to his amazement, he took to thriller writing like an old seasoned hack, revelling in his newfound voice. He would often write late into the night, hammering out page after page after page. When he'd completed the first few scenes, he shared them with Richard, who punched the air and leapt around the flat with childish glee, screaming at the top of his lungs, 'You got it, baby! You got it, baby!'

Soon they were living and breathing their project; bouncing ideas back and forth, carving, polishing, and fine-tuning scenes until they were tight as a drum. By the end of the month they had the bones of a completed screenplay. Paul wasn't done with it yet, but it was a workable draft. The next stage was the videos, and once again, Richard had a plan, and Paul's heart sank further into the pit of his stomach.

About a week later, Richard re-surfaced with rough edits of three short videos he had coerced his old drama school mate James into helping him put together. To Paul's surprise, the results were surprisingly good and he was forced to admit that Richard and James had worked some kind of miracle on the production. The location, the lighting, and above all, the acting, were highly professional, especially Richard as a deranged executive. Paul was also rather taken aback by how much the video looked like a glossy, eighties-style Hollywood thriller. Richard, uncharacteristically, let James take the credit for that.

"He's bloody good, isn't he. Totally wasted as a wedding photographer." Richard said.

"And he didn't want paying?"

"He owed me."

"He owed *you*?" Paul rolled his eyes. "Has there been some sort of tear in the space-time continuum? And where did you find that swanky office for the location?" he asked suspiciously.

"Let's just say we escaped a prison term by a ball hair." Richard smiled.

After a few quick re-edits and adjustments, Richard uploaded the finished clips to social media, along with completed script extracts. Within hours, they'd racked up thousands of views and comments. The *Agency O* project was going viral.

2

Zurich, 12th July, 7:30 a.m.

Hans Gleiber, chief executive of the Swiss banking conglomerate *Strasse*, steps out of his eighteen-bedroom mansion in the super-rich Zurich suburb of Meilen. On the doorstep, his beautiful, kimono-wrapped wife, Julienne, twenty years his junior, leans over, kisses his balding pate, and straightens his silk tie. His car, a top-of-the-range, gleaming silver Mercedes, sits in the driveway, its engine purring. Hans' driver, the portly Klaus, who usually waits obediently by the open rear passenger-side door, is today inside, tapping impatiently on the steering wheel. Julienne waves her husband off and checks her watch, shivering involuntarily. Hans fumbles with the door handle – does it go up or down? – until it swings open and he clambers over the pristine, squelchy upholstery.

'In a hurry, are we?'

Klaus ignores his boss' sarcastic comment and sets off down the long drive, past the immaculately manicured gardens and overly ornate fountain bedecked with Roman nymphs and pissing cherubs.

Hans leans forward. 'I said, in a hurry, are–?' A loud burst of Beethoven's piano 'Sonata No. 32' fills the back of the car.

'No music, please, Klaus,' says Hans, irritated. 'Turn it off.' He clicks open his briefcase and lifts out a handful of papers. The music increases in volume. Hans drops his papers and leans forward again. 'Klaus!' He taps the back of Klaus' seat. 'Please. I have a lot of work to do and I need–'

A glass screen slowly rises, separating the two men.

Hans bangs on the window. 'Hey, Klaus! What are you doing?'

The music grows louder, and the doors click shut. Hans thumps harder on the glass, but Klaus only has eyes for the road, accelerating onto the approaching autobahn. Hans glances nervously out the window. The car is racing way above the speed limit, lane-jumping and weaving between vehicles. They drive past the exit sign to the city centre.

A panicky Hans hammers his fist against the reinforced pane. 'Where are we going, Klaus?' he yells.

The car speeds on towards the mountains in the distance. Hans fumbles for his phone and stabs at it. *Shit!* There's no signal. Furious and frustrated, he flings it across the back seat.

PSSSSSSS. The pungent odour of lavender seeps into the car through the air-conditioning duct. It's now very warm in the back seat, and Hans is sweating. He takes his jacket off and yanks at his tie. He thumps the glass with the heel of his hand.

'Klaus, please! What are you doing? I can give you money, if that's what this is?' He's growing drowsy, his thought processes failing. He sits back. The lavender smell sticks to the back of his throat, and he coughs. It's as though the oxygen is being sucked from his lungs. It's a struggle to reach for the door handle, an invisible force pushing him further into his seat. His eyes roll back into their sockets, and he quickly loses consciousness.

Hans wakes to the sensation of being hauled out of the car by his shoulders. He's flat on his back, and all he can see is blue sky. A deep paralysis prevents all but his head from moving. His gaze tilts sideways. There's a pair of shoes in his eyeline: shiny black brogues. They drift out of view, and now someone is on top of him. He forces his head around. *Is that Klaus? I don't pay him enough to afford designer brogues.* Whoever it is has a ski mask on and is tying a rubber cord around Hans' arm, tightening it until the veins pop.

'No …' Hans tries to scream, but his throat and tongue are numb.

Hans' abductor has a syringe, filled with a dark-amber liquid. Hans makes a final attempt to kick himself free, but he can't. Nothing can stop the liquid being slowly injected into his arm. As it enters his bloodstream, Hans' body soars with a euphoric rush. But then the rush becomes a barrage of exploding missiles inside his crumbling brain. Before his body can go into shock, Hans is dragged back to the car and bundled, limb by limb, into the driver's seat.

Hans is frothing at the mouth now, and his muscles spasm. He's close to death, the heroin keeping him alive just long enough to appreciate his final ride to the great tax haven in the sky. His abductor leans over and releases the handbrake. The door is slammed shut. The car trickles forward and rolls off the road between a narrow gap in the barrier, snapping the wing mirror in the process. With a dull *CLUNK*, it disappears.

Hans' abductor runs to the cliff edge and watches the car summersault and batter against the rocky mountainside, shedding its skin and disintegrating as it falls. When it finally comes to rest, upside down and barely recognisable as the half-million-dollar car it was a couple of minutes before, there's a split-second of quiet, then the twisted remains explode in a colossal fireball, a mushroom cloud of smoke soaring skywards.

A thin hand lifts Hans' jacket from the side of the road and rummages through the pockets. The large wad of Swiss francs and the impressive collection of gold and platinum credit cards are ignored, the flicking fingers stopping at a small photograph of a child – Melissa, Hans' two year-old albino daughter – which is quickly removed and tucked into a pocket. The thin hands roll the jacket into a tight ball and toss it over the edge, where it drops to join the burning, broken body of its owner. The shiny brogues then leave the road, climb a splintered fence, and take the walkers' path back down the mountain to civilization.

3

Richard dropped down onto the sofa next to Paul. 'I now understand why the Nazis burned books.' He groaned, red-faced from the walk home from work.

'So, a good day then?'

Richard kicked off his shoes. 'This guy comes in. Geeky. Specs. Deep-fat-fryer hair. Asks me if we had Rowling's latest. He asks *me.*'

'Oh dear. Bad move. What did you say?'

'I suggested, politely, in a calm and measured manner, that reading may not be for him and that he should consider a hobby more fit for a turd.'

'I can't believe they haven't sacked you yet.'

'They recognise my value and contribution to their growth strategy.'

'Nothing to do with you being the only slave in the village, then? What is it, three quid an hour?'

'Three-fifty.' Richard pulled his socks off and rubbed between his toes, releasing a long, contented sigh.

Paul's nose wrinkled at the smell. 'Well, I'm glad that's a relief for you.'

'Indeed.'

'No, seriously, it's good to have revolting Richard back. I thought we'd lost you there for a bit.'

Richard looked at his friend for the first time since arriving home. 'So … did you have a creative day?'

'Pretty good. I tweaked Harvey's interview scene a little. You want to see it?'

Richard slid himself reluctantly off the sofa. 'Let me have a shower first. I smell like a book jacket. And I'm in a Lynx Africa mood tonight.' He stopped at the door. 'That reminds me, there's been another super-rich suicide. According to Dave at work anyway.'

'Dave the conspiracy geek?'

'The very same.'

'What happened?'

'Turns out some Swiss banker wanker was harbouring a secret smack addiction and embedded himself in the side of one of their giant Toblerone bars.'

'What?' Paul swivelled his neck round.

'Matterhorn, or whatever,' said Richard. 'His wife was banging his PA when it happened.' He grinned. 'You've got to shoehorn in that murky plotline. It's got everything: sex, drugs, money, and a bloody great explosion at the end. Ooh, and we should buy some Alpen.' Richard's brain flip-flopped like a hyperactive three-year-old feasting on a bucket of M&M's. 'I haven't had a bowl of that since I chucked up all over–' A ringing in his pocket stopped him mid-reminisce. He pulled out his mobile and flew a couple of fingers over the buttons. 'Fucking hell! Fucking hell! Fucking hell!' With each word, he seemed to leap higher and higher.

'What?'

'Ya fuckin dancer!' Richard roared at the ceiling. He grabbed Paul by the shoulders and ruffled his hair.

Paul pushed him away. 'Get off me! What is it?'

Richard shoved his mobile in Paul's face. 'Read that.'

Paul squinted, trying to focus. 'Read what?'

'The email. The one from Alice Lowe.'

'Who's Alice Lowe?'

'Just read the bloody thing! Oh, never mind, I'll do it.' Richard cleared his throat dramatically. '"Dear Mr Fleck,"' he began.

'Who?'

'Shush.' Richard cleared his throat again and continued. '"Dear Mr Fleck. My name is Alice Lowe, and I'm a senior talent scout for Omni Pictures International. We are currently seeking scripts for future productions and are very interested in your work."' He turned to Paul. 'Hear that? She's very fucking interested.'

'She never said "fucking".'

'It's what she meant. Can I continue?'

'Do you have to?'

Richard ignored him. '"I was very impressed by your short videos and accompanying script extracts and would very much like to meet with you to talk in more depth about your project. If you'd like to meet, please email to arrange a day and time that suits. Any evening this week or next would be most convenient, as next month I'm working out of our head office in Los Angeles and so will be unavailable, blah, blah, blah. Warmest regards, Alice Lowe, Senior Acquisitions Director, Omni Pictures International."'

Richard did a little dance on the spot. He looked like he either needed the toilet or was in the process of doing it. 'Los Angeles!' he shouted. 'I told you we had a winner.'

Paul took the phone from him and read through the email again. 'I think it's a scam.'

'What?' Richard stopped dancing and threw Paul an ugly glare.

'Working out of Los Angeles? Meet as soon as possible? Really?'

'Jesus Christ, Paul. Let's just savour the moment for a minute or two, please.'

Paul handed Richard his phone back. 'Our names and personal details are all online. We're just bait for con artists.'

'But we're Tor Fleck.'

'Who the fuck is Tor Fleck?'

Richard fumbled for the right words. 'He's … he's a … I just thought we should invent a fictional author.'

'A fictional author.'

'You know, some Scandinavian writer, with a dark past. Create a bit of intrigue. Something a bit more interesting than just us.'

'And when did you decide this?'

'I dunno. It just came to me. It was like a vision.'

Paul was puzzled. 'Wait. So, you've taken our names off the videos?'

Richard nodded. 'Tor Fleck is now the creative genius behind *Agency O.*'

'But he doesn't exist!'

'Exactly! But nobody knows that, except us. So he can be whoever we want him to be, even a woman!' Wink. 'And anyway, those Scandinavian depresso books and TV shows are all the rage.'

Paul was confused. 'So who, or what, are *we* in all of this?'

Richard shrugged. 'We're his UK representatives, or his old student buddies. I don't know. We'll come up with something. Leave it to me.'

'Now I'm even more worried.'

'Hey, I'm an actor.' Richard attempted a reassuring smile, but to Paul it just made him look like a condescending prick. 'I make up people all the time. Well, once upon a time.'

Paul still wasn't convinced. 'I don't know. What if this con artist actually *is* a movie exec? We'd be lying to her.'

'It's a harmless sting.'

'It's a fucking fraud! We're impersonating someone else.'

'Lighten up, for God's sake.'

Paul's sanctimonious tone was clearly getting Richard's goat.

'You can't impersonate a fictional character.'

Paul shook his head. 'You said this was going to be legit.'

Richard threw his hands up. 'All drama is legit! Let's just call this a dramatic conceit, an artistic pseudonym. Writers use them all the time. The thing is …' Big grin. '… she clearly loves our script, or at least what's she's read of it, so if she finds out about Tor, I reckon she'll love it – and us – even more.' He paused, studying Paul's face for a second. 'And if she's a con artist,' he added, 'then we've tricked a trickster. Game on, I say.'

Paul let out another long sigh. 'I can't believe you've roped me into this.'

Richard grinned. 'You recognise a sure thing. Let's just go and meet her, okay? If we think she's dodgy, we bail. And if any shit comes our way, we let Tor take the hit.'

'Before we decide anything,' Paul interjected, 'can we check this Omni Pictures mob and find out who they are, or even if they exist at all?'

'Fair enough,' agreed Richard. 'Christ, I hope they don't do that with Tor.'

It only took a couple of seconds to find the website: Omni Pictures International dot com. Despite the name, they were small and independent, the films cited on the site mostly European Arthouse. But one or two were English-language productions. Paul recognised one of them.

'I know this film,' he said. 'It was pretty good. Picked up a few awards.'

'See? Mr bloody sceptical.'

'Yeah, but …' Paul had already found another potential hole. '… how do we know this woman has anything to do with this company? She could have plucked the name out of thin air.'

'Jesus!' roared Richard, finally losing his patience. 'Stop being so fucking old!'

He stabbed angrily at the Contacts tab and scrolled down the list of employees. Alice Lowe's name appeared halfway down. *Click*. The link took him to her company profile page. There was no photo, but a short bio summarised her stratospheric career to date: a media degree from LSE, followed by a stint as a publishing assistant. Then a move to film production at Omni Pictures International, where, in the course of five short years, she had risen to the rank of Senior Director of Acquisitions.

'That's quite impressive,' conceded Paul.

'I feel so turned on right now,' Richard quipped.

Paul shook his head. He'd run out of arguments. 'Okay, you win. We'll go. But I'm still not happy about the name thing.'

'Fuck it. It's all a game.' Richard lifted his hand to high-five his friend.

Paul scratched his arse instead.

4

Paul left the library just before eight. He'd been there since two-thirty that afternoon, hunting down stories on executive suicides and mysterious deaths in the city, his time spent disappearing down one search engine wormhole after another. One story in particular grabbed his attention. It concerned a Marcus van Wooter, the chair of a multinational mobile phone company who'd thrown himself into a snow blower whist attending the World Economic Forum in Davos the previous January. The company he'd headed up had been doing exceptionally well, and there were no signs of any mental health issues. In fact, van Wooter was considered to be the sole reason the company was thriving, and he was well loved by all.

His wife, Emily van Wooter, vehemently disputed the coroner's verdict, at least initially, claiming her husband had been pushed into the snow blower and that his death was an assassination. Later, to the surprise of everyone, she suddenly changed her tune, supporting the coroner and insisting her husband was a secret drunk and manic depressive. All very strange.

And then – to add a final, macabre twist to an already sorry tale – a few weeks after whatever was left of her husband was cremated, a cleaner found Mrs van Wooter's dead body floating facedown in their rooftop swimming pool. This time, the same coroner recorded an open verdict, and the case remained unresolved.

A journalist who'd taken it upon himself to investigate the case – Pedro Silvestre (aka 'Oregon Pete' for some unspecified reason) – was later found dead, the victim of a botched home invasion; botched, presumably, because the unknown assailants were forced to flee empty-handed, scared off by a neighbour's garage alarm. And yet the perpetrators had still found time to stab Oregon Pete multiple times and mutilate his body almost beyond recognition. Again, all very strange.

The initial police investigation assumed it was the work of deranged drug addicts, but a number of details didn't quite add up. Accusatory fingers were soon pointing at van Wooter's business partners, with talk of Silvestre's murder being a contract killing. Silvestre's newspaper was also implicated in burying evidence the journalist had unearthed, with accusations being bandied around of huge hush-money payments. All very, very murky indeed, and excellent fodder for script rewrites and improvements.

Paul continued to search around the story but couldn't find any actual hard evidence of the dirt Silvestre had dug up on van Wooter or his business. It was clearly there but hidden too far down the rabbit hole for Paul to reach.

Out on the street, the temperature had dropped. Paul shivered and buttoned up his coat. Time to get home. Get warm. As he walked, he noticed someone keeping pace with him opposite, half hidden by the failing light, a flat cap pulled low over the brow. A man, age indeterminate. Curious, Paul slowed down. The man changed his pace to match Paul's. Paul stopped abruptly. Bent down. Pretended to tie his shoelace. The man hovered nonchalantly by a bakery window.

What the hell?

Paul stood up and changed direction, heading off at speed. The man turned and followed. At a crossing, Paul ignored the red light and dashed across, a car horn blasted and the driver swerved to avoid him. He glanced back. Nothing. He'd lost him. When he reached the underground station, out of breath and shaken, he stopped and checked behind him again. There was just a thinned-out mob of late commuters and early drinkers. Not a flat cap in sight.

You bloody, paranoid idiot, he thought. *Who'd want to follow you?* He bought himself an evening paper and headed down the escalator to the platform.

Squeezing into a packed carriage, Paul found a seat by the door. As the train shunted forward, he glanced through the bodies and bags and spotted a cap-wearing figure at the far end of the carriage. His head was hung low, his hand on the straphanger. The train lurched sideways, and the passengers shifted en masse, blocking Paul's view. When he was able to look again, the man had gone, the straphanger taken up by a tall woman with an afro. Paul's brain raced. Had the man followed him onto the train? Who would do that? And why?

The next station prompted an exodus from Paul's carriage. Although it wasn't his stop, he followed the passengers out onto the platform, scanning the sea of faces. No flat caps. He leapt back onto the train and the doors closed behind him.

Didn't Pacino do the same thing in Carlito's Way? *Richard would know. I'll ask him, if I ever get home alive.*

Paul sat back down, sweat gathering between his shoulder-blades and trickling down his spine. His eyes raced up and down the carriage in both directions.

Christ, how suspicious do I look?

But there was nothing to see. No flat cap. No menacing gaze. No hand stuffed in a pistol-shaped pocket. He sighed in relief and unfolded the newspaper he'd bought. The headline, in bold, prophetic, capital letters, declared *CHAOS IN THE CITY!* Paul couldn't read it. His brain was still reeling. He got up and stood by the door, willing the train to reach his stop. A group of young drunks were visible through the window between carriages, prancing around, laughing loudly and swearing. One of them tried to pole dance on a handrail and fell into the aisle, causing uproar and drawing Paul's attention to the figure the drunk had bumped against; a figure with his back to Paul; a figure wearing a distinctive flat cap.

'Fuck!'

An elderly woman sitting opposite the door glanced over at him and frowned. Paul ignored her.

'C'mon, c'mon, c'mon,' he muttered and the train finally pulled into his station.

The doors opened, and he leapt out, running towards the exit, pushing commuters out of the way. Once outside the station, he legged it across the main road and took a shortcut through a couple of side streets to his flat, everyone he passed a possible flat cap-wearing assassin. He reached his tenement at last and bounded up the stairs, his underarms sodden. His whole body shook, and he struggled to fit the key in the lock. Get *in*!

Footsteps. Footsteps on the stairs behind him. *Oh, fuck!* Paul dropped his keys. 'Shit!'

The footsteps sped up. *CLUMP! CLUMP! CLUMP! CLUMP!* Paul scooped the keys up and stabbed the key at the lock *Yes!* It clicked, and the door swung open. Paul jumped inside and slammed it shut behind him. A split-second later –

Ding-dong!

Paul's heart all but leapt into his throat. He held his breath.

Ding-dong! Ding-dong! Ding-dong!

Slowly, he leaned into the door and peered through the spyhole.

The landing was empty. Not a soul. He counted to twenty and gently opened the door.

'Boo!' Richard yelled, springing up from the floor.

Paul instinctively flung out a fist, narrowly missing Richard's grinning face.

'Jesus, Paul!' Richard jumped back in fright.

'What the fuck are you doing?' Paul shouted, his nerves shredded.

'What the fuck are *you* doing?' replied Richard. 'You could have had my head off, you fucking maniac!'

Mrs McGilvray appeared on the landing, a liver-spotted hand gripping the lapels of her padded housecoat.

'Would you two please mind your language? I can hear your obscenities from the kitchen.'

'So sorry, Margaret ...' said Richard, bowing his head in fake reverence.

Mrs McGilvray glared at him, not quite sure whether to believe him or not, then returned to her flat, slamming the door behind her with a ferocity unheard of in a five-foot-one octogenarian.

'... you crack-faced old trout.' Richard turned to Paul. 'Did you see what she was –?'

But Paul was nowhere to be seen. Richard eventually found him, in the dark, at the kitchen window, feverishly checking out the street below.

'What the hell's going on?'

'Someone's following me.'

'Who?'

Paul spun round. 'I have no fucking idea. When you arrived, was there anybody suspicious hanging around?'

Richard raised his eyebrows. 'You mean apart from the fist-waving lunatic at our front door?'

Paul shot him a glance. This wasn't the time for jokes.

Richard lowered his eyebrows and changed tack. 'What did he look like?'

Paul poured himself a glass of water and gulped it down. 'I don't know. He was wearing one of those Peaky Blinders-style flat caps, pulled down over his face.'

'And you didn't just imagine it?'

'No, I didn't fucking imagine it. Jesus!'

'Okay, okay,' conceded Richard. 'Calm down.'

'He followed me all the way from the library. He got on the same Tube. I think he followed me here, too.'

'Could it be, I don't know, somebody who lives round here? You know, a coincidence?'

'I slowed down, I stopped, I practically ran away from him. But he was still behind me, all the way to our street.'

Richard grinned and shrugged. 'Glasgow. The friendliest city in the world.'

'It freaked me out.'

'Acht, I wouldn't worry about it,' Richard reassured him. 'It was probably just one of the fucked-up mates I owe money to. Either that,' he laughed, 'or you've been helping yourself to my Lynx Africa!' He nudged Paul in the ribs.

'You're probably right,' said Paul and downed a second glass of water. But something in his gut, something he couldn't yet fathom, told him Richard was deadly wrong.

5

Richard arranged to meet the Omni executive on the other side of the city, in a wine bar neither he nor Paul had ever been to before. Less chance of bumping into any of his '*savant*' friends and blowing their cover, he told Paul with a wink. But the incident a few days before had rattled Paul's cage, and he protested about going somewhere unfamiliar, beyond their comfort zone, but, as usual, Richard got his way.

They arrived ten minutes late, the result of Richard's flawed map-reading skills and a spilled coffee, their cheap suits surprisingly in keeping with the pseudo antique furniture and décor, clearly shipped in – at little cost – from the Far East.

'Perfect,' whispered Richard, scanning the tables.

Most were taken up by stern-faced middle-aged couples, busy ignoring each other and grateful for the chance to do so away from home.

'There,' said Paul, spotting a young woman at a table on her own, glancing at her watch. He set off across the room.

'Slowly,' Richard cautioned, grabbing Paul's arm and cleverly overtaking him. 'Ms Lowe?' he smiled as they approached her table.

Alice stood to greet them. She was well-dressed, with an elegant beauty that belied her age. Paul had her down as late-twenties, if that. Long auburn hair curled over the lapels of her tight-fitting two-piece suit, and her Gucci watch was a far cry from the Apple Watch Paul had fantasised over since it first came out.

Alice Lowe certainly looked the part, and Paul fancied her immediately. It was clear from Richard's smarmy grin that he did, too.

'Yes,' she said, shaking both their hands in turn. 'Good evening, gentlemen.'

'Sorry we're late,' said Paul. He sat opposite and dragged his chair in closer to the table.

Richard sat beside him and dragged his own chair in even closer.

'We've just come out of a long, tiresome meeting,' said Richard, raising his eyebrows. 'You know what it's like.'

Paul shot him a frown. *Jesus.*

'That's okay,' said Alice. 'I've just arrived myself. So …' She smiled, and Paul swore he heard a 'Ping!' bounce off her perfect white teeth, '… which one of you is Tor Fleck?'

'Oh, er … neither of us,' Richard replied and coughed awkwardly. 'We're his representatives, his agents in the UK. He doesn't do abroad. Never leaves Norway. He hates flying. And water.'

'This is Richard Gann,' Paul interrupted, before Richard could say too much. '... and I'm Paul Grant.'

'Pleasure to meet you both at last.' Alice's smile seemed genuine, and infectious. She turned to Richard. 'So you're also the actor, in the movie shorts?'

'Yes. I studied at RADA, in Glasgow,' Richard lied.

'I have to say the videos are very impressive. You're a good actor, Mr Gann.'

'Why thank you. I'll take that.' Richard's grin was so wide you could have slid a banana in sideways.

'Oh, Christ,' Paul muttered.

'Perhaps a drink before we start?' Alice did a little drumroll on the table with her fingertips. 'What would you like?'

'Oh no,' said Richard, the banana grin now fixed, 'let me get them. What would *you* like?'

Alice thought for a moment. 'Oh, what the hell, it's Thursday. Could I have a small white wine spritzer, please?'

'And I'll have a tonic water and lime,' said Richard. 'And whatever you're having, Paul.' He nodded towards the bar.

Paul threw his so-called friend a sneer and sloped off for the drinks. From the bar, he watched Richard prattle on and prayed to God he wasn't trying to chat Alice up. An experience like that would scar the poor woman for life. Not to mention scupper their chances of selling her the script.

As Paul returned with the tray of drinks, Richard broke off from his conversation and leaned back.

'I've just been telling – may I call you Alice?'

Smarmy git.

'Of course.' Alice smiled.

'I've been telling Alice about how we came to acquire Tor's manuscript.'

Paul's stomach flipped like a fortune-telling fish. 'Uh-huh …'

'And how you were best friends at University.'

'That's right,' Paul recovered. 'We studied creative writing together.'

'So, he *used* to like travelling?' Alice asked.

Paul nodded. 'Yeah. Back before–'

'– the accident,' Richard added, quickly stepping into the breach. 'He was on his way to Espoo in Finland in a chartered plane when it went down in the Baltic Sea. Apparently, he was out there for days – pelvis broken, collarbone shattered – stranded on an iceberg. The rescue services said it was a miracle he survived.'

'Oh wow. I can see why that might leave a scar.' Alice winced at the thought.

'Indeed. Physical scars, and …' Richard's voice dropped half an octave to emphasise the gravitas of Tor's condition. '… deep, deep, psychological scars.'

'Anyway …' Paul jumped back in. 'Tor and I shared a flat.'

'So was he fluent in English, then?' Alice asked.

'Well, he loved our theatre and writers, didn't he?'

'Don't we all.' Alice sipped at her drink with the dreamy seductiveness of a wartime spy.

Paul continued. 'Some of my friends found him a little eccentric, but that's why I liked him.'

'How so?'

Shit. Paul felt himself teeter on the edge of a sinkhole. 'He was … er … ten years older than the rest of us, so … he had a life going on beneath the surface. More experience. You know?' Paul was unaware his foot was tapping against the table leg until Richard kicked him and he stopped. 'He liked to write about the darker side of the human mind. I think it freaked some people out. His favourite book was *The Strange Case of Dr Jekyll and Mr Hyde*.'

'A man of good taste.' Alice nodded in approval. 'So, what happened next?'

'Next, he went back to Sweden. Got a job with the government. Some hush-hush project I was never made privy to.' Paul was beginning to enjoy this game.

'You said Norway.'

'I said what?'

'Earlier. I think it was Richard who said Tor never leaves Norway.'

'Bloody Scandinavian countries,' scoffed Richard. 'They all look the same. If they're not covered in snow they're covered in tourists.'

The remark seemed to appease Alice.

'And you don't know what he did for the Norwegian government?'

Christ, she's persistent, thought Paul. He shrugged. 'I didn't see him much after uni, to be honest.'

'But you stayed in touch, didn't you?' Richard prompted clumsily. 'Didn't you visit him a couple of times in his ... what was it, a log cabin?'

'Log cabin?' Paul had to mentally think if they had log cabins in Norway. 'I'm not sure it was a log cabin, though he did live out in the country, near ... eh ... some trees.'

Alice laughed. She clearly thought Paul was kidding. He ploughed on regardless.

'We never talked about his job. I don't think he was allowed to. He thought he was being followed.'

'By whom?'

'Mercenaries.'

'He said that?' Even Richard was buying into Paul's shite.

Paul nodded. 'Oh, yes. Not out loud. On account of the bugs. But he'd whisper it. He'd say ...' And here Paul leaned over the table and slowly licked his lips, ratcheting up the tension.

As one, Richard and Alice leaned over, too, eager to hear just exactly what the fictional Tor Fleck had whispered to Paul out there in his ice-cold Norwegian wood.

'*... fucking Congolese.*'

Alice and Richard stared back, stunned. It was Alice who broke the awkward silence.

'Isn't that racist?'

Paul sat back and scratched his neck. 'I'm guessing his reaction would have been the same if he'd thought Scotsmen were targeting him. Or the English.'

'Especially the English.' Richard downed his tonic water and lime in one.

Paul was far more relaxed now. *Let's see Richard act better than that.* 'But we talked quite happily – and talked a lot – about his writing,' he added. 'After all, it was our mutual passion.'

'That's clear from the script,' said Alice, back in smiling mode, all thoughts of racism sent back where they came from.

Paul acknowledged the compliment with an almost imperceptible nod. 'You have to understand, he was a very complex guy. After all,' he explained, 'the Nordics are, historically, a deep and conflicted bunch, full of mystery and intrigue, and very difficult to pin down, psychologically speaking.' Paul took a large gulp of beer to refuel the yarn-spinning machine. 'He definitely rubbed people up the wrong way. He was blunt and said it like it was, and some folks gave him a wide berth because of it. But he was always there for me, even though he remained, as I said, a bit of an enigma.'

'Can you elaborate?' Alice had pulled a notepad from somewhere and was scribbling frantically.

Paul took a breath. 'There were hints that things weren't good with his family. There was also a woman he spoke of his great love. I never met her, and we only spoke about her when he chose to bring the subject up. She'd clearly caused him great pain.' Another long gulp of beer. *Think, think.* 'But then one day I got the news that–' He paused. 'He had died.'

'I know,' replied Alice sadly. 'Richard just told me.'

Paul shook his head, his eyes lowered in faux respect. 'Tragic,' he said, desperately racking his brains trying to recall the plotlines he and Richard had previously agreed on. 'Suicide, apparently,' he added hesitantly.

Alice looked up from her writing. 'Richard, didn't you say he'd been murdered?'

'I did,' said Richard, paddling like mad beneath the surface. 'I certainly did. And I'll tell you why.' He glanced at the bar and grimaced. 'His body was recovered on the Finnish-Russian border.'

'Of all places.' Paul was enjoying his friend's discomfort.

Richard returned the sneer thrown at him earlier. 'Authorities said his death had been made to *look* like suicide,' he clarified to Alice. 'Hence Paul saying *apparently*. Isn't that right, Paul?'

'Yep.' *Well played.*

Richard continued. 'The police investigation discovered that Tor had been involved in classified cross-border activities for a long time. This time, however, was the wrong time.'

'That is so mysterious.' Alice leaned forward. 'And do they know why he was there?'

Richard shook his head. 'It remains an unsolved crime to this very day. It's all very sad.'

'Wow,' said Alice. 'That's quite a story. But what about the script?'

Paul stepped up to the fiction plate once more. 'Well, about three months after I heard he'd died, I received a parcel, postmarked Norway.'

'Not Sweden?' Richard's eyes bored straight through his coconspirator.

Paul ignored him and ploughed on. 'Of course, I knew it was from him. And I have to tell you, it scared the bejesus out of me.' He took another sip of beer, replacing the glass carefully on top of the coaster. *Crumpsall Brewery.* He looked up at Alice, his eyes serious and unblinking. 'Inside was the script for *Agency O*, along with a letter from his solicitor saying Tor had left the script to me in his will.'

Alice gulped and fought back a shiver. 'And do you still have the letter?'

'Of course he does,' Richard interrupted. 'Not with him right now, obviously, but we can provide it, if necessary.'

Alice exhaled. 'Okay, good. We may need to see that at some point, just to establish your intellectual rights to the work.'

'That's not a problem,' Richard assured her, shooting Paul a fierce look.

'And thank you for letting me read Tor's original script,' said Alice, taking a sip of wine.

'Wait, you've read it? How?' Paul was puzzled. The script was back at home. Wasn't it?

'I sent it over last week,' explained Richard breezily. 'I thought it might speed things up.'

'It does need quite a bit of work. But you know that, right?'

'It was his first draft,' Paul offered lamely.

'But it has potential,' Alice continued. 'In fact, I would say it has great potential. The script has all the ingredients for a brilliant movie. It races off the page at breakneck speed. That's absolutely critical for any decent action thriller. And considering what's going on right now, the themes Tor explores are super-contemporary and bang on the money. Your late friend's knowledge and insight into this secret organisation–'

'Agency O,' Richard interrupted.

'– and their terrifying grip on the levers of power is compelling, utterly convincing, and an absolute winner as far as I'm concerned. I am very, very impressed.'

'He did just make it all up, though,' Paul reminded Alice. 'He had a very vivid imagination.'

'But one perhaps influenced by his mysterious, parallel life in Norway?' Richard suggested.

'I can see that.' Alice nodded thoughtfully and took another slow sip of wine.

'Well,' Richard broke the momentary silence. 'This is all just fantastic news, Alice. We couldn't have asked for better.'

'Before we get carried away, though,' Alice cautioned, 'I'll need to present it to my production team. Our policy on potential projects is to make a collective call, and even if we do get the script through this stage, there are a few more hurdles to overcome, including a thumbs-up from our executive board. However ... I'm confident that Omni will love Tor's script just as much as I do.' Another flash of those fantastic gnashers. *Ping!*

Richard took a breath. 'Thank you, Alice, for your belief in our project. Genuinely.' And he meant it. Genuinely.

'One step at a time, horsey,' she half-slurred, tackling the remains of her spritzer. Its warmth dripped down her chest to her legs.

Horsey? Paul tried to conceal a smile. She couldn't know it, but Paul had mistakenly ordered her a *large* spritzer.

'A question.' Paul asked, and Richard glared at him. 'Your production company makes mainly European Arthouse movies. So why are you interested in this more commercial-type kind of thriller? Isn't that a bit … downmarket for you?'

Alice tried to focus, searching her booze-addled memory bank for non-equine-related vocabulary.

Richard butted in. 'What my colleague means is, are you expanding and diversifying your brief?'

'That's right.' Alice flattened her trousers and regained her composure. 'What you just said.' She stopped, waiting on a response, before realising they were waiting on *her*. 'For the last five years we've been developing a stronger presence in Hollywood, and that means we have to diversify into more bloodstream – *main*stream areas, including thrillers such as yours. It's a slow, slow, slow, slow, slow …'

His eyes began to close.

'…process, but we now have a foothold in a few ongoing productions we believe will eshtablish … eshtablish … that's such a funny word.'

'It's "establish",' prompted Paul.

Richard booted him under the table, and Alice's eyes sprang open again.

'Anyway, they'll eshtablish ush as a major player in the coming years. That … my young friends … is Omni's ambition.' Her grin had taken on the appearance of Nosferatu. 'So … we still on board with this?'

'Absolutely,' said Richard enthusiastically.

Paul was a little more cautious. *Why was she so pissed on a few sips of spritzer – a hard day?* 'Let's see where it takes us.'

'Great,' said Alice. 'Let me check some dates.' She lifted her phone from her bag and promptly dropped it. She giggled.

Richard stifled a chuckle.

'Our next monthly script review is a week on Friday.' Alice was on her knees scrabbling for her phone. 'I can brief the team before then, so that should hopefully save some time and move things forward. C'mere, phone!'

Richard peeked under the table. 'And if your team approve?'

'Got it!' Alice grabbed the back of a chair and hauled herself up, holding her phone out in front of her like a pair of shitty pants. 'Bloody GPS doesn't work when you drop the bugger, does it?'

'If your team approve,' repeated Richard. 'What then?'

'Then we call you in. And you can pitch to the senior team. Is there a toilet in here?'

Paul looked around. 'I think there's one next to the–'

Alice shook her head. 'The car's waiting. I'll just go.'

'In the car?' Paul screwed his face up at the thought.

Richard elbowed him in the ribs.

Alice made her way unsteadily to the door. 'All being well,' she said over her shoulder, 'We should aim for a pitch to the senior team on Thursday eighteenth October. How's that sound?'

Richard walked her out.

'We'll double-check our schedules and email you tomorrow,' he confirmed.

'It's been a pleasure meeting you both.' Alice stopped at the door, reached for Richard's hand, and grabbed Paul's by mistake. Then she was gone.

As soon as she'd left, Richard raced to the window. 'Let's check out her wheels.'

'Oh, God,' moaned Paul, returning to the table and finishing his pint.

Richard rejoined him, shaking his head. 'She must be parked around the corner,' He sat, then immediately jumped back up again, singing, 'We're in the money! We're in the money!' at the top of his voice.

The landlord told him to button it or he'd be 'oot oan his fuckin' erse.' A Scotsman behind the bar of an upmarket wine emporium is still a Scotsman behind a bar.

'You were on fire, buddy.' Richard used Paul's arm as a mini punchbag. 'You ever considered acting as a career?'

'Why the fuck did you send her my script?' Paul spat.

'*Your* script?'

'Okay, *our* unfinished, first draft, mess of a script.'

'Sorry. I guess I got a bit carried away. It's just so brilliant, and I didn't want to lose her while she was in such a good mood.' He grinned.

'Fucking arsehole.' Paul thew back a deep mouthful of beer. 'Don't fucking do that again. We're supposed to be in this project together. That was the deal.'

'Looks like it's paid off though, eh?'

'I'm serious, Richard. Otherwise the deal is off. D'you know what I mean?'

'Whatever.' Richard's agreement was given grudgingly 'Listen, let me get you another drink to apologise and to set us up on the road to superstardom.'

'Not in this godforsaken place,' complained Paul. 'Can we please just get back to civilization? Somewhere I don't have to listen to you fucking singing again?'

As they packed up and left, Richard turned, bowed, and blew theatrical kisses at the barman, who glowered back at him with murderous intent. Much like a Congolese mercenary.

SCRIPT EDIT 7 - THE INTERVIEW SCENE

FADE IN:

EXT. STREET - DAY

A silver-rimmed wheel SCREECHES to a halt.

HARVEY CLARKE - late 30s, wearing a too-tight thin suit and a nervous expression - steps forward.

The rear door of the blacked-out Mercedes is open. Harvey climbs in.

INT. MERCEDES - DAY (MOVING)

A blacked-out screen separates Harvey from an unseen driver.

Harvey sits in the luxurious back seat in silence, glancing distractedly outside, as 'Lara's Theme' from Dr Zhivago is PIPED quietly from hidden speakers.

Beyond the glass, almost in slow motion, reams of grey, depressed, rain-drenched PEDESTRIANS trudge along grey, depressed, rain-drenched streets.

EXT. INDUSTRIAL WASTELAND - DAY

The Mercedes SPLASHES through a puddle and pulls up alongside a high metal gate with a barbed wire crown. Harvey climbs out and TAPS the driver's window, but the car ROARS away. Harvey stands alone, confused. He glances at the letter in his hand.

EXT. COMPOUND - DAY

Harvey's stubby forefinger presses a buzzer urging PRESS ME.

Almost instantly, the gate next to the buzzer CLICKS and swings slowly open. SCREEEEECH.

Up ahead is a sparse compound housing a large, unmarked warehouse. Harvey approaches it cautiously.

As Harvey nears a small metal door, it swings open, and he steps inside.

INT. WAREHOUSE - DAY

The sound of INDUSTRIAL CHURNING merges with Harvey's HEAVY BREATHING. A sudden flash of white light illuminates the warehouse interior. Harvey shields his eyes from the glare.

A long, empty, white-walled corridor fades off into the distance, halogen strip lights running along the centre.

At the far end, barely visible, sits a solitary FIGURE behind a white desk. Harvey swallows.

The stone-faced RECEPTIONIST, a gaudy lanyard hung over a conservative suit, SCRAPES back his chair and stands. He doesn't offer his hand.

RECEPTIONST

Good morning, Mr Clarke.

HARVEY

Agency O?

Harvey glances at the receptionist's chest.

The lanyard houses a photo of the receptionist wearing the exact same clothes and expression he currently wears. Beneath the photo, a barcode and a number: 1398790.

HARVEY (CONT'D)
I wasn't sure, as it's all a bit …

Harvey glances around. Smiles nervously.

HARVEY (CONT'D)

… you know.

The receptionist tilts his head. Clearly he doesn't.

RECEPTIONIST

Thank you for agreeing to attend the interview, Mr Clarke. Do you have your signed consent form?

HARVEY

Oh yes, sorry.

Harvey fumbles in his pocket and pulls out a folded A4 piece of paper.

HARVEY(CONT'D)

I have to say, some of the questions were a little … unusual.

Harvey hands the form over. The receptionist unfolds it.

RECEPTIONIST

We follow a holistic approach in our recruitment process, Mr Clarke. This ensures we select the most *ideal* candidate for the post every time.

The receptionist slowly checks over Harvey's form.

Harvey runs a finger under his tight, tide-marked collar.

The receptionist lifts his head. Smiles for the first time.

RECEPTIONIST(CONT'D)

Everything seems to be in order. Thank you.

The receptionist refolds the form and places it inside a drawer in his desk. He locks the drawer with a miniature key, which he then drops into his shirt pocket. It makes a tiny CLANG as it lands amongst a pile of other keys.

RECEPTIONIST(CONT'D)

If you'd like to follow me, please?

The receptionist steps away from his desk and PUNCHES a code in a door nearby. The door SLIDES open, and he steps aside. Harvey enters.

INT. MEDICAL EXAMINATION ROOM - DAY

An examination table dominates the room. It's surrounded by wall charts and a variety of medical tools and instruments.

DR SOFIE MALLING - 30s, glasses, blonde hair tied back - appears behind Harvey, startling him. She has a strong Scandinavian accent.

DR MALLING

Please remove your coat and any outer garments, and roll up the sleeve on your left arm, please.

Harvey lays his jacket and shirt neatly on a nearby bench.

Dr Malling pulls a small side table over beside Harvey.

DR MALLING (CONT'D)

Please sit. I am going to take some bloods. Okay?

HARVEY

Why?

DR MALLING

brusquely)

You signed the consent form, yes?

HARVEY

I thought I was here for an interview.

DR MALLING

We like to have a full physiological profile of our applicants in order to ascertain levels of aptitude, stamina, and resilience.

Dr Malling tightens a piece of tubing around Harvey's arm.

Harvey winces. It's too tight, but he won't admit it.

Dr Malling taps Harvey's vein vigorously.

DR MALLING (CONT'D)

This is common practice now for large organisations such as ours.

From her pocket, Dr Malling produces an oversized syringe with a fat needle.

DR MALLING (CONT'D)

This may sting a little.

Harvey turns away, closing his eyes and biting his lip.

Dr Malling quickly pushes the needle deep into Harvey's arm.

A small object appears in the tube of the needle and disappears into Harvey's vein. A bulge shoots up Harvey's arm.

Harvey MOANS and scrunches up his face, fighting back tears.

DR MALLING (CONT'D)

I am sorry. Your veins are very narrow. I will have to attempt insertion again.

Harvey INHALES sharply but doesn't move his arm.

Dr Malling finds another vein. Inserts the needle again.

Harvey's fist balls tighter and tighter, turning purple.

A WHOOSH of blood flows through the syringe.

Dr Malling pulls out the needle and steps back.

DR MALLING (CONT'D)

Good. Now I need you to stand on the scales.

A dizzy Harvey stumbles over to a set of scales. Dr Malling marks off his height and checks his weight. She then pulls hard on his chin, exposing his teeth.

DR MALLING (CONT'D)

Open, please.

Harvey instinctively opens his mouth wide. Dr Malling explores the back of his throat with a penlight.

DR MALLING (CONT'D)

Good. But please stay open.

Harvey's jaw shakes. The pressure to keep his mouth open is taking its toll.

Dr Malling casually swabs the inside of Harvey's cheek and drops the stick into a clear bag.

DR MALLING (CONT'D)

One more, please. For good luck.

Harvey's eyes widen in pain and fear.

DR MALLING (CONT'D)

I am joking.

(SLAPPING Harvey's cheek) Relax. Harvey's face folds in on itself, and he rubs his jaw.

Dr Malling crosses the room and stands in front of what looks like a metallic chrome version of a medieval torture device.

DR MALLING (CONT'D)

When you are ready.

HARVEY

What the hell's that?

DR MALLING

A simple eye check. Come on. Look through the lens, please.

Harvey approaches hesitantly.

DR MALLING (CONT'D)

Big baby. Come on!

Dr Malling hauls Harvey over to the machine and sticks his face against the binocular-shaped eyepiece.

DR MALLING (CONT'D)

Can you see a small black dot?

HARVEY

A what? Yes. Yes, I see it. Hang on, there's more of them.

DR MALLING

Please follow one of the dots only.

INT. EYEPIECE - DAY

A flurry of dots flicker over the surface of the eyepiece.
As they move, the light surrounding them pulses and intensifies rapidly.

INT. MEDICAL EXAMINATION ROOM - DAY

Harvey yanks himself away from the machine. Rubs at his eyes.

HARVEY

The light. It's like daggers.

Dr Malling grabs Harvey and pushes him roughly back against the eyepiece.

DR MALLING

It'll pass. Just a few more seconds.

Harvey grabs the metal handles either side of the machine. His body tenses. He stares again into the eyepiece. Behind him, Dr Malling presses a sequence of buttons on a rectangular panel.

INT. EYEPIECE - DAY

A needle suddenly fires out of one of the dots, and just as quickly, retracts again.

INT. MEDICAL EXAMINATION ROOM - DAY

Harvey jerks back in pain, cradling his wounded eye.

HARVEY

Something stabbed me! That fucking hurt!

Harvey tries to open his eye but can't.

DR MALLING

A reflex test. That is all. These drops will relieve the discomfort. Lean your head back, please.

Dr Malling holds Harvey by the shoulder and applies two drops to the wounded eye. Harvey blinks slowly, then opens his eye fully. The pain has gone.

HARVEY

Well, that wasn't pleasant.

DR MALLING

Pain is subjective. For some applicants this is routine.

Harvey rubs the last of the liquid from his eye. He didn't like that at all.

DR MALLING (CONT'D)

Your physical examination is now complete. Please get dressed.

Harvey mis-buttons his shirt, his co-ordination still off. Dr Malling waits patiently until he's done.

DR MALLING (CONT'D)

This way, please.

Dr Malling gestures to a door at the rear of the room. It eases open soundlessly. Harvey picks up his jacket and steps through the doorway.

INT. WHITE ROOM - DAY

The room is square and compact, the floor, ceiling, and walls pure white.

Three black hardback chairs are lined up in the centre. 'Lara's Theme' is again being PIPED in from somewhere. A calm female voice floats in over the music.

AMERICAN FEMALE (O.S.)

Please sit down.

Harvey looks around, searching for the voice's origin. Not finding it, he sits on the middle chair. The chair arms are sticky, as though coated in a thin film of glue. Harvey unsticks his hands. Places them back down.

Harvey waits. And waits. As he waits, he fidgets. Just as it seems he's about to lose patience, the music fades away. Harvey checks once more.

HARVEY

Hello?

Over to Harvey's left, a tiny hatch in the wall near the floor opens, and a mousetrap SLIDES into the room. The hatch SLAMS shut behind it.

To Harvey's right, another hatch opens. A white mouse appears from the hole. It runs along the edge of the wall towards the trap on the other side and then stops, as though considering turning back. Then it carries on.

Harvey grins nervously at the mouse's predicament.

The mouse approaches closer. It sniffs at a tiny morsel of bait poised on the trap.

Harvey winces. He knows if the mouse takes the bait, it'll die. He doesn't want the mouse to die.

The mouse nibbles. The trap shifts a little. The mouse stops and cleans its whiskers. Sniffs again. Stops. Glances in Harvey's direction. Then turns and runs back along the wall.
The hatch door reopens, and the mouse runs in and escapes.

Harvey SIGHS.

Different music is PIPED into the room. The theme from 'Ryan's Daughter' this time.

HARVEY(CONT'D)

(under his breath)

Fuck's sake.

The main door OPENS, and a BROAD-SHOULDERED MAN (30s) with side-parted hair and a waistcoat appears. A second candidate? The man nods at Harvey and sits next to him. They wait.

The door OPENS again. A PAINFULLY THIN WOMAN (20s) with a haunted face and a neck tattoo enters. She's like a coiled spring, all nervous energy and pent-up anger. She sits next to the broad-shouldered man. Harvey leans over, his palms clasped between his thighs.

HARVEY (CONT'D)

Are you here for the interview?

The woman suddenly directs a stream of aggressive-sounding, untranslatable WORDS towards the broad-shouldered man. He responds in a DIFFERENT LANGUAGE entirely, again not English. They argue, their hostility towards one another escalating.

The woman leaps to her feet and points at the broad-shouldered man, and then at Harvey.

Harvey, surprised, can only shrug. *What?*

The woman moves towards the man, making threatening gestures. She's SHOUTING now, and he's SHOUTING back, neither of them understandable. She turns her attention to Harvey, delivering the same incomprehensible diatribe.

Harvey holds his hands out, palms up.

HARVEY (CONT'D)

Whoa, whoa, whoa. Hold on. I don't know what you're -

Without warning, the woman attacks the man, PUNCHING and knocking him backwards off his chair. She looms over him, PUMMELING his face with her fists.

The man PUNCHES back, connecting with the woman's nose. She falls back, clutching her bleeding face. They grapple on the floor, fists flying. Someone SCREAMS. Someone GROANS. The two bodies stop moving.

Harvey stands in shock, in two minds as to whether to help or not. Who are these people? And why are they so angry?

The woman prises herself free from the man's clutches and slowly backs away. In her hand is a bloodied knife. The man is still sprawled out on the floor, unmoving. A widening pool of blood spreads outwards from his torso.

HARVEY (CONT'D)

Oh, fuck. What the fuck's going on?

Harvey raises his hands in surrender and addresses the woman.

HARVEY(CONT'D)

I don't know who you are, or what this is about, but I just came here for an interview. I don't want to get involved in any of … whatever this shit is, okay?

Harvey edges away from the woman and BANGS on the door.

HARVEY (CONT'D)

Hey! Open the door!

The woman moves closer to Harvey, the blade glistening beneath the artificial light. Harvey shakes his head.

HARVEY (CONT'D)

This has got nothing to with me. It's none of my business. I didn't see anything.

Harvey BANGS on the door again. Three times.

HARVEY (CONT'D)

Hey! *Hey!*

The woman stops a few feet from Harvey, the knife outstretched, almost in his face. Her menacing expression turns slowly to a smile. Behind her, the man stands, wipes the fake blood from his face, and joins her, grinning.

The door OPENS. The man and woman push past Harvey and leave. The door CLANGS shut again.

HARVEY (CONT'D)

You're kidding me!

The calm voice returns.

AMERICAN FEMALE(O.S.)

Please sit down.

Harvey paces the room, addressing the ceiling, the corner, everywhere.

HARVEY

What the hell is going on here? Some kind of psychometric bullshit crap is what it feels like. But whatever it is, I don't want it. I'm not interested, okay? I don't want your fucking job.

(under his breath)

This is so fucked up.

(to the ceiling)

Fuck you! Just fuck you! What you did, that was sick. Just let me out. Please. Let me out.

Harvey THUMPS on the door with both fists.

HARVEY(CONT'D)

Let me out! Let me out!

The door CLICKS open, and Harvey bolts through it into …

INT. CORRIDOR - DAY

… a corridor of pure white. Harvey races towards the exit as the MAIN THEME from 'Lawrence of Arabia' fills the air.

At the end of the corridor, Harvey PRESSES repeatedly at the green EXIT button until the door finally swings open.

EXT. COMPOUND - DAY

Harvey stumbles out into the rainy compound, dazzled and disorientated. Staggering through the open gate into the deserted industrial wasteland, he collapses onto the ground.

6

Richard ran from his room, yelling, 'The girl from Del Monte … she say yes!'

'Really?'

'Bloody hell, Paul … yes, really. Apparently, the production team gave it a resounding thumbs-up. Woop-woop! That's us booked in for our pitch to the senior execs on the eighteenth!'

'Fuck me, we're actually in.'

'Foot in the fucking door!' Richard galloped around the flat on a pretend horse, slapping his thigh. 'You are a genius, my friend.'

'Team effort.'

'Yeah, but you drove those eight-inch nails right through it. You've got it, baby!'

Paul shrugged. 'It's all just shit, really.'

'Platinum fucking shit,' Richard corrected. 'We're going to be rich and famous and get to drink and screw all day long. Whether we like it or not!'

'Yeah, right.' Paul laughed. *As if.*

Richard suddenly stopped waving his arms around and lost his Cheshire-wide grin. A deafening silence engulfed the room. Paul wondered if it was something he'd said. He was about to apologise when Richard cleared his throat.

'It's Pete's birthday today,' he said, his voice breaking. 'He would have been twenty-eight.'

'Oh shit,' said Paul. 'I totally forgot. I'm so sorry.'

He reached over and offered a supportive hand, but Richard shrugged it off.

'Come on,' said Richard. He reached for his jacket. 'Let's go get shit-faced and shout from the rooftops.'

'I'd love to,' said Paul, 'and I know that's exactly what your brother would want us to do, but aren't you forgetting one critical flaw in your plan?' He rubbed his fingers together to signal *moolah*.

'Ah, but that's where you're wrong,' grinned Richard and whipped a credit card from his pocket as though it were a set of nunchucks. 'I got the golden ticket!'

'How the hell?'

'I'm an employee, remember? I am now legally entitled to contribute to the national debt crisis.'

'Can I read her email?'

'Later. The grape and the grain doth call.' Richard tossed Paul his coat. 'To pub we go!' he decreed.

And they were out of the flat faster than a Jack Russell down a rathole.

7

Paul heard Richard come in around two and thump about the flat, moaning to himself. At some point in the course of the evening, Paul had abandoned his hyperactive flatmate and retreated to the quiet of the flat to work on the script. Saving his edits, he went to see what sort of drunken state Richard was in.

'Hey, Rich, what's up?' he asked, entering the kitchen.

Richard had his hoodie up over his head. 'Do we have any paracetamol?' he mumbled.

'Sounds like you need more than paracetamol,' replied Paul. 'Where'd you end up?'

Richard pulled his hood down. His left eye was swollen and partially closed, and his nose dripped a viscous crimson gunk. Further down, his lower lip, cut on the diagonal, bulged like an over-blown balloon. It wasn't a good look.

'Jesus!' Paul gasped. 'What the fuck happened to you?'

'I got jumped.'

'Where?'

'Southside. One minute I'm walking home, the next I'm on the ground with some ned laying his boot into my face.'

'Bloody hell. It's a right mess. We need to get you to A and E.' Paul found his phone.

Richard shook his head. 'I just need some paracetamol. And ice. We got any ice?'

Paul scrutinised at his friend dubiously. 'You sure you don't want it checked out? You might need stitches.'

Richard nodded, and Paul reluctantly pocketed his phone.

'Did you at least get a look at the shit who did this to you?' Paul asked, opening a freezer drawer and passing over a bag of frozen peas.

'It was too dark,' said Richard, pressing the bag to his lip. 'And too fast. All I remember was his hat. He had one of those flat caps from the thirties pulled down over his face.'

'Fuck!' Paul exclaimed. He popped a paracetamol caplet from its foil casing. 'That's the same guy who followed me.' He handed the painkiller to Richard along with a glass of water.

'Could be,' said Richard, throwing his head back and swallowing. He touched an open wound below his eye and winced. 'The guy was strong. I mean, I tried to fight back, but the bastard got the better of me. Fucking psycho.'

'I told you I was followed.'

'And I should have believed you. I'm sorry.'

'Did he take anything? Money, or–?'

'I don't think so.' Richard checked his pockets. 'Oh great, my wallet's gone. Still got my phone, though.' He placed it on the coffee table. 'And it's fucking cracked. The wanker.'

'We should report this.'

'What's the police going to do?'

'We're being fucking stalked, Richard.' Paul shook his head in alarm. 'There's bound to be CCTV footage of the bastard … or witnesses … anything.'

'Fuck's sake, Paul,' said Richard. 'They're not TV cops. They haven't got time for low-level shit like this.' He hauled himself up off the couch and groaned as he tried to straighten up. 'I'll be fine. I just need to sleep it off.' Still pressing the bag of Bird's Eye to his face, he shuffled off to his room.

Paul sighed, checked the locks on the doors and windows, and went back to his room, an unfamiliar feeling of panic slowly growing in his chest.

It was just after eight when Paul knocked on Richard's door to wake him for his shift at the bookshop. There was no reply. Paul knocked again, then cautiously pushed the door open. Richard was sitting at his desk, peering at his laptop.

Paul entered and crossed the room. 'Hey. You remembering you got work?'

Richard's eyes never left the screen.

Paul leaned over and checked Richard's face. The swelling on his lip and nose had gone down, and there was only a hint of a black eye. 'Your face looks better. More like its usual ugly self.'

Richard pointed to the screen.

Paul stared at a list of emails. The top one was headed 'This is the End.'

'What's this?' Paul asked.

Richard clicked on it, and the message opened up.

Remove your videos, erase your script, terminate your files

Yesterday we warn – Tomorrow we end

'Who sent you this?'

'Check the time,' said Richard, shaking his head.

'Twelve-oh-three a.m. Oh fuck! The bastard must have sent you this right after he did you over!'

Richard sighed.

'The sick fuck. What the hell's going on?'

Richard pressed his finger onto the cut on his lower lip. 'Weird shit, that's what's going on. You want to see something weirder?' He hovered the cursor over the word 'end' in the message and clicked. The word expanded until it filled the screen, then burst into flames.

'Jesus Christ!' The panic in Paul's chest returned with a vengeance. 'I fucking told you not to put our details online.'

'I didn't,' said Richard. 'I set up a fake email address with Tor Fleck's name on it. It's the one Alice contacted me through.'

'That's even worse. They know who we are!'

'Oh, stop nee-nawing like a demented donkey,' said Richard dismissively. 'They're just trolls.'

'Richard, you were fucking set upon last night.'

'You know me and my eloquent way with words. I probably upset somebody in the pub.'

'He was wearing the same flat cap as the guy who followed me.'

'Maybe I got that bit wrong. I don't know.'

'You knew it well enough last night.'

'It's just one of those things.'

'"Tomorrow we end". That's pretty threatening,' Paul squeaked, his voice leaping a couple of octaves.

Richard cracked a painful smile. 'It's all a bit *Mission Impossible,* don't you think? Even our script isn't that bad. It'll be one of my idiot acquaintances winding us up.'

'I can't believe you're playing this down. We need to go to the police. Now.'

'For a stupid prank gone too far? Don't be daft.'

Paul sensed Richard was hiding something. 'Have you had any more of these?'

Richard hesitated just a fraction too long.

'Oh, Jesus Christ!' yelled Paul. 'When?'

'Last week.'

'Why didn't you fucking say something?'

'I told you, it's just trolls,' said Richard. 'They're not worth the energy.'

'We're being stalked. Were they all like this, the emails?'

'More or less.'

Paul was incandescent. 'I can't believe ...' He rubbed at his eye. 'And all demanding we pull our project, or else?'

'Yup.'

'But why?'

'I don't know,' admitted Richard. 'Because they're mischievous wankers?'

Paul shook his head. 'This is more serious than that.' He couldn't work out whether Richard was genuinely unfazed over all of this or just afraid to show how terrified he actually was.

'One other thing,' said Richard.

'What?'

'Look at the sender's name at the bottom of the email.'

Paul leaned in and scanned the message again. 'What the fuck? Tor Fleck?'

Richard nodded. 'Our mystery man from the tundra.'

Paul stared at his friend, totally confused. 'But that's just fucked up.'

'Your fictional best friend from uni, and our ticket to the stars, has turned out to be a saddo troll. We've quite literally created a monster!' Richard laughed, wincing again at the pain rippling across his cracked lips.

'We need to report this,' said Paul. 'It's fucking with my head. And the sooner we pull our stuff from the Internet the better.'

Richard scowled. 'Don't be so bloody stupid. We're two weeks away from our pitch. If we pull it now, we risk blowing the deal.'

'Fuck the deal! We're being threatened!'

'By who? Somebody we just made up? You need to calm down, Paul. This is just a bubble in a fart bag.'

'A what?'

'Whatever. We're sitting on the deal of a lifetime here. Are you going to let fucking Gollum fuck it up for us?'

'The email said "we", ie. more than one.'

'Of course it does. Him and his imaginary friends from Middle Earth. Just sit tight and he'll go away.'

'I'm not happy about this.' Paul clenched his teeth and shook his head.

Richard smiled. 'When are you ever happy? Just trust me. Okay? I know it goes against your better nature, but can you make an exception this one time? For me?'

Paul stared at the floor, refusing to answer.

'Paul,' Richard soothed, 'think about it. This only happens in the movies. You've been working on the script for too long. You're going la-la.' He put a hand on Paul's shoulder. 'Last night was a bar-room conversation gone wrong, that's all. These messages are stupid and harmless. Somebody pissed, firing them out in a fit of anger, end of.'

Paul glanced up. He still wasn't fully convinced, but what if Richard was right?

Richard grinned. 'There we are. Our boy has returned unscathed from Narnia.' He raised his arms in victory.

'Any more emails or threats of any kind,' cautioned Paul, 'and we pull the plug.'

'It's not going to happen,' said Richard. 'And besides, I could flatten Tor Fleck any day. Who is he anyway? A fucking nobody, that's who. And a fictional one at that.' He closed his laptop. 'Right, I need coffee. Some of us have to work today.'

Paul forced out an unconvincing smile. For the sake of their friendship, he'd carry on with this charade. For now. But in the pit of his stomach, he knew it wasn't over. Not by a long shot.

8

To Paul's immense relief, the next two weeks passed without a single threatening email. Maybe Richard was right after all; maybe it was just a nutter with a grudge who'd gotten bored when they'd ignored him. The return to a state resembling normality reignited Paul's creative spark, and as he worked furiously on honing the script, *Agency O* began to look more like the real deal, a fact Paul couldn't help but feel a little excited about.

He checked his watch. 2:47 a.m. He'd been working on Scene Twelve, a critical turning point in the story, for more than five hours, tightening the action and fine-tuning the plot. He stretched and yawned. He was done. He'd nail the scene tomorrow. He reached over to click Save, but something in the predawn soundscape of the house had him pausing and turning. Was that the door? Richard was spending the night with an ex – or, as Richard himself described her, an ex with severe memory loss – so it couldn't be him. And it was too late, or too early, for a visit from Mrs McGilvray. Was it even a sound at all? Paul rose from his desk, eased open the bedroom door, and peered into the gloom.

Nothing.

Of course it's nothing, he thought. *Who the hell would–?* A clatter from the kitchen cut short the thought. Paul pushed his head out further, his heart thudding, but it was still too dark to see. Moving into the living room proper, he stuck his head round the corner into the kitchen. There was a sudden crash, as though a saucepan had been dropped.

'Shit!' He edged his way back out of the living room.

Reaching his bedroom door, he caught a glimpse of a shadow moving across the hallway. He quickly ducked into the bathroom and locked the door. He scanned the room for any kind of weapon he could defend himself with, but all he could find was a toilet brush. *Fat lot of good that'll do.*

Pressing his ear to the door, Paul listened for the intruder. His heartbeat was more like a dance beat: *DOOF-DOOF-DOOF-DOOF. If I ever get out of this alive,* he thought, *I'm never listening to Calvin Harris again. This is fucking killing me.*

The door handle turned with an agonising slowness. Paul jumped back and grabbed the toilet brush, prepared to administer a soft-tipped, but cleansing, beating. The door handle was let go. Paul leaned in, straining to hear the slightest sound. Something struck the door with force – *BOOM!* – sending him stumbling backwards. Another violent boom. And another. And another. Whoever was out there was trying to kick the door in. Paul was panicking now, cornered and trapped like a slaughterhouse hog. There was no way out. No window or hatch to climb through. In desperation, he yanked back the shower curtain and clambered into the bath. *BOOM!* Another kick. The door shook in its frame.

Paul opened the storage cabinet beneath the eaves and squeezed inside, pushing aside towels and toilet rolls and a foot-high blue plastic penguin. *What the fuck?* The battering of the door continued. Shards of plaster and wood flew out in all directions. Tucking in his legs and arms, he forced his body into the impossible space. *Jesus.* Just as he pulled the shutters closed, the door flew off its hinges and catapulted sideways into the bath, taking the shower curtain down with a crash. Paul's hand flew to his mouth.

Do not breathe!

An ominous quiet descended in the bathroom. Calvin Harris cranked up the BPM in Paul's chest. *DOOF-DOOF-DOOF-DOOF-DOOF-DOOF-DOOF!* Paul fought the urge to scream.

Where the hell is the fucker? Did he leave?

A pair of black-trousered legs climbed over what was left of the door and entered the bathroom fully.

Nope. The fucker didn't leave. The fucker's in the bathroom. My bathroom! And I don't think he's here to do a shit!

Paul couldn't see his face, the cupboard's air vent was too low, but he could hear the fucker's breathing. Kicking the door in must have taken it out of him.

He should get himself a Bannatyne's membership, Paul thought randomly.

The black-clad legs moved further in and stopped. Paul looked down. A pair of black, shiny brogues pressed up against the door. Whoever he was, he was listening for signs of Paul's whereabouts. The feet reached the cupboard. Paul clenched his fists to defend himself, still gripping the toilet brush. The feet stopped. A flat cap appeared at the vent. Paul pulled back further into the darkness. The door rattled. *Fuck!* He was about to kick out – *one good shot to the goolies should do it* – but then the front-door chime rang like the bell on the *Titanic* and the intruder fled. A loud commotion erupted in the close, and then the voice of Mrs McGilvray shouting at the top end of the sound spectrum.

'Manners, young man!'

Paul pushed himself out of the cabinet, stumbled over the debris, and ran to the front door, toilet brush in *en garde* position.

'What in God's name is going on?' asked a shocked Mrs McGilvray.

Paul lowered the toilet brush and caught his breath. 'I am so glad to see you, Mrs McGilvray.'

'One of your rude friends nearly knocked me down the stairs.'

Paul nodded. 'We had an intruder.'

'Oh my. Are you okay, son?' There was genuine concern in Mrs McGilvray's voice. 'I thought the whole tenement was going to fall down with all that noise.'

'I was hiding in the bathroom. He kicked the door in.'

'And you were going to defeat him with that?' Mrs McGilvray nodded to the toilet brush and shook her head. 'Come away in. I'll call the police, then make you a nice cup of sweet tea. You'll be in shock.'

Paul followed Mrs McGilvray into her flat, lurching against her door as exhaustion kicked in.

'Now don't break *my* bloody door in as well,' she said.

Paul could swear he caught the hint of a smile.

About twenty minutes later, Richard appeared at Mrs McGilvray's door.

'Why are the police outside our flat?'

'Somebody broke in,' said Paul. 'I thought you were out for the night.'

'What? Oh, that didn't work out,' said Richard. 'I got these, though.' He opened up a large holdall and produced two tartan suits. 'For our pitch.'

Paul didn't respond.

Mrs McGilvray appeared at Paul's back. 'Your flatmate's in shock, Dick,' she said. *Dick?* 'He's been attacked.'

'Oh, Jesus. Are you okay?' Richard laid a hand on his friend's shoulder.

'I'm fine,' said Paul, forcing a smile. 'Luckily, Mrs McGilvray heard the banging, and when she rang the bell, they legged it.'

'There was more than one?'

'Oh aye, son,' said Mrs McGilvray. 'There was at least two o' the wee bastards. One in the flat and one down on the landing, waiting.'

'Bloody hell,' said Richard. 'Are you okay, Mrs McGilvray? It must have been terrifying for you.' It was his turn to show genuine concern.

'Och, no. They'd soon know all about it if they came near me.'

Richard didn't doubt it.

All three heads turned swiftly at a *CLUMP-CLUMP* on the stairs.

A uniformed policewoman appeared at the top of the landing. 'Mr Grant?' she asked.

Paul nodded.

'My name is PC Betts. Can I come in?'

The briefest hint of dawn crept through the curtains and into Mrs McGilvray's 1960's time warp of a living room as four hands reached over the coffee table at the same time and lifted four mugs of tea.

PC Betts took a sip and lowered her mug. She turned to Paul. 'I need to take a statement from both you and–?'

Mrs McGilvray's smile showed three missing teeth. 'Mrs Margaret McGilvray, here to help.'

'I'll take Mr Grant's statement first, then we'll do you.' PC Betts said.

Margaret nodded. She knew the drill. She'd been interviewed by CID just after her late husband had fallen down the stairs.

'Just when you're ready,' PC Betts reassured Paul.

Paul took a deep breath. Then another.

'Did you get a good look at them?' Richard interrupted, earning himself a glare from PC Betts.

'No,' Paul replied. 'Just the hat. It was the same flat cap, pulled down over his face.'

PC Betts leaned over. 'You just said, *the same* flat cap. What do you mean by that?'

Paul glanced over at Richard. Richard nodded.

Paul continued. 'A couple of weeks ago, I was followed home by a man wearing one of those nineteen-thirties' prohibition-type caps.'

'Oh,' said PC Betts, 'like on that TV show, you mean?'

'*Peaky Blinders*,' said Richard.

'That's the one.' PC Betts grinned. 'My partner loves that show. So, when exactly did this incident occur?'

Paul mentally worked the dates back. 'Third … eleventh of ,' he said. 'I was coming back from Charing Cross Library. He followed me all the way to the flat.'

'And did you report it?' PC Betts scribbled a couple of lines in her notepad.

'No,' said Paul. 'I didn't think much of it.' *Liar*. 'But then a few days later …'

PC Betts glanced up. 'A few days later … what?'

'A few days later I … er …'

Richard was gesturing behind the constable for Paul to shut the fuck up.

PC Betts swivelled round, but she wasn't fast enough to catch Richard quickly drop his hands by his sides.

'Nothing,' said Paul. 'I guess I should have reported it at the time.'

Mrs McGilvray noticed that Paul's hands were shaking. 'Drink your tea, son, and I'll get you another biscuit.' She pulled herself up from her armchair.

'Before you do that, Mrs McGilvray,' said PC Betts. 'Could you tell me what you saw?'

'There were two of them,' said Margaret. 'One came running out and nearly knocked me down the stairs. Another was waiting for him on the landing next floor down.'

'Did you see their faces at all?'

'As Mr Grant said, one was hiding under his hat. The other was wearing a balaclava. I'll give him balaclava!' Margaret's lips tightened at the thought of painful retribution.

'So they were both male?' PC Betts asked.

'I really don't know,' Margaret admitted. 'I didn't have my glasses on.'

'Thank you, Mrs McGilvray.' PC Betts smiled. 'You've been very helpful.'

Margaret nodded again. They'd said the thing same after her late husband's death.

PC Betts turned back to Paul. 'Just one more thing. Has anything been stolen from the property?'

'I didn't get a chance to look,' said Paul. 'I came straight over here.'

'I'll go and check,' Richard offered and rose from his chair. When he was gone, PC Betts cleared her throat.

'Have you lost a set of keys recently?'

Paul pulled a laden key-ring from his pocket. 'Nope.'

'You see,' said PC Betts, 'there's no sign of forced entry.'

'No?'

'Are you in the habit of leaving your door unlocked?'

'In Glasgow? Are you kidding?'

Richard poked his head back in. 'I can't see anything missing.'

'Have you got your keys?' Paul asked.

Richard checked his trouser pockets, front and back. Nothing. He checked his coat. Nothing. Lastly, he unzipped the holdall lying at his feet. Again, nothing. Confused, he felt around his trousers again. 'I seem to have …'

Paul let out a long frustrated sigh.

'It would appear the intruder or intruders may have used your key to enter the property,' said PC Betts.

'But I had them earlier,' Richard protested. 'Oh god,' he said, a hand flying to his mouth.

'What?' asked Paul, fearing the worst.

'I was over at the theatre I used to work at, you know, trying on some suits. I know a girl who works in props.' Richard paused. 'I tried on a couple. Then we went for a drink – oh, shit.'

'Oh shit what?'

'I think I might have left them in the pub.'

'For fuck's sake!' exclaimed Mrs McGilvray, the other three staring at her in astonishment. 'I mean … which pub?'

'The Beehive.' Richard squinted at Mrs McGilvray's bouffant. 'You know, at the back of Buchanan Street Bus Station.'

'That'll do for now,' PC Betts said, rising to her feet. 'Oh, just one more question. Do you have contents insurance?'

Paul and Richard looked at each other blankly.

'No,' they said in unison.

Okay,' said PC Betts, tucking her notebook into her top pocket. 'Probably just as well. An unlocked door and hastily damaged goods would probably invalidate your claim anyway.' She glowered at the flatmates, as though she knew they were hiding something. 'I think we have everything we need for now. If anything else pops into your head …' She continued with the hard stare '… even if you don't think it's relevant … pop into the station or give us a ring. In the meantime …' She stuck her cap on her head and adjusted it. '… I suggest you review your home security arrangements and change the locks on your front door.'

After PC Betts had gone, Paul turned to Mrs McGilvray and smiled. 'You've been very kind.'

'Och, away with you,' said Margaret. 'But as for that friend of yours over there …'

9

Back in the flat, Richard found Paul propping the bathroom door up against the wall. 'I really am sorry about the keys, mate.'

Paul turned on him. 'You were scoring some blow, weren't you? Don't deny it. That's what they do in the bloody Beehive.'

No answer from Richard. He couldn't deny it.

'And that was why you didn't want to tell the copper about the assault.'

Richard tried to squirm his way out of it. 'I just didn't want to complicate things. You know, with the script.' He grabbed Paul's arm. 'Jesus, the script! Was it on your computer?'

'The script!' Paul roared. 'Fuck's sake, is that all you can think about? I could have been fucking killed tonight.'

'Oh, don't be such a drama queen,' said Richard. 'A couple of druggies broke in looking for skank money and legged it the minute Hell's Granny arrived.'

'Listen,' said Paul. 'If it wasn't for Margaret–'

'Oh, it's Margaret now, is it? When's the wedding?'

'Fuck off!'

RAT-A-TAT-TAT!

'Aha! Perfect timing,' sneered Richard as he headed out of the room. 'It's never too early to discuss seating arrangements.' He threw open the front door.

It wasn't Mrs McGilvray who stood in the doorway facing Richard. Not unless someone had pumped her full of helium and dark net steroids in the past five minutes. Whoever it was stood in his own obese shadow, leaning against the doorframe and blocking out most of the light from the landing. His neck was slick with sweat, his breath heavy and rasping from the climb up the stairs. It was all he could do to flash his badge.

'Inspector Quinn, CID,' he wheezed. 'Can I have a word?'

Richard stared at the inspector for a moment, trying to take in the entirety of him. 'Why not?' he said sarcastically and stood back. 'Come in and join the party.'

Inspector Quinn straightened up, wiped his feet on the mat, and stepped into the flat.

'Paul!' shouted Richard. 'We've got a visitor. Inspector Quinn from CID. All we need now is the police commissioner and we've got the whole set!"

'I'm just following up on your break-in earlier this evening,' Quinn told Paul when he appeared. The Inspector spoke with a strange mid-Atlantic accent, somewhere between Glasgow and New Jersey.

'Follow up?' Richard asked. 'Already?'

Quinn wiped his sweaty forehead with a large, heavily stained handkerchief. 'We have a few loose ends, Mr Gann.'

Richard tilted his head. 'How'd you know my name?'

'I've been briefed on what happened, sir.'

'Bit OTT for CID to be involved in a run-of-the-mill break-in, isn't it?' asked Richard.

'Let him speak,' snapped Paul.

Quinn shifted his weight from one leg to the other.

'Would you like to sit down, Inspector?' Paul offered.

'Do you have a hard-back chair?' Quinn asked. 'I'm not on good terms with sofas.'

Paul brought a chair in from the kitchen, which Quinn cautiously lowered himself onto. The frame creaked ominously as his buttocks spread across the seat and down over the sides like lava.

'Thank you,' he said, now even more uncomfortable than he had a moment before.

'You said loose ends,' Paul prompted. 'Which ones exactly?' He glanced down with horror at the Inspector's overstretched and visibly stained underpants, which seemed to be trying to climb out from the crack of his arse.

'Do you have any enemies, Mr Grant?' Quinn asked.

Paul hesitated. He'd just seen what looked like a squashed chip stuck to the end of the detective's dangling coat-tail.

'Only his mother,' Richard cut in with a fake laugh.

Quinn turned, with monumental difficulty, to Richard. 'And what about you, Mr Gann? Anyone harbouring a grudge against you? Someone you've maybe crossed swords with recently?'

'Nope,' said Richard. 'I'm pretty much universally loved.'

Paul rolled his eyes.

'And what about your film project?' asked Quinn. 'How's that going?'

Paul took a step forward. 'You know about that?'

'The "I" in CID is there for a reason, Mr Grant,' Quinn smiled. 'It stands for "Intelligence".'

'You mean "Investigation",' Paul corrected.

'You seem to have quite a following on social media,' Quinn continued. 'A haven for trolls and the like. Or so I'm led to believe.'

'What's this about?' Richard interrupted. 'My flatmate's been through a traumatic experience tonight. He's not up to any more questions.'

'You don't think there's a connection between your break-in this evening and what you're up to online?' asked Quinn, pulling the waistband of his pants rapidly up and down in an effort to alleviate an itch on his arsehole.

'We're not "up to" anything,' Richard protested. 'The two things are unrelated.'

Paul threw up a hand. 'Stop!' he yelled. 'Just stop.' He turned to Quinn. 'I'm sorry, Inspector. My friend is a knob. Please ignore him. He won't go away, but at least you won't have to look at him.'

Quinn smiled. 'Is there something you'd like to tell me, Mr Grant?'

Paul drew in a breath. 'We've had a number of death threats. Online, and by email.'

'Unrelated,' Richard repeated.

Paul carried on. 'A couple of weeks ago, Richard was attacked. And we think it was the same person who'd followed me earlier that week.'

'My flatmate is misinformed,' said Richard. 'Yes, I was attacked, but it was likely the consequence of a heated conversation I'd had in the pub earlier that evening.'

'Bollocks!' said Paul. 'What about the cap?'

'An unfortunate coincidence,' Richard insisted.

Paul shook his head. 'You're unbelievable. Next you'll be saying tonight wasn't a real break-in.'

'What was the name of the pub?' Quinn interrupted.

'I can't remember,' Richard lied, looking away.

'Could you describe what happened?' asked Quinn, his patience waning. 'Or have you forgotten that as well?'

Richard held Quinn's stare for a moment before lowering his gaze. 'I was walking home. Someone pushed me to the ground and started beating the crap out of me. I managed to escape before any serious harm was done. End of.'

'And what time was this?'

'I don't know,' said Richard with a smirk. 'My watch was covered in blood.'

'It was around midnight,' said Paul. 'I was up working when I heard Richard come in.'

'And did you get an ID on your assailant?'

'Jesus Christ,' said Richard. 'Why are you are so interested in something completely unconnected to tonight?'

A bead of sweat dripped off Quinn's nose. 'It's important for us to establish a clear and accurate picture, to assist in any subsequent investigation.'

'Whoa, wait a minute!' Richard held up his hands. 'Investigation? I don't want to be investigated.'

Quinn eyed Richard suspiciously. 'I'm not suggesting you're under investigation, Mr Gann. Like I said, I'm just tying up a few loose ends.'

'Calm down, Richard,' said Paul. 'The Inspector's only doing his job.' He turned to Quinn. 'So, do you think this is all connected to our videos and the script?'

'I'm not at liberty to discuss any ongoing investigation,' said Quinn, trying to stand, 'but you can rest assured …' His body teetered dangerously to one side. '… that we are investigating all aspects of the case.' Quinn's arms spun like windmills as his legs gave out and he crashed back down onto the chair. *THUD!* Frustrated, he looked up at Richard and Paul. 'Don't worry. We'll keep you informed of any developments.'

'Hang on,' said Richard. 'You can't just come in here and allude to some so-called wider investigation and then just leave it at that. If we're in danger, we should know.'

'Whoever's doing this wants us to take it all down and delete our files,' said Paul. 'Are you saying that's what we should do?'

'Let's just say the case is close to completion,' replied Quinn, 'so it's more a matter of sitting tight.' He made an embarrassingly poor second attempt at leaving his chair.

'Let me,' said Paul, offering Quinn his arm.

Quinn batted it away and pushed himself up with an almighty groan. Finally on his feet, he took a moment to make sure he wasn't going to fall back down again. 'Sit tight for now. If anything changes, call me.'

'So that's it?' said Richard. 'Sit tight?'

'That's right. Do nothing for now. I'll be in touch.' Quinn shuffled to the door.

Richard shook his head. 'Unbelievable. You come in here and tell us we're being stalked, then expect us just to "sit tight"?'

'What's the problem?' asked Paul. 'Isn't it all "unrelated"?'

'It's not that, it's him.' Richard pointed to Quinn. 'With all his scare-mongering shite.'

'You can sleep tight, Mr Grant. Everything's in hand,' Quinn said.

Paul walked Quinn to the door. 'What if this guy comes back?'

Quinn stopped. 'It's important that for now, you hold your nerve. You understand?'

Paul nodded.

Quinn headed down the stairs, gripping the bannister tight. 'And tell your shit-for-brains friend to cool the beans!' he bellowed over his shoulder. 'I can't guarantee his safety.'

In the morning, Richard knocked quietly on Paul's door. There was no reply. He tried again.

'Piss off!'

'I need to talk to you,' said Richard, his ear against the door. 'Can I come in?'

Heavy footsteps thudded across the room. Suddenly, the door was flung open, and Richard almost fell into Paul's arms.

'What do you want?' growled Paul, pushing his friend away.

Richard straightened up and reached into his back pocket. He pulled out a half-folded A4 sheet of paper and stuck it in Paul's face. Paul took an instinctive step back and grabbed the paper. Unfolding it, he read it to himself, his lips moving silently.

When he'd finished, he glanced up at Richard in fear. 'When did you get this?'

Richard reached back into his pocket and removed a second sheet of paper, similarly folded. 'That one was last Saturday. This one–' He handed Paul the second sheet. '– I got on Tuesday.'

Paul read the second sheet, shaking his head as it became clear what was happening. 'Richard, these threats are escalating. This one says "soon".' He glanced up. 'What the fuck does that mean?'

Richard fumbled in his pocket a third time.

'Tell me you don't fucking have another one,' groaned Paul.

'Naw,' said Richard. 'I've got an itchy arse. Of course I've got another one.' He handed it over. 'Four-oh-nine this morning,' he said. 'I don't know what's worse: him being a psychotic, or him being an insomniac.'

Reading the third message, Paul shook his head in disbelief.

'I know,' said Richard. 'It's fucked up, right?'

Paul's head jerked up. 'No, Richard. *You're* fucked up. Quinn was right, you are a shit-for-brains arsehole.'

'He said that?'

'You knew it was all connected and yet you stood there and lied. To the policewoman … to Quinn … to me. Why?'

'It's this deal,' said Richard. 'We can't jeopardise it. If the film company find out, they'll think we're trouble.'

'Oh, for fuck's sake, you have definitely lost–' Paul paused. Controlled his thoughts. 'No, not perspective,' he corrected. 'You've lost your fucking *mind*. Fuck the deal and fuck the film company. I was fucking assaulted, you fucking fuck!'

'That's a lot of fucks for one sentence,' said Richard. 'I counted at least six.'

'FUCK! OFF!' How many in *that* sentence?' Paul spat back. 'Don't you fucking dare play this down. We need to do as they say.'

'Paul, this is a chance in a lifetime for us.'

'And one we won't be alive to appreciate. You heard Quinn. This is much bigger than us. Something is seriously terrifying about all of this, and we need to get out, before it's too late.'

'Yeah, but Quinn also said we should sit tight.'

'Well, fuck that.' Paul turned and headed back into the bedroom.

A desperate Richard followed him. 'But it's two days away,' he pleaded. 'We can't pull out now. We've put so much into this. The pitch is ready, the script is so fucking tight, and I even got us a couple of sharp suits.'

Paul snapped the curtains shut and swivelled round, his face barely an inch from Richard's. 'You honestly think I can go and pitch our shitty film to some bigwig producers now?'

Richard's eyes were like beach balls. 'But those trolls are after me, not you.'

'What?'

'Some arsehole's got a grudge against me. He'll have seen me in the videos and somehow, I don't know, got my email off social media.'

Paul was flabbergasted. 'Can you hear yourself? Can you seriously fucking hear yourself?'

'I bet they thought it was me in the flat,' said Richard. 'I have enemies.'

Paul slapped Richard across the face. 'Shut the fuck up!'

For a split-second, Paul thought Richard was going to cry. *Don't fucking cry.* But then whatever switch had been flipped by the slap suddenly righted itself, and it was as though nothing had happened.

'Listen,' said Richard, back in full-on obsessive mode. 'We've got two more days. If you don't want to do it, I'll pitch on my own. If it's a goer, we come clean with the production company and the police. If it sinks, we pull everything and walk away.'

'I've heard enough.' Paul pushed his way past Richard to the door.

Richard ran ahead of him and blocked the doorway. 'But in theory, you're okay with me doing the pitch on my own?'

Paul's anger had gone. Now there was only pity. 'Do what you like,' he said. He bent down under the bed and yanked out a holdhall. 'If you want to throw yourself to the wolves,' he said, stuffing the bag with clothes from the bedside drawers, 'then you go for it, buddy.' He had to get away from this madness. His nerves were shot. The new emails, threatening all sorts, were the last of last straws.

'I'll let you know how it goes!' Richard shouted after Paul as he left the flat.

'I couldn't give a shit!' Paul shouted back, almost falling down the stairs in his hurry to escape. 'And I'd change the locks if I were you!'

When he reached the city centre, Paul thought about carrying on to his parents' house but changed his mind. Instead, he rang Aunt Doris and asked if he could stay a couple of nights in her caravan up at Loch Gilpen. He'd stayed there before as a kid, and also with Richard, so figured it was a familiar and safe place to hide until the chaos subsided and he could put his head back together. Twenty minutes later, he was on a train to Oban.

10

'Well, well, well, look what the cat dragged in!' The balding, six-foot landlord, his sleeves rolled up to his elbows, grinned. He ran a dishcloth around the inside of a pint glass as Paul approached the bar. 'We don't normally see you up here this time of year.'

'Aye, well, a change is as good as a rest, as they say.' Paul dropped his holdall onto the floor and reached over the bar for the man's hand. 'Plus, I needed to get away from the city for a while. Good to see you again, Duncan.'

The two men shook hands.

'Always a pleasure, Paul.' Duncan drew his hand away. 'Now, what would you like?'

'Just the keys for the caravan. I need to dump my bags and sort myself out.'

'Gimme a minute.' Duncan disappeared through a side door.

Paul scanned the cosy but run-down lounge. It was quiet. A roaring log fire in the corner tempted him over, but he resisted. An elderly man with a sheepdog practically the same age as him lying at his feet raised his glass in Paul's direction.

Paul smiled. 'Hey, George, how's tricks?'

'Och, ye know. Life in the fast lane as usual.'

'Can I get you a pint?'

'Well, I wouldn't want to offend you, son. 80 Shilling, ta.'

The side door opened, and Duncan reappeared.

'Mary's put the lights on for you. If you don't have enough gas,' he said, handing Paul the keys, 'let me know and I'll bring a new bottle over.'

Paul shoved the keys into his pocket. 'Thanks. I'll be back later for a pint. Are you still doing food?'

'I'm sure we can find some roadkill for you.'

'Just a wee bit of bother back in the smoke, you know?'

'So you thought you'd come *here* to escape trouble. You'll be lucky.' Duncan smiled.

Paul picked up his holdall. 'Oh, and a pint for George. Keep him hydrated.' He rustled up some change and dropped it onto the bar.

'I'm sure if he sat there long enough,' said Duncan, 'somebody would buy him his tea and pay his rent. Old codger.' He palmed the coins and headed back to the pumps.

The small caravan park was tucked away at the end of a narrow path along the edge of the loch. There were eight caravans in total, but only one near the entrance was lit: Aunt Doris'.

The caravan was freezing. Statics are not designed for Scottish weather. And, if anything, it was even colder inside than out. Dropping his holdall in the compact kitchen, Paul traipsed back outside and turned the gas on. Movement in the shadows on the far side of the park caught his eye. *Probably a deer looking for scraps*. Back inside, Paul fired up the hob and turned the gas heater up full. The caravan warmed up quickly. It was an old-fashioned static, but his aunt had maintained it well, and once it rose above arctic temperatures, it was always a welcome retreat from whatever shit the city had thrown at you. He'd sleep in the living room by the fire tonight, but first he needed a wash and a change of clothes. And something to eat.

'I hope you don't mind me saying,' said Duncan, handing over a pint to a freshly cleansed Paul, 'but you don't look too good. Is something bothering you?'

'Trouble in the city,' said Paul, gulping down his beer.

'Aye, trouble magnets, those cities.' Duncan grinned. 'But if ye need tae share, I'm no going anywhere.'

'It's just some idiot giving me grief,' said Paul.

Duncan noticed the way Paul's hand shook as he picked up his pint. 'It's not like you to let arseholes ruin your day.'

'There are arseholes,' said Paul, 'and then there is *this* arsehole.'

Duncan nodded. 'Ah, King Arsehole. El presidente de bawbags. That kind of arsehole can be very trying indeed.' He wiped imaginary dust off the bar with a cloth.

'I just needed to get away and think it through.'

'Well, if it's thinking you're after,' said Duncan, 'you've come to the right place. There's bugger all else to do here, unless you're into sheep.' He threw Paul a wink. 'The key is to never give in to the arseholes. If you roll over, arseholes like whoever these arseholes are that are bothering you, will never stop doing their arsehole things, because that's what arseholes do.'

'Never a truer word.' Paul laughed. 'And may I say, a very elegant and liberal use of the word "arsehole". Cheers.' He raised his glass.

Paul ordered fish and chips and found a table in the corner, by the fire. George and his dog had gone, and the bar was deserted, allowing Paul to enjoy his meal in peace. He definitely felt a lot calmer about the threats and the attack now, although that may have had something to do with the three pints he'd just downed. He'd been through a nightmare, no question, but hopefully if Richard pulled the videos from the web then that would be an end to it.

In some ways, Richard's demented obsession with fame and fortune had caused Paul even greater anxiety than the stalking and the break-in, so there was a relief to be had in being rid of him for a while. They had been sharing each other's space for too long, and perhaps the events of the past few weeks would prove the catalyst Paul needed to make some big changes to his life. Finishing his pint, he bid Duncan goodnight and trudged back to the caravan.

In the morning, Paul headed out of the village and up the forestry road towards Gilpen Point. It was a long walk up a steep and winding hill, but it was worth it for the spectacular views and the space to breathe and think. Over the years, the cliff tops had helped Paul solve all sorts of problems in his life, from breakups and bad decisions to lost opportunities and the endless stream of rejection letters. They were literally his rock, his reliable old friend, and he was in dire need of one of those right now.

Climbing over the worn stile at the bottom of the path, he made his way slowly up the hill, going over everything that had happened to him and Richard since they'd started their project. He sieved through the details in his mind, trying to work out who might have it in for them. Continuing on, the path became steeper and narrower. The clean, crisp, autumnal air flowed into his lungs, and he felt more alive and relevant than he had in months. The higher he climbed, the stronger he felt. Whoever was behind both the threats and the burglary was trying to scare them off and force them to stop. But why? Maybe Richard was right, and it was a jealous enemy of his who'd taken things too far. He climbed higher, and Paul's resolve hardened.

Duncan's right, he thought. *I shouldn't be running away. When did I become so fucking timid?*

At the top, Paul found a flat slab of rock that pushed out over the glistening loch far below and plonked himself down on it, dangling his legs over the side, like he'd done so many times before. The visibility was unusually good, and he could see all the way up the length of the loch, past the village, and out to the firth beyond. To his left, the snow-tipped mountain range extended upwards like a great sleeping beast, gathering its strength for future battle. He took a long, deep breath and roared into the wind.

'Fuck off!'

A seagull swooped down and wailed as though agreeing with the sentiment. Paul smiled and lay back on the rock, and as he stared into the emptiness above, his crushed personality sprang back to shape and reformed.

'I'm not going to just roll over and take this shit from a troll like you,' he said, kicking his feet against the side of the outcrop. 'Threaten me again and I'll fucking end *you,* you tosser.' He leaned out over the edge. 'Wanker!' he bellowed, his defiance resounding across the estuary.

He was furious. Furious that someone could back him into a corner and force him to run away. He sat up. *No,* he thought. *I'm not going to let the cunt get away with this.* He stood. *Why should we give it all up for this creep? No fucking way.*

He lifted a rock and lobbed it over the side of the cliff, sending it on its way with a hoarse 'Ba-a-a-asta-a-a-ard!' and watching it smack the surface of the loch before sinking. With renewed vigour, he set off back down the path to the village. He wasn't going to run anymore. He'd return to Glasgow and track down the bastard or bastards threatening him. Make them pay.

That evening, at the hotel, Paul checked his phone. He had two texts, one from Richard – 'I'm going in, wish me luck' – and one from a private number. Paul opened it up. 'Last chance to save your skin,' it said. 'Wipe your files now.'

Paul's rage returned. The stalker had his mobile number now, confirming what Paul had known all along: that this wasn't about Richard's past coming back to bite him. It was far more serious. Paul downed his pint and told Duncan he was heading back to Glasgow first thing. He had some unfinished business to take care of.

'That's more like it, Don Corleone.' Duncan grinned. 'Don't forget to batten down the hatches tonight, though. It's going to be a bit wild. Hopefully, we'll all still be here by the morning.'

Back at the caravan, Paul did a quick tidy-round and gathered up his stuff. He had an early start in the morning and needed to sleep. The wind was already picking up, rattling the windowsills and doorframe, getting louder by the minute. It didn't seem to Paul as though it would die down anytime soon. *Shit.* He grabbed his jacket.

Outside, he shone his torch beneath the caravan. It looked secure enough, but who knew how strong this wind would get? Once again, movement on the far side of the park caught his attention. There was a figure shifting in and out of the shadows.

Paul shouted into the wind. 'Hello?'

The figure disappeared into the trees. Paul followed the path down to the edge of the forest and peered into the black. He was about to venture further when a young doe suddenly burst from the undergrowth and careered past him. Paul yelled and almost lost his footing.

'Fuck's sake!' he roared. When he'd calmed down, he returned to the caravan and a warm bed.

A loud thump startled Paul awake. The lamp had gone out, and the room was pitch-black. Outside, the wind sent thin shrieks through the caravan's ageing sides. Another thump, louder this time, had Paul jumping up and fumbling for his trousers. It was coming from the back bedroom. Scrambling in the dark, he rummaged under the sink for the torch. *Fuck.* He must have left it outside. He gave up and edged towards the bedroom. Through the half-opened door, he watched a figure shake the window frame from outside, trying to force it open. *Not again!* Paul ducked down and retreated to the living room in search of a weapon. A flash of lightning and a deafening crack of thunder rocked the caravan sideways, taking Paul with it. He steadied himself, grabbed a broom handle, and inched back towards the bedroom. The window flew open, and a body plunged through the flapping curtains. Paul raised the broom, poised to strike.

'Wait!' a muffled voice cried.

But it was too late. Paul brought the handle down on the back of the intruder's head. His body slumped forward, half in and half out of the window. When he groaned and tried to get up, Paul raised the handle again, a second strike imminent.

'Paul!' the intruder moaned. 'Don't! It's me!' Staring wide-eyed up at Paul from the confines of a zipped-up hoodie was his terrified best friend.

Paul lowered his weapon. 'Fucking hell, Richard! What the fuck are you doing?'

'Help me in,' said Richard.

Still stunned, Paul dragged him through the window and onto the floor, where he lay slumped like a half-drowned rat.

'What the fuck, Richard?' said Paul, battling with the window. *SLAM!* 'I mean, seriously!'

Richard rubbed the back of his head. 'You could have fucking killed me.'

'You stupid bastard. What were you doing?'

'I was trying to get in.'

'There's a fucking door. That you knock on.'

'I tried the door, but–' He winced. A searing pain shot through his head. 'Christ, it's hellish out there. I thought I was going to die.'

The power came back on with a *click*, and the caravan lit up. Richard's condition genuinely shocked Paul. He looked to be in the early stages of hypothermia.

'You need to get warm,' said Paul. 'Come on.' Helping his friend to his feet, he guided him over to the fire. 'How did you know I was here?'

'It's where you always go when you're in trouble,' said Richard. 'I got worried when I couldn't reach you. I wanted to tell you how I got on yesterday.'

'It's the middle of the fucking night,' said Paul, crossing to the sink and filling the kettle from the tap.

'I wasn't expecting a bloody hurricane. The taxi driver had to change route about three times just to get round fallen trees.' He glanced up. You got anything stronger than coffee?'

Thirty seconds later, and Richard was sipping brandy from a chipped East 17 mug.

'I need to tell you what happened,' he said between shivers.

'Before you do,' interrupted Paul, 'I want to say I've been thinking about everything that's happened lately. Why should we pull the plug? Who are they to tell us what to do? This is our one chance at success. We should fight back. Bring the fuckers down.'

Richard raised his eyebrows. 'Them's fighting words.' He nodded at the brandy bottle.

Paul took the hint and topped up his friend's glass.

'What made you change your mind?' asked Richard.

'I'm just tired of being a victim and a coward,' said Paul. 'You know, running away from opportunities.'

'Okay,' said Richard. 'I get that. So what now?'

'Well, now you tell me about the interview. How did it go?'

'It was strange, to say the least.' Richard paused to take a large gulp.

He looked edgy, but Paul put it down to having been lamped with a broom handle.

'I met Alice,' Richard continued, 'and she introduced me to all the bigwigs at Omni. Eight of them. They all just sat there staring at me, waiting to be entertained. So … I went all in. Proper hardcore. Oscar-winning, it was. And at the end of it they were still sitting there, staring at me. Alice thanked them, we left, and she took me for a coffee. I thought it was game over, but apparently, silence is a good thing, and they always play it cool when they love something.'

Paul nodded. 'That sounds promising.'

Richard took another gulp of brandy and winced as it hit the back of his throat. 'It'll still be a month or so before we get any kind of official word back, but it's all good.'

'Well, that settles it,' said Paul. 'We can't give up.'

'There's still the chance they'll say no,' cautioned Richard. 'Alice says nothing's certain with these guys.'

'Understandable,' said Paul. 'Have you pulled the video yet?'

'No,' said Richard, 'but I still can if you want me to.'

A grin crawled over Paul's lips. 'No. Fucking leave it up. We need to let these bastards know we're going nowhere.'

'You sure you're up for this?' asked Richard. 'I mean, you were bloody shitting Lego a couple of days ago. I've never seen you so agitated.'

'Attack is the best form of defence,' said Paul. 'Always. I realise that now. I didn't before.' He refilled both their glasses. 'So tomorrow, we go back to Glasgow and we start digging. We'll track these bastards down, Richard. Don't you worry about that.'

'And if they come at us again, and it gets worse? Are you prepared for that?'

Paul raised his glass defiantly. 'Bring it on. I'm done running.' He clinked his glass against Richard's. 'Let the fight back begin.'

SCRIPT EDIT 12 - THE BALLROOM SCENE

FADE IN:

INT. BALLROOM - NIGHT

A lavish party is in full swing. On a raised stage, an effortlessly cool JAZZ BAND TINKLES and PARPS its way through timeless classics, as black-tied and be-frocked GLITTERATI mingle beneath a huge, sparkling chandelier.

Harvey enters, his tight suit the wrong size and the wrong price. He is nervous, feels out of place. He snatches a glass of champagne from off a WAITER'S tray and weaves through the throng, eliciting disapproving looks.

ANNE MAXTON - middle-aged, overly made up, and heavily Botoxed - approaches. She somehow manages to raise an eyebrow.

ANNE

And who have we here?

Harvey glances over his shoulder, instinctively looking for a way out. There isn't one. *Fuck.*

HARVEY

(extending a hand)

Harvey. Mr Ballatine's new assistant.

ANNE

Oh. I thought you seemed a little wide-eyed and innocent. I'm Anne.

Anne takes Harvey's hand but doesn't shake it.

ANNE (CONT'D)

It's a pleasure to meet you, Harvey. So … are you going to be a good boy or a bad boy?

Harvey, aware that Anne still has his hand, prises it back.

HARVEY

Sorry?

ANNE

Oh, come, come. You know what I mean. There are good boys, there are bad boys, and there are very bad boys. Which one are you?

Despite his nervousness, Harvey manages a smile.

HARVEY

What do you do, Anne?

ANNE

Oh, change the subject, why don't you? Okay, I'll play along. What do I do? Well, let's just say I take care of things and people that need taking care of. Do you need taking care of, Harvey?

Anne touches Harvey's hand. He pushes it away.

HARVEY

Please excuse me.

Harvey shoves past Anne brusquely, and she pouts.

ANNE

Bye, Harvey.

Anne suddenly smiles, turns, and joins another GROUP.

ANNE (CONT'D)

Well hello, Bob. Surviving those alimony payments?

Harvey stops the waiter from earlier.

HARVEY

Where are the toilets?

INT. LARGE OSTENTATIOUS BATHROOM - NIGHT

Harvey stares at his reflection in the mirror above the sink. He INHALES deeply. Runs the tap. Washes his hands.

Two tuxedo-wearing EXECUTIVE TYPES BURST into the bathroom, TALKING and LAUGHING. EXEC 1, flush-faced and sweating, produces a packet of white powder and sprinkles a small pile onto the black marble surface of the sink.

Using a credit card, Exec 1 cuts the powder into two lines.

EXEC 2 rolls up a $100 bill and SNORTS his line. Wiping the residue from his nose, he ROARS with delight.

Exec 1 takes the rolled-up bill and leans over. About to snort, he stops. Turns to Harvey. Offers him the bill.

EXEC 1

Care to indulge?

HARVEY

I'm fine, thanks.

EXEC 1

All the more for me then!

Exec 2 LAUGHS MANIACALLY and rubs again at his nose. Exec 1 SNORTS his line.

The cubicle door behind them OPENS, and a dishevelled, DRUNKEN COUPLE appear. He's tucking in his shirt. She's wiping her mouth.

EXEC 1 (CONT'D)

So that's where you got to.

DRUNKEN FEMALE

We had some unfinished business to attend to.

DRUNKEN MALE

A healthy exchange of ideas. And bodily fluids.

Everyone LAUGHS. Harvey takes the opportunity to leave. At the door, he turns and watches as the drunken female bends over the sink and SNORTS a line. Exec 1, grinning, presses himself up against her rear.

INT. BALLROOM - NIGHT

An ever-more anxious Harvey steps back into the fray.

The jazz band stops playing. Ballatine is up on stage, grappling with the microphone.

BALLATINE

How do I …?

The saxophonist comes over and frees the mic from its stand.

BALLATINE (CONT'D)

Ladies and gentlemen!

A loud SQUEAL of feedback. The saxophonist adjusts the mic.

BALLATINE (CONT'D)

If I could have your attention, please!

Guest CHATTER continues. Ballatine turns and nods to the drummer, who responds with a *RAT-A-TAT-TAT* on the snare.

The CHATTER dies away. Ballatine pushes out his chest.

BALLATINE (CONT'D)

I'd like to thank you all for coming tonight.

GIGGLING and LAUGHING, the group from the toilet stumble back into the room, where they're immediately SHUSHED.

Despite the apparent calm, Ballatine has clearly been annoyed by the group's disruption.

BALLATINE (CONT'D)

Where was I? Yes. It gives me great pleasure to announce that NLightN Industries' annual net profits for the year ending in May have soared to sixty-two million dollars.

LOUD CHEERS.

BALLATINE (CONT'D)

This represents an increase of twelve-point-three percent on the previous year, and a 485 percent increase since I became CEO five years ago.

More CHEERS.

BALLATINE (CONT'D)

In the past twelve months, we've secured eighteen major contracts with governments and organisations across twelve countries. We've become a world leader in cutting-edge data analytics, overtaking all our rivals. We're now working with at least four intelligence agencies on vital security software projects. In other words, we - NlightN Industries Incorporated - are the masters of the fucking universe!

ROARS of approval.

BALLATINE (CONT'D)

Our success, all of this, is down to you. Your brains, your sweat, your work ethic, your dedication, all the hard, painful sacrifices you made to get us here. Believe me, I know there have been many long days and nights along the way and many neglected loved ones, wives, husbands, and children.

Ballatine's comments elicit nods from his audience.

BALLATINE (CONT'D)

But here's the payoff. We dream big. Again and again we surpass impossible targets we set ourselves. We have triumphed in battle and we have slaughtered our enemies. We are invincible!

More CHEERING.

BALLATINE (CONT'D)

Victorious!

The CHEERING intensifies.

BALLATINE (CONT'D)

Triumphant!

ROARS, WHOOPS, and CLAPPING. Ballatine nods proudly and LAUGHS, waiting for the applause to die down, which it does.

BALLATINE (CONT'D)

So … with that in mind, I've instructed my finance director … where are you, Bleekes?

The gaunt, skeletal BLEEKES, standing close to Harvey, raises a bony hand.

BALLATINE (CONT'D)

(shading his eyes)

There he is! Blink and you'd miss him.

Ballatine's statement incites a ruckus of LAUGHTER. Not from Bleekes, though, who looks far from amused.

BALLATINE (CONT'D)

I have instructed Mr Bleekes to issue all employees with a twenty percent bonus, to be added to this month's salary …

The CHEERING and HOLLERING is now off the scale.

BALLATINE (CONT'D)

… including yours, Mr Bleekes.

More LAUGHTER. Bleekes, however, remains corpse-like.

BALLATINE (CONT'D)

So … here's to victory!

Ballatine raises his glass to the ceiling.

CROWD

(together)

To victory!

Ballatine steps off the stage. The band RESUMES PLAYING.

Ballatine ignores the employees who surround him, eager to shake his hand. He's looking for Harvey. Then … he sees him.

BALLATINE

Harvey!

Harvey turns. Makes his way over to his new boss.

BALLATINE (CONT'D)

Glad you could make it.

HARVEY

Thanks for the invite. Good speech.

BALLATINE

Hollywood bullshit. It never fails.

Ballatine becomes aware of the confident, power-dressed young woman - Sarah McConnell, the late Martin Jameson's former secretary - standing next to them.

BALLATINE (CONT'D)

Harvey … this is Sarah McConnell.

Harvey and Sarah smile and shake hands.

BALLATINE (CONT'D)

Sarah is our media and communications director. She's the eyes, ears, and voice of our organisation. She knows more about us, and about me, than even I do, so be careful what you say.

(leaning in and whispering)

She's probably wearing a wire.

Harvey LAUGHS. Sarah just shakes her head.

BALLATINE (CONT'D)

You'll be working together over the coming months. Sarah is your mentor. Your guru. I suggest you get to know one another.

Ballatine slips diplomatically away, leaving Harvey and Sarah to their awkward silence.

HARVEY

So … nice party. Have you tried the - ?

SARAH

Let's get something straight. You work *for* me, not with me. I tell you what to do, and you do it. I say jump, you jump. Understand?

HARVEY

Sure. No problem.

Harvey sips his champagne. Looks at Sarah closely.

HARVEY (CONT'D)

May I ask a question? Or do I have to request an extraordinary meeting?

SARAH

Is that supposed to be funny?

HARVEY

I thought it was.

SARAH

It wasn't. What's the question?

HARVEY

Who's Anna?

Sarah LAUGHS and shakes her head.

SARAH

Oh my, she's a fast worker. I take it she's invited you to play tennis at her club?

HARVEY

No, she didn't mention tennis.

SARAH

Then she must really like you. Oh boy, you *are* in trouble.

HARVEY

What does she do? Aside from seduce new employees.

Sarah checks her watch, her social graces exhausted.

SARAH

That's more than one question. I'll see you at seven-thirty a.m., my office, tomorrow. Don't be late. And don't drink too much.

Sarah walks abruptly away. She glances back briefly.

Harvey grabs a glass from a passing WAITER'S tray and raises it to Sarah, smiling.

Ballatine returns.

BALLATINE

Impressive, isn't she?

Harvey nods, still watching Sarah's departing rear.

BALLATINE (CONT'D)

If you want to get on, keep in with her.

HARVEY

I intend to.

BALLATINE

But watch her. She'll burn you alive.

Ballatine raises his own glass.

BALLATINE (CONT'D)

Cheers!

Ballatine and Harvey CLINK glasses.

FADE OUT:

11

Once safely back in Glasgow, Paul set to work. First on his suspects list: the mysterious Alice Lowe. Her enthusiasm for their project was a little too good to be true, and something about her just didn't square with the goody-goody image she was trying to project. There was no use confiding his suspicions in Richard; he'd only brush them off as irrelevant at best and dangerous at worst. Richard had no time for anything that threatened to jeopardise their future success.

Paul fired an email off to Alice, suggesting they meet. Then he headed to the library. He could work from there on a non-traceable computer. *Christ,* he thought, as he clicked into the anonymous PC's search bar, *I'm living in a fucking John le Carré novel.*

Omni's homepage listed two office addresses: Glasgow and London. London was clearly the administrative office. Glasgow? Well, he'd check that out later. For now, he was more interested in Alice's bio. It mostly covered what Paul already knew: her hiring by the London office three years earlier, her two successive promotions in the same year, and her current position of Head of Acquisitions in Glasgow. Nothing new there. But to his surprise, her profile image was now present on the page: a stark and unflattering shot, taken from a low angle, presumably to give her a sense of importance.

Zooming in, Paul noticed something odd. There was a slight blurring around her head, as though the image had been tampered with. Above her head, on the wall behind her, a small section was pixelated. Paul enlarged the image to max, but the distortion increased, and he couldn't make anything out. He leaned in closer and squinted. There seemed to be some kind of plaque or display in the middle of the distortion. Paul readjusted the screen and squinted again, but it was still too fuzzy. He jumped at a sudden tap on his shoulder.

An elderly man, rain dripping from the rim of his trilby and soaking Paul's trouser leg, nodded at the screen.

'If yer no planning on marryin' that lassie,' he said gruffly, 'then I'd suggest you gie somebody else a go.'

'Sorry,' said Paul, moving his leg away and brushing off a small pool of water, 'I was just–'

'Aye. I know exactly whit you were just,' the man sneered.

'No, no,' Paul laughed. 'I'll let you on, no bother. Just let me log out.'

'Am no sure ah want tae pit ma hons onywhere near it efter you've been droolin o'er it,' spat the man and wandered off to the large-print section over by the issue desk.

What the hell was all that about? Paul shook his head and turned back to the screen. He tried interrogating the image again but felt too self-conscious. He logged off and headed back to the flat.

Alice's reply came the following morning. She was happy to meet up. Paul suggested they get together at her office – he wanted a closer look around the mysterious Omni Productions – but Alice preferred the pub they'd met in previously. Paul agreed, albeit reluctantly. He told Richard he was going to the library to do some more anonymous online searches. No point worrying him unnecessarily.

Paul was surprised to find Alice at the same table as before. This time, however, was different. She'd clearly been crying.

'Hello?' Paul felt awkward and slightly uncomfortable, as though intruding in some way.

Alice wiped her face with the back of her hand. 'I'm sorry. 'I've just had some sad news.'

Paul sat opposite. 'We can cancel, if you like.'

'No,' said Alice. 'It's fine. It's just a family bereavement.'

'I'm so sorry,' said Paul.

'Thank you.' Alice looked at her hands. 'It's quite a close family member actually.'

Paul leaned in. 'Seriously, we can cancel. It's no bother.'

Alice smiled. 'You are kind. But I need a distraction right now. And a brandy.'

Paul watched her from the bar, searching her behaviour for a crack in her defences. All he saw was a young woman, vulnerable and lost. Could that really be all she was?

'Sorry you had to see that,' said Alice as Paul handed her the glass.

'Not at all.'

'Why did you want to meet?' asked Alice.

Paul sat and sipped his pint. 'I wanted to fill you in on some developments.'

'Where's your partner?'

'He's busy tonight. He sends his regards.'

Alice nodded, her eyes fixed on Paul, waiting.

'I needed to get something off my chest,' said Paul. 'About *Agency O*.'

'Okay.'

'The thing is …' Paul hesitated and took another drink. *Dutch courage.* 'The thing is, Tor Fleck didn't write our script. We did.'

'Go on.' Alice didn't flinch or even break eye contact.

'Tor Fleck,' said Paul, 'doesn't exist. He's a fiction. A figment of our imagination. We invented him to make our project seem more mysterious. Or glamorous, take your pick.'

'So the work is all yours?'

Paul nodded. 'Richard came up with the original idea, we developed it together, and then I wrote it.'

Alice sipped her brandy. 'What about the murder? And the will?'

'All made up.'

'Interesting.'

'I'm sorry we lied to you, Alice,' said Paul. 'I couldn't go on with it.'

'Does Richard know you're telling me this?'

'No, not yet. I just wanted to be honest with you.'

'I appreciate that,' said Alice. 'I mean it.'

'There's more.'

'Oh?'

'Over the past couple of months,' said Paul, 'we've been receiving some threats.'

'What kind of threats?'

'It started off just comments on our videos, threatening all sorts if we didn't remove them. Then it was emails. And then last week we had a break-in, and I was attacked.'

'Oh my God!'

'Just after that we got another email threatening that worse was to come.' Paul examined Alice closely, looking for anything that might give her away.

'That's terrible,' said Alice. 'You must be really shaken.'

'I was at first. But the thing is, I think I know who's behind it.' It was a blatant lie, but Paul wanted to see how Alice would react.

'Who do you think it is?' asked Alice, her face a mask of concern.

'I'm not going to say anything until I'm sure,' lied Paul again.

'That's so upsetting,' said Alice. 'Why would anyone do these things? And for what?'

'Jealousy, maybe? Whatever it is, they want us to stop this project.'

'Have you been to the police?'

'Not yet, no.' Paul shrugged. 'We don't really have what they'd consider hard evidence.'

Alice reached out and took Paul's hand. 'Are you okay?'

To Paul, her voice was like honey dripping off a soft pillow.

'Bearing up,' said Paul. He let her rest her hand on his. 'It'll be all over in a couple of days anyway.' Again, he tried to find a flicker of deceit in Alice, but all he saw was genuine concern. *If she's lying,* he thought, *she's good. She's very good.*

Alice slid her hand off Paul's and smiled. 'How about another drink?'

Two hours, and four drinks, later they were out on the street, shoulder to shoulder for warmth. Their conversation had veered into more personal territory, and Alice had opened up about her sudden bereavement, the death of an ex-boyfriend. It felt natural for Paul to comfort her, holding and stroking her hand. Alcohol had lowered his defences quite significantly, and he was now pretty sure Alice had nothing to do with the threats. Whispers of paranoia, however, still fluttered around him.

'Do you have your driver?' he asked, buttoning up his coat.

Alice shook her head and did his top button for him. Leaning in, she kissed him gently, taking him by surprise. He pulled her in close, and for a moment, she let him.

'Coffee at mine?' She whispered.

Paul hesitated, his head reeling. 'Are you sure that's a good idea? I mean, with everything that's going on?'

'I could do with some company.' Alice smiled.

Paul sensed the urgency in her and looked around for a taxi.

He woke with a start, a door slamming somewhere distant. The bedroom was unfamiliar, the bed a little less so. He couldn't remember much of the night before. A couple more drinks, his hands all over her body, and then nothing.

What the fuck were you thinking? Like that's going to make things less complicated.

He pushed himself up and scanned the room. It was all soft palette whites and greys, with a forgiving blind over a large bay window saving his head from the glare of the morning. His clothes were strewn all over the wood-panelled floor. When the carousel in his head had stopped spinning, he picked up his trousers and got dressed, shuffling from the bedroom into a wide hallway. There were three doors ahead of him. The first revealed itself as a bathroom. Inside, he splashed cold water on his face, avoiding eye contact with the hungover idiot in the mirror. Down the hall was a second bedroom, full of boxes and clothes. The third door led into a modest open-plan living room and kitchen. There was a pink Post-it lying on the kitchen island.

Gone to work, help yourself to coffee and breakfast.

Alice x

Paul let out a sigh of relief. He wasn't sure if he'd made a mistake last night, partly because he couldn't remember exactly what had happened. Had she manipulated him, or was it the other way round? The complexities of the situation hurt his head.

Alice had laid out bread and jam, a box of cereal, and some ibuprofen. Paul poured himself a coffee from the still-steaming pot and walked with it around the room. Considering her occupation, Alice's tastes were surprisingly modest: modernist prints, the odd coffee-table book, and a wide variety of ornaments, mainly Eastern. Wandering back through the hall, Paul peered into the small office. A desk by the window housed a pile of papers. Above it was a shelf filled with box files marked *Omni – in production, Omni – post-production,* et cetera.

Paul glanced quickly back at the front door before stepping into the room. He picked one of the papers up from the desk and skimmed its contents: it was a thank-you letter from some catering company. Then he noticed another pink Post-it, stuck to the desktop PC. He leaned in to try and decipher the tiny, scribbled words. *Tor-izon?*

A noise outside the room. He set the letter down and headed back out into the hall. A loud clattering then led him into the kitchen.

'Good morning!' he said cheerily, expecting to see Alice.

Instead, there was just a cat, up on the work surface, licking its way through the butter. When it saw Paul, it hissed and jumped down, running past him and disappearing beneath the coffee table.

Time to go. Paul gathered up his things and was about to head off when his phone pinged. It was a text from a private number, listing his parents' names, with an attachment. Paul's heart stopped. Shaking, he clicked on the jpeg. It was a photo of his parents' house, taken from their front gate. His phone pinged again. Paul almost dropped the handset in fright. He fumbled frantically with the buttons and clicked the message.

With love from Tor x

'Evil bastards!' roared Paul. He quickly dialled his parents' number, then hung up.

His father was a retired squaddie, and the last thing Paul wanted was to get him riled. Years ago, George Grant had stopped a burglar from making off with their telly by fracturing his skill with a baseball bat, snapping the bat clean in two in the process.

They've definitely picked the wrong guy to mess with, Paul reassured himself. But he needed to be sure they were both safe, especially his long-suffering mum, who'd had to put up with the best part of a lifetime of her husband's off-the-scale shenanigans. Grabbing his coat, Paul slammed the door behind him and hurried off to the station.

12

Paul's mum and dad lived out in the sticks, just beyond the city boundary. It took him the best part of an hour and three buses to get there. Approaching their bungalow, he noticed all the lights were on, as usual. He automatically searched his pocket for his key before remembering he'd lost it walking the West Highland Way a couple of years ago. He knocked on the door. No answer. He thumped on it hard.

'Mum? Dad?' he cried. Still no answer.

Paul ducked round the side of the house to the back door. It was wide open.

'Fuck!' he shouted, running in.

Apart from a potful of potatoes boiling away on the stove, the kitchen was deserted. Paul was about to check the living room when he was grabbed roughly from behind.

'Boo!' the assailant cried.

Paul spun round.

'Dad!' yelled Paul. 'What the fuck?'

George Grant stuck his hands on his jeaned hips, looking childishly pleased with himself.

'You scared the shit out of me,' said Paul. 'What are you doing?'

'I was oot the back,' said George, 'havin' a quick puff.' He leaned forward conspiratorially. 'Don't tell yer mithir.'

'Where is Mum?'

'She's havin' a wee lie doon,' said George. 'We're no the party animals we once were, son.'

'Aye, righto,' said Paul. 'I'm sure you could give most clubbers a run for their money.'

George rubbed at his stubby, broken nose. 'So … where's yer washin'?'

Paul raised his eyebrows. 'I'm thirty-two, Dad. I have a washing machine.'

'Then a wee loan, maybe?'

'No!' Paul shoved his dad playfully in the chest. 'You make me sound like a scrounging bastard.'

'And?' George laughed, rolling back on the balls of his feet.

'I just thought I hadn't been over in a while, and what with all these burglaries …'

'You can't kid a bullshitter, son,' said George, 'so don't even try. Whit's the matter?'

A small figure in a crocheted wrap shuffled into the kitchen. 'Who was that at the door, George?' she asked. The sight of her son woke her up instantly, and she grinned. 'Oh, well, well, look who it is.' She threw her arms out. 'Come and give your wee mammy a hug, or are you too big for all that now?'

'Never too big for a hug, Mum,' said Paul. He wrapped his arms around her and giving her a long, affectionate squeeze.

'Paul's got a big bag a washin' for ye, Jean.'

'Oh, that's good. I was just about to put a load on.'

'Dad!' shouted Paul. 'Don't listen to him, Mum. I'm here to make sure you're both okay.'

'Oh aye,' said Jean. 'And why would we no be? Did you think we'd both popped our clogs?'

'A suicide pact, Jean,' quipped George. 'That's whit we agreed, remember? An you're takin' your pill first.'

'Och, George!' Jean laughed. 'Yer father's an awful man, Paul. Do ye no think?'

'Open wide,' said George. He grabbed his wife, pretended to shove a pill into her mouth, then kissed her on the cheek.

'Hands like bloody shovels,' said Jean, pushing him away. 'Anyway, son, ignore him. Have you had yer tea? Yer probably starvin'.'

'He's always starvin', Jean,' said George. 'He's a human hoover.'

'I'm okay, Mum,' said Paul. 'But thanks anyway.'

Jean placed a palm on her son's cheek. 'Yer lookin' a bit peely-wally. Ye need to come back more and I'll feed ye up.'

'Don't fuss, Mum,' said Paul. 'I'm fine. A cup of tea would be nice, though.'

'A cup of tea coming up,' said Jean.

Paul went through to the living room and slumped down on the sofa. George followed him.

'So whit's aw this nonsense about break-ins?' George asked quietly so Paul's mother couldn't hear.

'It was in the *Record*,' said Paul. 'Apparently, this area's been targeted. You need to be careful.'

'I didnae see that,' said George. 'When was it in the paper?'

'A few days ago. And it was on *Reporting Scotland*.'

George rubbed at his nose again. 'Well, we huvnae heard anything. An' the neighbours huvnae mentioned it either, an' they'd use ony excuse tae come roon an' drink me dry.'

'You need to make sure you're safe, Dad. You know, check your home security's sound.'

'Get you, home security. Don't you worry about that,' said George. 'I've got all the security I need.' He held up his fists and took a playful swing at Paul, narrowly missing his face.

'Dad!'

'Are ye forgettin' I was the Springburn boxing champion five years on the trot?'

'But you're not now,' said Paul with a scowl.

'I also have backup,' said George. He pushed himself off the sofa with a groan and gestured for Paul to follow him upstairs. In the bedroom, he rummaged in the wardrobe before emerging with an ominous-looking long black case.

'Are we going fishing?' quipped Paul.

George lay the case down on the bed and, with a quick squint at the door, flipped the lid. 'Ye mess wi me, ye mess wi this cunt,' he said, removing a twelve-bore shotgun.

'Jesus Christ, Dad,' said Paul. 'What the fuck is that?'

'It's a fully functioning antique shotgun. Gorgeous, isn't she?' He turned it over to inspect it.

'I can see what it is,' said Paul. 'I meant what the fuck are you doing with it?'

'I got it from an old pal. He thought I might want tae update ma 'home security'.'

'Fucking hell,' said Paul. 'Is it loaded?'

'Of course not.' George opened a flap in the case and removed a cartridge. 'The shells are–'

'Don't load it!' yelled Paul. 'Jesus.'

George uncocked the barrel.

'Dad, I mean it!' Paul said.

'Spoilsport,' said George, snapping the gun shut.

'Put it away,' pleaded Paul. 'It's making me nervous.'

Jean shouted up from downstairs. 'Tea's ready!'

George replaced the gun and returned the case to the wardrobe, covering it with an old blanket. He looked over at Paul, his expression serious for once. 'Don't tell yer mither.'

Back downstairs, Jean handed Paul a plate with enough biscuits on it to induce a diabetic coma.

'I've put a couple of Jaffa Cakes on there for you, son,' she said with a wink.

'Thanks, Mum. That's plenty.'

When Jean returned to the kitchen, Paul turned to George.

'I'm being trolled, Dad.'

'Trolled?' asked George. 'What the fuck is that?'

'I've been getting these texts and emails, you know, threatening messages.'

'Who's dein' that?'

'I don't know. It started a few weeks ago. I wrote a film script and put it online, and somebody's taken the hump with it.'

'Ah didnae know ye'd started writin' films,' said George. 'Christ, that'd be something, eh? Turnin' up at yon Oscars.'

The thought of his dad hassling A-listers on the red carpet had Paul smiling despite himself. But this was no time for levity. He looked his dad in the eye. 'Then Richard got attacked.'

'Whit? Jesus. Is he all right?'

'He was a bit shaken up,' said Paul, 'but basically he's okay.'

'So whit happened?'

'Somebody jumped him in the street. Then we got a follow-up text. Here, I'll show you.' Paul got his phone out, found the text chain, and handed it over. 'You've got it upside down, Dad,' he said and flipped the phone the right way round.

'Och, Jesus,' said George. 'I canny be dein' wae this shite. How dae ye–?' He peered at the screen.

'Use your finger to move the – oh, never mind, give me it.' Paul snatched the phone back and read the texts out one by one, checking over his shoulder to make sure his mother wasn't nearby.

'Whit sick heid-the-baw wid dae this?' asked George, unable to conceal his fury.

'You can see why I came over,' said Paul. 'I thought you needed to know.'

George turned his anger onto Paul. 'Exactly whit the fuck huv ye been dein'?'

'I told you,' said Paul. 'I wrote a film script. Just a crappy thriller. A load of bollocks, really.'

'An' are ye gonny dae as they say an' remove it?' asked George. 'Destroy the incriminating evidence?' He cracked a smiled. 'Christ, it's like an episode o' *Line o' Duty*.'

Paul looked a little sheepish. 'Well, things are escalating … an' I wouldn't want you two to–'

'Stop right there,' interrupted George. 'There's nae way yer dein' whit they say. If this thing ye've written is windin' folk up, then ye must be dein' somethin' right. Ye need tae tell them tae fuck right off, in nae uncertain terms.'

'I'm worried that they might come after you,' said Paul.

'Do I look worried?' asked George with a shrug. 'I fought in the fucking Falklands. These wee cowardly shites don't frighten me.'

'But what about Mum? She'd be terrified if she found out.'

'She's been living wae me fur over forty years, son. She's seen plenty, let me tell you. She's harder than she puts on. I'm a pussycat compared to her when she gets goin'. An' whit ye huv tae understand, son …' George's eyes took on a steeliness Paul couldn't recall seeing before. '… is that these cunts are gettin' aff on scarin the shite oot o' ye. Ye need to take charge, show them yer a fuckin Grant, an' that Grants are no threatened withoot consequences. An anyway,' he sneered, 'I've got Little Nellie upstairs waitin' tae unleash fuckin' hell if they care tae try me.'

'Whit are you two jabberin' aboot?' asked Jean, entering the room. 'On second thoughts, don't answer that. Whit happens in Balloch, stays in Balloch.' She wiped her hands on a floral apron. 'I've put some mince on fur ye, son. Ye'll be stayin' fur yer tea?'

With the local bus situation, staying for tea meant staying over, and Paul hadn't thought that far ahead. 'I haven't brought any clothes or a toothbrush or anything.'

'Acht, ye can borrow something from yer father's wardrobe,' said Jean. 'I'll go have a wee look.' She turned to the door.

'NO!' shouted Paul and his father in unison.

Jean halted.

'It's okay, Mum,' said Paul, 'I'm used to wearing clothes two days on the trot.'

'You bloody students.' Jean shook her head. What are you like?'

'I left uni six years ago, Mum.'

'Aye, righto,' said Jean with a knowing smile. 'I'll just go make up yer bed.'

'I can do that,' said Paul.

'I know,' said Jean, 'but I like looking after you. I don't get to do it that often anymore.' She yanked his head down to her height and kissed his forehead.

'Mum,' said Paul, pulling back.

'You're still my wee laddie.' Jean smiled and headed for the stairs.

'An' yer ma wee laddie an' aw.' George grinned. He grabbed Paul's cheek and squeezed it.

'Jesus!' Paul recoiled.

Later, returning from the off-licence armed with a rattling bag of booze, Paul took a shortcut across the nearby playing fields. It was already dark, and the streetlights barely lit the path that wound slowly towards the bungalow. As he drew closer, a car crawled past and stopped about four or five doors from his parents' front gate, its engine still running. Paul tried to catch a look at the driver but the windows were blacked out. He hurried up the garden path and banged on the door.

'Hawd yer fuckin' horses!' yelled George. He unbolted the locks from inside.

'Lock the door,' said Paul, pushing past his dad into the hallway.

'Whit?'

'Lock. The. Door.' Paul dropped the booze in the hallway and ran into the living room, his dad trailing him, nonplussed. 'See that car?' Paul held the lace curtains open just enough for George to see out.

'Aye?'

'Do you recognise it?'

'It's an Audi S4. Nice motor if you've got the cash tae splash. Zero to sixty in–'

'I mean, is it one of the neighbours' cars?'

George peered out. 'I've no seen it afore. Naebody roon here's flush enough tae afford wan o' they. Could be a mate o' wee Boab's boy, though. He's intae aw sorts.' He stopped and looked over at Paul. 'Ye dinnay think this is yer stalker, dae ye?'

'We can't take any chances,' said Paul. 'Not if–'

BRRING, BRRING! BRRING, BRRING!

George grabbed his chest. 'Fuck me, ah nearly shat masel.'

The ringing of the phone brought Jean through from the kitchen. 'I suppose I'll answer that myself, shall I?' she said tartly and passed through into the hall. A moment later she was back. 'Paul, it's for you. A Tom Fleck?'

'*Tor* Fleck?' Paul asked, his voice far higher pitched than he'd intended.

'Aye, that might be it,' said Jean. 'He sounded a bit foreign.'

Paul's chest tightened as he entered the hall and picked up the receiver.

'Hello?' The line hissed with static.

'Hello?' Paul repeated, more agitated this time. 'Who is this?'

The line crackled, but there was still no answer.

'Listen to me, you fucking bastard!' raged Paul. 'You threaten my parents again, and I will fucking end you, you cunt!'

The line clicked and went dead.

'That car's away,' said George when Paul rejoined him in the living room. 'It just buggered off a minute ago.' He looked closely at his son. 'I heard ye rantin' an ravin' at yer man on the phone there. Whit did he want?'

'Nothin'.'

'Fuckin' coward.'

'George!' Jean scowled at her husband. 'Language.' She turned to Paul. 'Who is this … whit's his name … Tor?'

'Just some clown I can't be bothered with,' said Paul.

'Well, you sounded right annoyed with him.'

'He borrowed some LPs from me and never gave them back,' Paul lied. 'He's a bloody thief.'

Paul's room was pretty much as he'd left it the day he'd started uni. His parents had preserved it, almost like a shrine, and it made him feel a little sad and nostalgic. It had been his castle when he was younger, and now he had to defend that castle, and the occupants in it. He'd intended to sit up all night at the window, but the Himalayan-sized plate of mince and tatties he'd had for dinner, followed by his mum's artery-curdling apple pie and ice cream, had totally drained him. He climbed into his old bed and squeezed under the tightly tucked duvet. The mattress wrapped around him like an old familiar friend, and within seconds, he'd lost himself to sleep.

He awoke to a presence in the room. It was his dad, standing over him, shotgun in hand.

'Jesus, Dad, what are you doing?' Paul mumbled through the fog of sleep.

'There's somebody in the gairden,' whispered George. 'C'mon.' He gestured for Paul to follow him.

Paul dressed quickly, his adrenaline pumping, and padded downstairs after his dad.

'Who is it?' he asked, hoping for a simple answer. *Wee toerags raiding the crab apples, maybe?*

'Shh!'

When they reached the kitchen, George stopped. 'Listen.'

Paul held his breath. Other than the ticking of the clock above the fridge, he couldn't hear a thing. 'Dad, I don't think–'

George stepped fully into the kitchen. 'Right, that's it!' he hollered, his patience worn. 'I've got a weapon here! Ye've got ten seconds tae git the fuck oot o' ma gairden! Whit's it tae be?' Again ... nothing. George crossed to the back door and eased back the bolt.

'What are you doing?' whispered Paul in alarm.

George turned and put a finger to his lips. He threw open the door and pushed his shotgun out into the garden. 'A'm tooled up, ya bastard!' he roared. 'So get tae fuck!'

There was nobody there.

'Where'd the wee cunt go?' George muttered, stepping out onto the path and swinging the gun from side to side.

Paul ran across the kitchen in a crouch and peered out into the night. 'Dad! Come back!' There were no lights in the back garden, and no sign of his dad. *Christ, what if he* – Just then the front door rattled violently. 'Dad!' Panicking, Paul ran back across the kitchen and into the hallway, running into his mum at the foot of the stairs.

Jean tightened her dressing gown. 'What in God's name is all this commotion?' There was another sudden banging at the door, and she jumped. 'Who's that at this time o' night?'

'Get back upstairs, Mum,' Paul insisted.

'Will I hell,' said Jean. 'Whoever that is, is getting a piece o' my mind.'

'Mum, no!' Paul shouted, but Jean opened the door.

Paul leapt in front of her, just as his dad stepped in.

'It's me, ya bampot!' said George.

'Jesus Christ, George,' said Jean. 'What the hair oil are you doing out there?' In times of crisis, Jean liked to invent new phrases. 'And what's that?' she asked, pointing at the gun.

Before George could answer, a brick smashed through the living room window, spraying glass all over the sofa and the floor and landing on the TV.

'Fuckin wee bastard!' roared George and ran out the front door.

'Get upstairs, Mum!' Paul insisted, 'Go!'

Pushing Jean out of the way, Paul rushed after his dad. He found him in the middle of the road, aiming the gun at the tail-lights of a car racing away from him. A couple of hundred yards down the street, the car screeched through a handbrake turn and came racing back towards the bungalow, its headlights blinding. George raised the gun and pointed it directly at the windscreen. He was about to pull the trigger when Paul tackled him to the ground. The shotgun blasted into the air, the pellets peppering the branches of a neighbour's tree. The car screeched past, narrowly missing them both as they rolled across the tarmac. The car squealed to a halt. With a crunch of gears, it reversed back up the street towards them again.

'For fuck's sake,' groaned George.

Paul hauled his dad to his feet, just as the car screamed past them, reversing all the way to the end of the road. It carried out a manic three-point turn, George cocked the shotgun and loaded up again.

'No, Dad!' Paul pleaded.

But his father was like a man possessed. He aimed at its tyres. But before he could fire, the car bumped over the kerb, careered out of the street, and it was gone.

'Bastards!' hollered George.

The neighbour whose tree George had hit – Danny McLintock - chose that moment to open his front door and peer out, a fur coat thrown over his XXL pyjamas.

'Is that you, George?' he shouted across the street.

'Aye, Danny,' said George. 'It's me all right.'

Danny crossed the road. 'Whit's goin' on?' he asked, doing up his buttons.

'Some bampot's tryin' tae dae us over. Nice coat, by the way. Somethin' ye want tae tell us?'

'Shut it,' said Danny. 'Oh hello, Paul. I didnae recognise ye there.'

'Hey, Danny.'

'Are ye both okay?'

'We saw them off,' said George.

'Aye, you did that,' said Danny through a yawn. 'An' ye shot ma bloody tree.'

'Sorry about that,' said George. 'I was aimin' for the bastard in the car.'

'Christ, they Argies must have been shittin' themselves when they saw the Balloch tree killer comin'.' Danny laughed.

'Did you get a look at them?' asked Paul, eager to interrupt this absurdly casual banter.

'No really,' said George. 'He was wearin' wan a they bunnets, ye know, pulled aw the way doon. But I bet he saw ma little friend.' He held up the gun.

Danny ducked.

'There must have been two o' them, though; wan drivin' and wan shittin' himself runnin' awa. They'll no be back in a hurry, believe me.'

'I'm so sorry, Dad,' said Paul, his hands shaking. 'This is my mess.'

George shook his head. 'Och, awa wae ye. Tae be honest, this is a lot mair interestin' than vegetatin' in front o' *Coronation Street*. C'mon. Ye look like you could use a wee snifter. We'll see ye in the mornin', Danny. We'll git the rest o' the troops the gither fur a powwow, eh?'

'So am no gettin' a snifter, is that it?' said Danny. 'Despite bein' totally bereft efter ye murdered ma tree.'

'Nice try, neebur,' said George. 'Noo … fuck off!'

'Hasta manana, then.' Danny grinned and crossed to his house. In the doorway, he glanced back over his shoulder. 'It wis gid seein' ye again, Paul!' A second later, he'd slipped back inside.

Paul found his mum in the living room, sweeping up the broken glass with a dustpan and brush. 'Let me do that, Mum,' he said, but she pushed him away without a word. He wandered over to the TV. There was a dent in its side, but the screen was okay.

George came in with a large whisky.

'Get that doon ye,' he said, handing Paul the glass. 'I've one here for you, too, Jean.'

Jean ignored him and carried on sweeping.

'Jean!' George repeated.

'I don't want that thing back in the house, George,' said Jean, not looking up.

'Och, awa wi ye, wummin,' said George. 'It's no a real wan. It only fires blanks. It's fur scarin' the craws mair than onythin' else.' An outright lie, but a necessary one.

'Yer father still thinks he's in the forces,' said Jean. She turned to her husband. 'Well, you're too old, George. *I'm* too old. I'm done worryin' if the man I love is going to come home in one piece.'

'They're toerags, love!' George laughed. 'The Argies would have eaten them fur breakfast.'

'Well, I think we should call the police.'

George held up his hands. 'Jean, Jean, listen. Me an' Danny are gettin' the troops the gither the morra tae sort oot our home security. It'll aw be fine. I promise.'

'No the bloody neighbourhood watch, surely? You lot are like *Dad's Army*.'

'The Home Guard,' agreed George. 'Exactly!'

Jean laid the pan and brush down. 'I'm going to bed. Goodnight, Paul. Your dad's aff his bloody heed.' Halfway up the stairs, she stopped and turned. 'I'll let you and Captain Mainwaring there tidy up the rest o' this mess.'

'Everything's fine, Jean,' said George, hoping to reassure her. 'I'll be up in a minute.'

'And lock the bloody doors!' Jean shouted back as she slammed her own behind her.

'She'll be fine,' said George with a nod.

Paul was unconvinced.

When Paul stirred, it was past lunchtime. George was already in the kitchen, brewing up.

'Ah,' he said with a grin, 'the living dead finally arise.'

'Afternoon,' said Paul through a yawn. 'Sorry, I must have passed out.'

'Yer mither's no in, but she's left us some bacon butties.'

Paul snatched up a sandwich from the plate and bit into it. 'God, Dad, she's a bloody slave.'

'Aye,' agreed George, 'but a bloody guid yin.'

Paul sipped at the tea George had nudged in front of him.

'I can't go on with all this shit, Dad,' he said, putting the mug down. 'It's doin' ma nut in.'

'Listen, pal,' said George. 'These arseholes are bullies. Two fingers and two barrels, that's whit they need.' He bit into his own sandwich. 'Dinny worry.

We can look after oorselves here. We've been through a lot worse. Remember they dealers that took over number thirty-three?'

'Aye,' said Paul, 'but that was a while ago. You're not a young soldier anymore.'

'I'm an old an' wise soldier.' George smiled. 'An' there are four o' us on this street. An' anyway … a brick? Come on. Total fuckin' amateur hour. If they think I'm aff ma heed, just wait till they meet the McRae twins. An' then there's Mr Grearson … and his wife!'

They both laughed.

He leaned closer to Paul. 'You keep going, son. Don't let those bastards destroy yer dream.' He glanced down at Paul's half-eaten sandwich. 'D'ye want that?'

Before Paul could reply, he'd snaffled it up.

Paul didn't wait for his mother to get back. Instead, he said his goodbyes to his dad, promising to ring every night.

'Ocht, awa an don't be daft,' said George. 'Just ring yer mithir later on, otherwise she'll be oan at me aw night fur lettin' you go.' He took a hold of his son's shoulders. 'Noo listen. No surrender, okay?'

Paul shook his head and gave his dad a hug, and for once, his dad let him.

At the gate, Paul turned. 'Thanks, Dad,' he said, raising his fist.

'You'll miss yer train!' George shouted back and shook his own.

13

Moscow, 5th October, 7:08 p.m.

Convinced the security arrangements for the oligarch's unexpected visit are water-tight, Dimitri Pasternak, the flustered manager of the Moscow State Opera, checks his watch for the umpteenth time, takes a deep breath, and steps out to face the waiting crowd and huddled paparazzi. A burst of camera flashes momentarily blinds him, and for a split-second he wishes he was at home with Yuri, sharing a hot bath and a bottle of Stolichnaya. But he has a job to do, and so he smiles and waves and descends the red-carpeted stairs like the paid lackey he is, engaging in mindless small talk with local dignitaries and bug-eyed fools lined up to greet the great Oleg Petrov.

He's interrupted by the arrival of a long black limousine, from which steps an inscrutable and immaculately dressed driver, who opens the door for Russia's third-richest man and most eligible bachelor.

Petrov is rocking his smart suit-and-sneakers attire, his heavily bleached Hollywood smile well practised. The crowd of mostly young women scream and cheer – 'He looked at me!' 'No, he looked at ME!' – as the paparazzi click incessantly to catch a half-decent shot of the icon.

Two shaven-headed brutes, shaped like fridge-freezers, exit the car behind Petrov and flank him as he approaches Dimitri. The flimsy barrier separating Petrov from the rows of perspiring, oestrogen-fuelled WAGS threatens to topple any second, a fact the fridge-freezers pick up on immediately. They sweep Petrov brusquely towards the opera house entrance where he greets Dimitri with a firm, farmer-like handshake.

'It is a pleasure and a privilege to meet you, Mr Petrov,' says Dimitri, trying not to sound too ingratiating. 'Thank you for coming.'

'Where do we go?' asks Petrov, expediency trumping politesse.

'Please.' Dimitri directs Petrov into the opera house, leaving the fridge-freezers to guard the door.

Inside, he introduces Petrov to the hastily assembled staff, some of them still tucking in their creased uniforms. Petrov shakes their hands perfunctorily and moves along the line quickly, eager to get to his seat and get the evening over with. At the bottom of a grand, gold-leaf-covered staircase, Production Director Sven Edberg rushes from a side door, heading straight for Petrov. From nowhere, a third fridge-freezer – this one wearing sunglasses and a Schwarzenegger scowl – appears and manhandles Edberg to one side.

'No, no,' says Dimitri, intervening. 'This is the director of tonight's opera.'

Schwarzenegger seems reluctant to let Edberg go but eventually does. Flustered, Edberg straightens his bow tie and flattens his hair. Petrov, meanwhile, unleashes a torrent of abuse, in Russian, at his unbowed guard.

'My apologies,' he tells Edberg with the smallest of nods. 'My men, they are not usually so … how do you say … pig-headed.'

'That's quite all right,' replies Edberg, although it clearly isn't.

'There are many people who wish me ill will,' continues Petrov. 'I fear my life parallels one of your wonderful operas, Mr Edberg.'

He laughs and is joined by Dimitri, but Sven is not impressed.

'If you will excuse me, Mr Petrov,' he says. 'I have some last-minute preparations to attend to.' Retreating with a curt nod, he returns backstage.

Dimitri ushers Petrov and Schwarzenegger upstairs to the Royal Box. It's usually reserved for heads of state and other high-ranking officials, but Dimitri feels its usage tonight is justified. A nervous usherette bows repeatedly as the entourage approaches.

'The curtain please!' Dimitri clicks his fingers, snapping the usherette out of her star-struck trance.

She pulls back the curtain, and Petrov slips inside, followed by Dimitri. Schwarzenegger pushes the usherette away from the entrance and takes her place.

'The finest seats in the house, Mr Petrov,' Dimitri says proudly and invites Petrov to sit.

The audience, Moscow's glitterati, file in, jewellery and teeth gleaming under the lights of the giant chandelier. There are gasps and murmurs, nods and pointing when Petrov is spotted high above them. The three Romanov sisters, direct descendants of the last Tsar, are perched on the edge of their seats in the less showy Grand Box opposite Petrov. One of them raises her champagne glass in Petrov's direction, smiling seductively at the oligarch. The identical triplets, much to Petrov's dismay and growing impatience, have pursued him with romantic intent for more than five years. He waves them away dismissively, sighs, and flops back in his seat. He'd offered the theatre a substantial sum for a private performance of Edberg's opera at his country estate, but the temperamental Swede had refused to play ball.

'Champagne and caviar is on its way, sir,' purrs Dimitri.

'No caviar,' snaps Petrov. 'I can't stand the stuff. Do you have any fries?'

'You mean French fries?' Dimitri isn't sure he heard the oligarch correctly.

'That's right. Preferably McDonald's, but Burger King will do.'

'Certainly,' says Dimitri, wincing a little at Petrov's Luddite tastes. 'I'll see to it personally.'

A waitress appears with an ice bucket containing a bottle of Dom Perignon. She sets a glass on a side table and carefully pours, spilling a little in the process.

'Leave it!' Petrov roars.

The waitress sets the bottle down.

'You need to pour slowly,' says Petrov. 'Take your time. It needs to be seduced out of the bottle, not raped!'

The waitress bows. 'I'm sorry, sir. Please forgive me.'

Petrov doesn't. 'Tell my man to come in.'

The waitress scuttles off.

Schwarzenegger reappears. 'Yes, sir.'

Petrov hands him the half-filled glass. 'Test this.'

Schwarzenegger unrolls a black cloth and removes from it a dropper and a brown, label-less bottle. He takes a sample of the champagne and squirts it into the bottle. He shakes it, waits, and then nods. 'Clear.' He packs away the equipment and rolls the cloth back up.

'Stand behind me, please,' says Petrov. 'I'm feeling … nervous tonight.'

'Yes, sir.' Schwarzenegger positions himself at the rear of the box. Petrov pours the champagne himself, downing the glass in one.

The lights dim, and the opening strains of 'La Boheme' – Petrov's mother's favourite – float up to the Royal Box. As patron, he'd pumped millions of roubles into this crumbling dump, yet this was his first visit. The place stank of piss and poverty, but it was worth it to remember his mother. If it wasn't for her, well ... even at the age of forty-two, Oleg Petrov – oil magnate extraordinaire – can't bring himself to go there. He pours himself another drink, sits back, and closes his eyes.

The tenor rips into the first aria. The soprano responds in kind. Already Petrov's eyes are welling up. He wipes at them discreetly. The last thing he needs is for someone to see him crying. He carries on drinking. The music swells and voices soar, and soon the bottle is empty, and Petrov is drifting off, sinking into a dark hole of stoic mothers and vicious fathers.

A tap on Petrov's shoulder hauls him from the hole and back into the light. For a second he doesn't know where he is. *Mother?*

'McDonald's fries, sir,' the waitress whispers in his ear.

Petrov jerks back, insulted at having his personal space invaded.

'Away!' he yells, throwing up a hand.

The waitress mumbles an apology and steps back. She replaces the Dom Perignon with a bottle of vintage red, its label faded and indecipherable.

Petrov stares at it. 'What's this?'

The waitress pulls a note from the pocket of her apron and hands it over with shaking fingers. Petrov takes it and holds it up to the light.

Enjoy the opera, Comrade Petrov

Sergei Topov

State Minister of Culture

Petrov lays the note on the table and picks up the bottle. He has to hold it close to read the label. *Romanee*

Conti 1971. It's the rarest of burgundies, worth over 800,000 roubles, but of this Petrov is ignorant. He smiles. As one of the president's closest allies, the culture minister is Petrov's golden ticket, his means of securing an invite to the G20 summit in February. He fills the glass, swirls it around as he's seen others do, and sticks his nose in. The aroma is intoxicating. He didn't expect that. He sits back, refocuses on the opera, and gorges on three or four mouthfuls of burger and over-salted fries. Che Gelida Manina', La Boheme's famous and emotionally charged aria, begins. Licking his lips, he's about to take a sip of the wine when he remembers he should check it first. He glances behind him. He can make out Schwarzenegger's shadowy frame and the sheen from his black brogues.

'Fuck it.'

Petrov sips slowly, savouring the wine's delicate notes. It's like nothing he's ever tasted before. As he swirls it around in his mouth the aria soars, sending Petrov's senses into overdrive. He takes a second sip, and then guzzles a third. The seventy-one is beyond delicious. It's irresistible. Before he can take a fourth sip, though, Petrov's windpipe clamps shut. He can't breathe. He drops the glass and claws at his throat. A searing white heat shoots down his neck and across his chest. He stumbles from his chair and retches violently, throwing up 20,000 roubles' worth of liquidised champagne and McDonald's fries over the edge of the Royal Box and onto the assembled fur coats and Armani suits below.

La Boheme's principal cast are so deep into their performance that the screams from the stalls go unnoticed. High above them all, Petrov tears at his tuxedo, his shirt buttons *pop-pop-popping*. His entire body explodes with pain. The audience are now on their feet, uncomprehending. Someone shouts for help. All are looking skyward, rather than to the stage, where the aria is reaching its heart-wrenching climax. A pair of ushers in matching red trousers burst through the Royal Box's curtain and race to Petrov's aid. But they're too late. Petrov staggers backwards, his mind addled.

Father, what have you done? Why don't you love me?

With a final unhuman scream, he tumbles over the side of the box, landing on top of the elderly Madam Ivankov thirty feet below, crushing her thorax and killing her instantly. Two deaths for the price of one. The dealmaker inside the poisoned Petrov would have approved.

Panic. Heels, jewels, jacket tails … they fly in all directions as escape becomes a priority. The orchestra, deep in their pit, carry on regardless. The on-stage stars – blinded to tragedy by the relentless spotlights – continue singing to a fleeing mob. But then someone must have come to their senses because now the houselights are up and an armed paramilitary unit are storming the theatre, waving Kalashnikovs and handguns, forcing patrons onto the floor while they secure the building and form a physical cordon around Petrov's contorted body.

Madam Ivankov's distraught husband, Aleksey, battles to reach his beloved, but is pushed away at gun point. An officer checks Petrov's pulse. It's weak, but he's alive. His eyes open, and his chemically charred mouth forms a pattern that may, or may not, be the forming of a word. The officer leans in, but there's only a dying breath left. Petrov – the fries-loving oligarch, the bath-sharing boyfriend, the loving son – is gone. But he won't be travelling alone. Within hours, the officer who bore testament to his final breath, the clumsy waitress who served him his wine, even poor Aleksey Ivankov, will also be dead, poisoned by the unidentified nerve agent found on the rim of Petrov's glass. Even Schwarzenegger can't cheat death. He'll later be found impaled on the lead soprano's dressing room door, a single crossbow arrow burrowed deep into his left eye socket.

14

'No fucking way!' said Richard, pouring out two coffees. 'How'd the bastards find out where your parents lived?'

'I've no idea,' said Paul. He took one of the offered mugs, 'but my old man saw them off.'

'Oh shit, what did he do?'

'Chased them up the street with a shotgun.'

Richard spluttered on his coffee. 'Seriously?'

'I'm not kidding. He let them have it with both barrels. Literally.'

'Fuck me!' Richard wiped at his stained t-shirt. 'He didn't kill anyone, did he?'

'He would have if I hadn't stopped him.'

'Your dad's mental. Where'd he get a gun from anyway?'

'No idea,' said Paul. 'But you're right, he's off the scale.'

Richard pulled a seat out from the kitchen table and plonked himself down beside Paul. 'I told you things would get nastier. Did you get a good look at them?'

'No, but I think it was our boy in the bunnet again.'

'Jesus. They don't stop, do they?'

'So you do accept that we're dealing with something more than a grudge match between you and one of your ex-mates?'

'Okay, okay,' Richard conceded. 'Things do seem to have escalated somewhat since my last assessment of the situation.'

'You think?' Paul shook his head. 'They've crossed the line, mate. As my old man said, you threaten a Grant at your peril.'

'Yeah, but–'

'Yeah, but what?'

'Your dad … he's ex-SAS, isn't he? I mean, what have you got, aside from a moleskin notebook full of well-armed free verse?'

Paul reached into his coat pocket and retrieved a memory stick. 'I've got this.'

Richard's eyes widened. 'Is that the master?'

'Don't be daft.' Paul dropped the stick back in his pocket. 'It's my working folder. Don't worry, the master's safe.'

'That's right,' said Richard. 'I forgot you'd secreted it away somewhere. It's up your arse, isn't it?'

'Fuck off,' said Paul. The Newspaper headline caught his eye.

Crisis Deepens as Markets Tumble

'What's this?' he asked, picking the paper up.

Richard rolled his eyes. 'Oh yes, and there's that. There's been a run on the banks, apparently. Stock market's fallen through the floor. Everything's in meltdown. So,' he sighed, 'that'll be another ten years of fucking doom and gloom and cereal for breakfast, lunch, and dinner.'

'See if there's anything on the TV about it,' said Paul, nodding to the antiquated portable.

Richard cycled through the limited channels until he found images of young, white-shirted men bickering on trading room floors, cutting to … snaking queues outside banks, then riots … and the inevitable looting.

'Actually, this is quite brilliant,' said Richard.

Paul was incredulous. 'What?'

'Our script's bang on the button,' said Richard. 'Who'd have guessed we'd be cutting edge?'

'Shh!' urged Paul.

The 'Breaking News' banner flashed up, and an ashen-faced newsreader announced that the London FTSE had dropped over ten percent within five minutes of opening. Investors were looking at an instant loss of almost three billion pounds.

'Oh my God,' said Paul. 'What if it's us?'

'What if what's us?'

'What if Agency O actually exists, and we've accidentally opened up a can of worms?'

Richard tried to interject, but Paul shushed him with a raised palm.

'What about the story in the news the other day,' he said, 'about that Russian guy killed at the opera. How's that any different from the stuff we're writing about?'

Richard couldn't argue with that. He knew Paul was right.

'Think about it,' Paul continued, determined to hammer his point home. 'All the shit that's happening right now ... the financial crash, the suicides, the murdered journo. Our script has driven a fucking steam train through of all of that. What if we've pissed off the wrong people?'

'Hey, we're anti-establishment!' said Richard, fist-pumping the air. 'Get in there!'

'I'm serious,' said Paul. 'This is heavy shit.'

'Okay,' said Richard, 'let's suppose, for argument's sake, that you're right, and that Agency O is a real organisation, operating in the shadows, running the world, blah de blah, just like how we wrote it. That'd make them a pretty formidable foe, right?'

Paul nodded.

'Well ... why would they bother playing with us? Wouldn't they just take what they wanted?'

'Ah,' said Paul, 'but we've still got the upper hand.'

Richard sighed. 'The memory stick.'

'As long as it remains safe,' said Paul, 'we remain safe.'

'And you don't think you should tell me where you've hidden it?' asked Richard. 'Just in case, you know, something happens to you?'

'No,' said Paul. 'That would put you in danger, too. It's best if only I know.'

'Oh my God,' said Richard. 'You really do believe this insane shit. This isn't a Bourne movie, you know. It isn't even a fucking Austin Powers movie.'

Paul didn't answer. To him, it felt more like a Tarantino movie. Where everyone dies in the end.

Back in his bedroom, Paul switched on his laptop. Nothing. He tried again. Nothing. He checked the plug, turned it off and on at the wall, and tried again. *Shit.*

'My laptop's not working,' said Paul, walking back into the kitchen. 'Have you been using it?'

Richard grinned. 'You tried switching it off and on again?'

'I'll switch *you* off and on again.'

'That doesn't even make sense.'

'Can I use yours?'

Grudgingly, Richard sloped out of the kitchen, returning with a silver HP under his arm.

'Thanks,' said Paul. But when he switched it on, he got the same result: a black screen.

'Fucking hell,' muttered Richard. He grabbed the laptop and turned it upside down.

'What are you looking for?' asked Paul.

'I don't know. Something. Anything.'

'Screwdriver marks? Evidence of tampering?'

'Stop thinking everything's fucking Agency O!' yelled Richard. He shook the laptop in Paul's face. 'My whole life's on this. How can you be so calm about it?'

'You backed up your files?'

'Of course not. Who does that?'

'Everybody?'

Richard wasn't listening. He was too busy hammering away fruitlessly at the buttons. Eventually, he gave up. 'Well, at least we haven't lost the script. That's still up your arse, right?'

'Yeah,' said Paul, 'all the writing's safely tucked away in my *semi*-colon.'

'How the fuck did they get in without our passwords? I mean, if it even is them behind this.'

'It's fine,' said Paul. 'We'll take them in to that shop on Byres Road. Get the young techie guy there to check it. He might even be able to trace who's responsible.'

'Will he be able to restore everything?' asked Richard. 'I mean, will he see everything I've got on there?

'Don't worry,' said Paul. 'He's seen it all and more, I'm sure.'

Richard scratched at his head. 'I'm not talking about porn. I mean personal stuff. You know, like letters. Stuff like that.'

'Letters? Are you a man of letters now?'

'Just personal communications with good friends.'

'Women, you mean.'

'That sort of thing, yes.'

'I'm sure he won't say a word,' said Paul. 'No matter what soppy, sentimental gush you've spewed out to get your end away.'

Richard smiled. 'I'm a sensitive soul really.'

'Yeah right.' Paul sighed.

'I tell you what,' said Richard, snapping the laptop shut. 'You go ahead, and if your man fixes yours, then I'll drop mine in, too.'

'But he might be able to find out more if he digs around in both,' argued Paul.

'It's okay,' said Richard, 'you go first. I can always watch porn on my phone.'

He smiled, but Paul wasn't convinced. Richard was hiding something.

15

The next day, Paul dropped his laptop in at the computer repair shop. Axel Rhodes, the geeky, bespectacled owner, gave Paul a rundown on what he was going to do to his beloved machine, but Paul could barely follow any of it and ended up staring at his own perplexed face reflected in Axel's lenses.

'So, is it salvageable?' Paul asked, when Axel finally stopped.

Axel rubbed at the pubes sprouting from the centre of his chin. 'Hmm ...' he pondered. 'It depends what you mean by salvageable. If, for example, you mean–'

'I mean ...' interrupted Paul, before Axel could fully launch into any more geekidigook, '... will you able to trace whether the machine's been hacked, and, if so, by whom?'

'Oh, that?' grinned Axel. 'Oh yeah, dead easy.' He winked at Paul. 'Takes one to know one.'

'Great. And we keep this between us, yeah?'

'Discretion comes with the territory, my friend,' said Axel, his voice taking on a strangely fey

American accent. He closed the lid and slid the laptop beneath the counter. 'I'll call you when I'm done.'

'Thanks, Axel,' said Paul. 'I owe you.'

While he waited on Axel getting back to him, Paul decamped to the library to use their computers. He needed to research psychometric testing; the dialogue he was writing around the subject lacked the authenticity of an insider. Or even someone who vaguely knew what the fuck he was talking about. A quick search unearthed a recent item involving Ipcress, a major data broker, and their dealings with an unnamed social media platform. Paul scribbled notes as he read, flabbergasted. He had no idea private data could be bought and sold, either legally or on the black market. Ipcress had been accused of brokering member profiles of up to thirty million users on the unnamed platform, and of selling them on to key establishment institutions such as governments and political parties.

Their unique selling point seemed to be a psychometric system so sophisticated that the data collected could be used to not only predict customer behaviour, but also to influence, and even control, emotional responses, feelings, attitudes, as well as aspirations, wants, and needs. Ipcress' software harvested all forms of online interaction, from emails and viewing habits to conversations, likes, and follows. It hacked telephone records and collected texts, voicemails, and even live conversations. It could also replicate individual profiles, enabling them to be re-formed, like emotional plasticine.

The more Paul read, the more frightening the implications became. The psychometrics acted like a giant sponge, soaking up personality traits and individual characteristics in order to hardwire the human brain to accept, conform, consume, and act the way Ipcress wanted them to. Charges of blackmail and extortion were inevitable, given the extraordinary reach of the company's data mining ability.

Paul stopped to take a breath. He'd thought that, with his script, he'd been writing fiction. Yet here it was being presented as truth. How was that possible? And who the hell were Ipcress anyway? He returned to the computer and found their website. He had to scroll through page after page of bland corporate nothingness – strange, considering the level of scandal the company had attracted – before finding the nugget of gold he never knew he was looking for. Tucked away on the last page, at the very bottom, was a line in extremely small print.

Ipcress is a subsidiary of Tor-izon Inc.

A hand clamped onto Paul's shoulder, and he leapt to his feet in fright. 'Fu-u-u-ck!'

'Shh!' whispered Richard, pushing Paul gently back into his seat. 'It's a fucking library, no a play park.'

The lank-haired librarian at the desk opposite glowered in their direction.

Richard clocked her and smiled back obsequiously. 'And we're no getting a ride aff her.'

'What are you doing here?' asked Paul, his head still reeling from his dive into the dark web of cyber brainwashing.

'I thought you might like to accompany me to the local hostelry,' said Richard. 'You look like you could do with a pint.'

'What time is it?'

'Twenty to seven.'

'I thought it was earlier.'

'Come on.' Richard picked up Paul's bag and handed it to him. 'I'm giving you an order, soldier.'

'But we don't have any money.'

Richard flashed a credit card. 'This'll do nicely.'

'Where did you get that?' Paul asked.

'It's a long story, and probably best I keep it to myself. But lucky for you I remembered I still had it tucked away under my mattress.'

Paul sighed.

Four pints later, they were back out on the street and heading home.

'So that's it sorted, then,' said Richard. 'We take down Agency O before they brainwash us all, then we take out the CIA, and then we establish a new social order, with me as the omnipotent demagogue leader serviced by a harem of nubile adoring followers. Correct?'

'Impotent, more like,' slurred Paul. 'Let's get a bag of chips.'

They stopped at the lights. As they waited for them to change, a car up ahead revved its engine.

'Alpha wanker,' Richard muttered.

The lights changed, and he and Paul crossed. Through the haze of alcohol, Paul thought the car seemed familiar.

'That car,' he said, 'it looks like–' Before he could finish, the car was careering towards them, its tyres squealing and spinning on the tarmac.

'Watch out!' Paul shouted. He slammed his body into Richard's, knocking them both to the side of the road.

The car sped past, missing them by inches. At the next set of lights, it handbrake turned and accelerated back towards them again.

'Run!' Paul yelled.

Scrambling to their feet, they sprinted down the street. The car raced after them, mounting the pavement and bouncing on its hydraulics like something out of *Mad Max*. Paul grabbed Richard's collar and shoved him through a gap in the railing, following him down a set of steps into a basement. The car screeched to a halt at the top of the steps, its engine rasping. Paul and Richard lay still, too scared even to breathe. Above them, the passenger-side door was pushed open, but before anyone could get out of the car it was shunted into the railings from behind. Twice. Three times. Avoiding a fourth time, the driver spun the wheel and tore off, tyres squealing.

Paul lay on top of Richard in a heap of shock. Slowly, they disentangled and sat up.

'What the fuck was that?' wheezed Richard.

'Bastards!' screamed Paul. He helped Richard to his feet. 'Are you okay?'

Richard checked his arms and legs for injuries.

'I think so. Thanks, pal,' he said and placed a hand on Paul's shoulder. 'You saved my life.'

Car headlights flashed down at them from the top of the steps.

'They've come back!' cried Paul, and he and Richard ducked back down into the gloom.

The driver's door swung open, and the large pumpkin-sized head of Detective Quinn appeared. 'Come on!' he gestured to them.

Paul and Richard stared at each other, not sure exactly how to react.

'Now!'

Quinn's order had the terrified pair scrambling back up the steps. They pushed through the railing and approached Quinn's car, the bumper hanging by a thread.

Quinn was squeezed into the driver's seat like an elephant trapped in a sardine tin, his gut engulfing the steering wheel. The interior resembled a mobile landfill site, with half-crushed wrappers, empty food cartons, and coffee cups scattered all over the seats and floor. A slice of half-eaten pizza lay on the dash. It was as though the entire inside of the car was smeared in congealed fat.

'If you want to stay breathing,' said Quinn, 'get the *fuck* in!'

Richard immediately jumped in the front, leaving Paul to handle the foul-smelling detritus in the back.

The engine roared, the wheels spun, and Quinn bounced the broken car off down the uneven street.

'What the fuck's going on?' shouted Paul from the back, the smell of sweat and rotting food invading his nostrils. 'Those were the same arseholes who terrorised my mum and dad!'

Quinn took a hard right, almost knocking Paul into a foil carton of discarded vindaloo. He careered on, crunching gears, ignoring signs and traffic lights, and hurtling round corners at breakneck speed. He seemed to prefer it to speaking.

'Stop!' Paul cried out again. *We're going to die! We're going to die! We're going to die!*

The car raced on, down to the bottom of Byers Road, then out towards the fringes of the city. Finally, it slowed, turned into a deserted industrial estate, and screeched to a halt.

'Okay,' said Richard, his throat rasping, 'so what the actual fuck is ha–?'

'Shut your hole,' Quinn barked, his mid-Atlantic twang lending him such an air of harsh authority it immediately clammed Richard up.

Paul watched from the back seat as the detective checked his mirrors, keeping an eye on the car park entrance and shuttered lock-ups beyond. The tension was too much for Paul, and he lost his patience.

'Look, Detective,' he said, 'you clearly know what that was all about back there, but if you don't start talking, right now, we'll–'

'You'll what?' growled Quinn. He twisted his fat neck round. 'What is it you think you'll do, dickhead?

Here's what you'll do. You'll shut that pussy hole of yours and fucking listen.'

Chastened by the detective's sudden personality transplant, Paul shrank back into his seat.

'You still have absolutely no idea, do you?' asked Quinn.

'About what?' Paul's voice was small and tinny, as though talking into a bin.

'You two fuckwits are up to your gullets in shit,' said Quinn, 'and you're utterly fucking clueless.' He let out a loud belch of a laugh, and the car's suspension squeaked in response.

'So enlighten us,' said Richard, playing the tough guy role.

The detective squirmed and groaned as he battled his bulging gut sideways to face Richard. 'Don't be a prick,' he snarled. 'It's extremely important that you listen to what I have to say.'

'So say it,' Richard replied defiantly. 'We're all ears.'

'You think I'm doing all this for you?' snapped Quinn. 'I couldn't give a gorilla's tiny cock about either of you.' He ran a hand over his face. 'I've been working myself raw on this investigation for two years – two whole fucking years – and then you two clowns stumble onto the set and jeopardise the whole fucking movie.' Beads of sweat trickled down his bloated, flushed cheeks.

'Forgive me,' Richard interrupted, 'but what the fuck are you talking about?'

'The script, shit-for-brains! The script!'

'Our script?'

'Is there an echo in here?' said Quinn. 'That piece of crap you posted all over the Internet.'

'What investigation?' Paul interrupted from the back.

'Oh, hello,' said Quinn sarcastically. 'Still cowering like a child in the shadows, are we? I almost forgot you were there.' He tried to turn further round, but his belly refused to budge.

'You talked before about an ongoing investigation,' said Paul cautiously.

'I work for the US Government,' said Quinn. 'That's all you need to know.'

'You mean like the IRS? No wait, I've got it, you're a federal librarian, aren't you?' Richard mocked.

'Yeah, go ahead,' said Quinn. 'You won't be laughing when the bastards stop playing.'

'What do you mean?' asked Paul.

'Your script kicked a hornet's nest,' said Quinn, 'and now they've sent their best soldiers out to defend their kingdom. You two bozos have made it damn near impossible for me to conclude my investigation, and I was this close.' He held up a fist and clicked his fingers in Richard's face.

Richard didn't flinch. 'Oh, come on. You expect us to believe that bullshit? So you're saying you're a CIA operative, is that it? You?' He looked down at Quinn's gut hanging over the steering wheel.

'Who said anything about the CIA?' said Quinn. 'I'm a librarian, remember? You lard-lumps have fucked my case over and now you owe me.'

'I am very particular about what or who I fuck,' Richard snapped back.

'Let him finish, Richard,' said Paul. He turned to Quinn. 'Are you saying some kind of organisation is behind the threats and attacks?'

'Join the dots, dipshit. Right now, they're just playing with you, but make no mistake, they want you gone.'

'But that's just crazy. Our script is bullshit fiction. It's total bollocks. We just made it up. Surely they must know that?'

Quinn wiped his brow with a pudgy hand. 'Your script cuts a little too close to the knuckle. They don't know how or why, but they think you know more than you do.'

'We don't know anything,' said Paul.

'Speak for yourself.' Richard sniffed.

'You're idiots,' said Quinn, 'but they don't know that. They see you as a threat. You're messing with some very bad people. Dangerous people. That's why you need me to help you.'

'What do you want from us?' asked Paul.

Quinn contorted his bulk a little more so he could look Paul in the eye. 'Right now, it's all about intimidation. They're just biding their time.'

'But why?'

'They want your script and they're trying to frighten you into handing it over to them.'

'What will they do with it?'

'Destroy it, of course. Remove all record of it, online or off. It will be like it never existed.'

'But what about everyone who's already read it?' asked Paul. 'Or watched the videos. What about Omni? We're about to close a deal with a production company.'

Quinn's expression hardened. 'That cannot happen. You need to give that up. You hear me? It's imperative you hand over to me everything you've written. Your drafts, your master, the video masters, all your notes, even the handwritten stuff, all of it.'

'Oh, now I get the picture.' Richard nodded. 'Now I see what's going on.' He opened the car door and turned to Paul. 'Come on, Paul, we're leaving.'

'Sit back down, shit-for-brains,' growled Quinn.

'Paul, come on,' insisted Richard. 'Move it.' He stepped out of the car.

Paul was torn. On the one hand, he knew Richard was right. They couldn't trust Quinn. But on the other … Quinn's story kind of made sense. He wanted to hear more.

Richard stuck his head back through the window. 'Come on!'

Shit. Mates before dates. Paul climbed over the fetid debris and out the other side.

'It's him,' said Richard as they headed towards the car park exit.

'Wait,' said Paul. 'Who's him?'

Richard stopped. 'Can't you see? He's our fucking lunatic stalker.'

'Quinn?'

'He's clearly after our script. Jesus, why did we even get in the car with him? I mean, where the fuck are we?'

'But look at him,' said Paul, 'He's not the guy who followed me or broke into our flat. He can barely walk, far less flee a break-in.'

'I'm telling you, he's the bastard who nearly broke my jaw.'

Quinn emerged from the car, holding onto the doorframe for support. 'They won't stop,' he wheezed, exhausted with the effort. 'They'll wipe your script and then they'll wipe you, too.'

'Fuck you, you bastard!' shouted Richard. 'You could have killed me!'

'Right now, I'd *love* to kill you, but it was the organisation that was most likely behind that.'

The comment took Paul by surprise. 'You know about the attack?'

'It's my job to know everything about you.'

'Yeah, stalkers are good at that,' fumed Richard.

'I can protect you,' said Quinn. 'I have the power to make sure you're safe.'

'I fucking bet you do!'

'It's your funeral.' Quinn smirked. He slowly lowered his expanse of buttock back down onto the seat and squeezed himself into the car, like toothpaste trying to get back in the tube.

'Wait!' said Paul. 'You can't leave us out here.'

As he walked back towards the car, Quinn started up the engine. With a squeal of tyres, it roared across the car park. Paul and Richard watched as it turned and came straight back at them at high speed.

'Fuuuuck!' Richard yelled and leapt out the way again.

The car was almost upon them when it swerved and screeched to a stop just yards away.

Quinn stuck his head out the window and looked straight at Paul. 'Watch your back, son,' he rasped. A final roar of the engine, and the car was gone, fleeing the deserted car park for the sanctuary of the night.

'Well, that's just fucking great,' said Paul with a scowl. 'Well done, Richard.'

'What?' Richard threw up his hands. 'The guy's a madman. I'm just glad he's gone.'

'Quinn's right. You *are* a fuckwit.' Paul stuffed his hands in his pockets and stomped off.

'Where are you going?' Richard called after him.

'As far away from you as possible!' Paul yelled back.

The bus shelter was a Turner Prize shoo-in, a mangled, dog-shitted bomb-site carpeted with beads of shattered glass. *Tracey Emin would kill to doss down in here,* thought Paul. He'd reluctantly let Richard catch him up, but neither had spoken for a good twenty minutes. All that was about to change.

'Duntocher? Jesus!' groaned Richard, half-heartedly punching the half- vandalised timetable. 'The good news is that there's a bus in …' He paused to check his watch. '… forty-five minutes.'

There were lights in the distance. Paul headed towards them.

'You're not planning on walking all the way, are you?' said Richard, pulling his coat in tight against the cold.

'Yup!' Paul replied and carried on doing exactly that.

'Suit yourself,' said Richard. He kicked away some of the glass and sat, wriggling against the remains of the back wall until he got comfortable. He closed his eyes. They flew back open again almost immediately. *Is that fucking dog shit I smell?*

16

By the time Paul found his way out of Duntocher and made it back to the West End, it was past midnight and he'd been walking for over two hours. He was exhausted, his brain fried from everything that had happened. Who was this Quinn character? Maybe Richard was right, and he *was* the man responsible for the threats. And what did he mean by 'watch your back'? What else hadn't he told them? At Byres Road, Paul decided he'd had enough of Richard's posturing for one day and kept walking.

As he stood outside the tower block, Paul's brain was still fizzing with questions, doubts, and rampaging paranoia. He rang the buzzer. No reply. He rang it again. And then a third time. Finally, there was a click. Someone had picked up.

'It's me,' said Paul. 'Can I come up?'

'It's late,' mumbled Alice. But then the buzzer sounded, and the door clicked open.

Paul took the overly bright lift to the third floor and gently rapped on the door of apartment thirteen. Alice opened up, her eyes half shut. Before the door had closed on him, his lips had found hers and he was kissing, fumbling, and falling into her. Wide awake now, Alice broke off and pulled Paul by the belt buckle backwards into the bedroom.

Later, in the quiet of the dark, Paul listened to the ebb and flow of Alice's breathing. 'Are you awake?' he whispered.

She stirred, turned, and lay an arm across his chest.

'I think I may be out of my depth,' he said.

Alice stroked Paul's cheek. 'You did okay.' She smiled seductively.

Paul ignored the joke. 'A car came at us tonight and almost killed us both.'

Alice sat up. 'What?'

'Out of nowhere. Just drove straight at us.'

'Jesus Christ, Paul.' Alice's face was full of concern. 'This is getting way out of hand. You need to go to the police.'

'I can't. We've got nothing on whoever it is who's doing this. It's just speculation.'

'But I thought you knew who it was?'

Paul remembered his lie and thought fast. 'I thought I did,' he said, 'but – oh, I don't know. I'm tired.' He sank beneath the duvet.

Alice followed him, squeezing in behind him.

'You should give it up,' she said.

'What?'

'Give it up. Stop. It's not worth losing your life over.'

'But then they win.'

'So what? It's better than being dead.'

'It's not that simple.'

'It's exactly that simple!' Alice's voice softened. 'I'm not saying destroy the script. Keep the script.' She smiled. 'You could keep it here. I could hide it for you. I could hide you.'

'I couldn't put you in the front line like that.'

'No one would know.'

'They seem to know everything else about me.' Paul shook his head. 'It's too dangerous. And anyway, the script's already in a safe place.'

'Not in your flat, I hope?' asked Alice.

'Of course not.'

'Listen,' said Alice. 'Stay here, if you don't feel safe in your flat.'

'I'm a liability.'

'You're lovely, is what you are.' She kissed him gently, and then with more urgency, until he let himself tumble into her again.

Paul woke to the sound of music drifting in through the open bedroom door. He pulled on a pair of boxers and shuffled through to the kitchen. Alice was at the cooker, singing along to the radio. Some god-awful pop tune Paul had never heard before. He was about to head back to the warmth of the bed when Alice whipped her head round.

'Morning, sleepyhead.' She smiled.

'What time is it?'

'Almost eleven.'

'Sorry,' said Paul. 'I didn't mean to sleep so long.'

'You needed it,' said Alice, still grinning. 'After last night.'

'It was pretty intense, wasn't it?'

'Not that!' Alice laughed. 'I mean almost getting run over.' She crossed the room and wrapped her arms around him, kissing him lightly. 'Though that was intense and lovely, too.' She kissed him again, then broke off. 'Coffee okay?'

Paul nodded and sat at the kitchen table.

'And some toast?' asked Alice. 'I'm having some. Or I could make you some eggs?'

'Coffee's fine.'

Alice brought two mugs over and sat. 'So what are you going to do now?'

'I've been thinking about it, and you're right. I have to go to the police.'

Alice sighed in relief. 'At last! You shouldn't have let it go this far. It needs to stop.'

'I'm still not sure they'll be able to do anything,' Paul said, sipping his coffee. 'I mean, apart from the emails and the online stuff, I don't have anything concrete. Last night could have been a drunken idiot who just lost control of his car.'

'But you don't believe that, do you?'

'No, but that's what they might say. There's nothing connecting the threatening emails with the break-in or the incident last night. Just paranoia. *My* paranoia.'

'But at least you're doing something about it,' said Alice. 'Before you get really hurt. Of course, if you just did what–'

Another terrible pop song blared from the radio.

'Could we turn that off, maybe?' Paul rubbed at his temples.

'Sure.' Alice got up and flicked the dial, catching the lead story of the eleven o'clock news.

'... international banking group, London Regal. A spokesperson for the bank said administration had been inevitable, given the severe losses sustained by the bank following the death, last July, of their CEO. The financial auditing firm, Tor-izon, has been called in to help find a rescue package to save the bank. This is the third time in eighteen months the Scandinavian firm has been involved in such a high-profile insolvency case. However, there appears to be little confidence in the city that London Regal will survive, its share value falling by over thirty percent since last Tuesday, as many of the bank's customers continue to queue at branches around the country in an attempt to close their accounts and withdraw savings while they still can. A spokesperson for Tor-izon was unavailable for comment this morning.'

Paul lowered his mug. 'Do you have a computer?'

'I've got a tablet in my bag. Why?'

'Can you look up Tor-izon for me, please?'

'You don't think you should rest a bit before–?'

'Please,' Paul urged.

Alice retrieved her device and logged on. 'What was that name again?'

You already know it. You wrote it on a Post-it note.

'Tor-izon,' said Paul. 'T. O. R. Dash. I. Z. O. N.'

Alice typed in the name and scrolled down the results until she found the company URL, which took them to a homepage in Swedish. She clicked on the English version, and the language switched. They scanned the page, but beyond some bland mission statements, glossy corporate video shorts, and a few sterile hi-tech images, there was very little detail. Alice scrolled down to a map of the world listing Torizon's global network of offices.

Paul leaned in. 'Check the UK.'

Alice zoomed in on northern Europe and clicked the icon hovering above Scotland. An address in Edinburgh popped up.

'Do you have a pen?' asked Paul.

'You're not thinking of actually going there, are you? To their office.'

'No harm having a look.'

'I'm not sure that's–'

'Just write the address down. Please.' Paul's irritation rose, and he struggled to contain it.

Alice shook her head and dug around in her bag for a pen. 'But you'll go to the police first, yeah?' she asked, scribbling down the address and handing Paul the scrap of paper.

'I will,' Paul promised, and of course, he didn't.

17

The Edinburgh branch of Tor-izon was located in the New Town, about a ten-minute walk from Waverley station. It was listed as number twenty-three, but the terrace Paul found himself on skipped from twenty-two to twenty-four. He checked the other side of the street. An uneven line of small shops stared back at him. He turned around and looked again at number twenty-two. *A law firm of some sort, by the looks of it..*

Paul rang the bell. The door clicked open, and he stepped inside. A young receptionist perched behind a polished mahogany monstrosity smiled as he approached.

'Can I help you?' he asked with a strong Edinburgh twang.

'I'm looking for the offices of Tor-izon,' said Paul. 'They should be at number twenty-three, but … there's no number twenty-three.'

'Twenty-two and twenty-three are the same address,' said the receptionist. 'Don't ask me why.' He shrugged. 'Something to do with the war, I think.'

'Okay. Thank you.' Paul turned to go.

'But you won't find anyone there.'

Paul stopped. 'Why's that?'

'Tor-izon only use it as a P.O. box address.'

A bespectacled middle-aged man in a light linen suit and tan loafers entered the reception area and dropped a letter onto the desk. 'ASAP, please,' he snapped.

The receptionist rolled his eyes at Paul.

'Are you are talking about next door?' the man asked.

'Yes, Mr Findlay,' replied the receptionist.

'Tor-izon. They're quite the outfit.' Mr Findlay removed his glasses and wiped them with his tie. 'Scandinavian, I believe.' He glanced up at Paul. 'I have an acquaintance in Norway. You don't need to know his name.'

The receptionist rolled his eyes at Paul again.

'He told me they pay their staff in Bitcoin. Did you know that? And that everyone is referred to by reference number, rather than by name.' Findlay smiled. 'Bloody foreigners.'

Paul cleared his throat. 'So … there's no one in the building, then. The one next door, I mean.'

'That's right,' said Findlay, 'although someone comes on the first Thursday of the month to collect the mail. Regular as clockwork.' He clicked his heels together. '*Vorsprung durch technik!*'

'Actually,' said the receptionist, turning to Paul, 'he's sometimes a day or two late. He usually pops in to say hello, but I didn't see him yesterday. Maybe you'll get lucky and catch him later.'

Paul nodded. 'Thank you. You've been very helpful.'

As he pushed through the door back out onto the street, Findlay bellowed after him.

'They make damned good bacon, I'll give them that!'

The façade of number twenty-two was a duplicate of next door's but with a more weather-beaten door and dirtier windows. Paul rubbed the grime off one of the panes and peered in. It was dark, but he could make out a corridor with rooms leading off on either side. He tried the door handle. Locked. *Shouldn't there be a plaque or logo somewhere with a name on it?* Paul checked his watch. There was still another six hours until the end of the working day. He was going to need a stakeout, and some help. That café he'd passed at the far end of the street, what about that? It was close enough to keep an eye on the building, yet far enough away not to attract attention. He rang Richard.

'Have you any idea how difficult it was to find this fucking café?' Richard slumped onto the chair opposite Paul. 'Where the hell did you go last night anyway?' He picked up the menu and scanned it.

'I went to see my parents,' Paul lied.

'You walked all the way?'

'I caught the night bus.'

'Lucky you,' said Richard. 'I spent my journey back to the first world in the company of three delightful young socialites who kindly offered to carry my wallet and phone for me on our long, dark journey home together.'

'So how come I was able to phone you?' asked Paul.

'The driver called the police and got the wee scrotal sacs arrested.' Richard sighed and leaned over the table. 'This better be fucking worth it. And before you start talking, I need coffee.'

'See that building up there?' said Paul, pointing, once Richard had returned with his latte.

Richard peered out the window. 'What about it? Bugger, that's hot.' He put his mug down.

'It's Tor-izon's office.'

'Who?'

'Tor-izon,' said Paul. 'Sound familiar?'

'I know a Tor Fleck,' said Richard. 'Don't think he has an office, though. Given that he doesn't fucking exist.'

'Tor-izon,' repeated Paul. 'As in … Tor's eyes on … us.'

'This is where we're at, is it?' Richard nodded. 'Actual people targeting us, that's not enough for you, we have to have words as well. Can you fucking hear yourself?'

'Listen,' said Paul. 'Tor-izon is a major financial auditing firm, okay? Those failing banks and corporations on the news? You know who they call when they're in the shit? Tor-izon are up to their necks in all of this. They're into everything. Data harvesting ... personality mining ...'

'Personality what?'

'All the bullshit conspiracy crap that's in our script ... turns out it's all fucking real.'

'Oh God,' groaned Richard. 'You're having one of your paranoid turns again.'

'Please don't start this shit again, Richard. Open your eyes and look around you, for fuck's sake. What about that first car, the one that tried to flatten us?'

'The guy saw me swear at him,' Richard said dismissively.

Ignoring the rage building in his chest, Paul handed Richard his phone. 'Look at this.'

Richard fumbled with the screen.' What?'

'Press fucking play,' Paul growled.

After more fumbling, Richard finally hit the right button, and a video started. A middle-aged man with long blond hair tucked under his cap talked silently to camera.

'Who's this?' asked Richard.

'Tor Torrensen. CEO of Tor-izon.'

Richard peered closer. 'Is that that same Peaky Blinders hat?'

'What do you think?' asked Paul. 'And that name? Tor Torrensen? Really?'

Richard handed the phone back. 'If a billionaire Abba lookie-likie wanted to kill me, he'd have a minion do it. They've all got minions, those bloody billionaires. They're minion-daft.'

'Maybe this is who Quinn's investigating.'

'Quinn's a fat lump of rancid cheese,' said Richard. 'He's a fucking fraud.'

'Maybe,' said Paul. 'But the only thing we know for sure right now is that that grubby little building out there is Tor-izon's main office in the UK. And they only use it as a P.O. box.'

'P.O. box addresses are all the rage these days,' said Richard. 'It'll be a tax dodge. Their actual registered office'll be in Luxembourg or the Caymans.'

'Something's not right,' said Paul. 'I had a squint inside. It's like no one's been there in years.'

Richard took a sip of his coffee.

'So what do you want to do?' he said, wearying of Paul's persistence.

Paul glanced round to make sure he wasn't being overheard. 'Once a month, a guy comes to pick up the post. There's a good chance he'll be there this afternoon. I thought if we waited for him, and you caused some kind of distraction, I could duck inside and take a closer look.'

'What kind of distraction?' asked Richard.

'Anything you want.' Paul shrugged. 'You're the master bullshitter.'

'So it's like *Miami Vice,* and we're on a stakeout?' Richard's enthusiasm suddenly piqued.

'If you want.'

'I very much want.' Richard grinned and rubbed his hands together. 'Oh, just one thing.'

'What's that?'

'All respectable stakeouts involve eating vast quantities of food.'

'Is that right?' Paul asked sarcastically.

'And this particular undercover cop is fucking starving after my night of the long knives.'

Paul scanned the room. 'I'll ask about the specials. Lunch is on me.'

Two paninis, a large slice of tiffin, and four cups of coffee later, there was still no sign of the Tor-izon mailman.

'Are you sure the target's coming today?' asked Richard, slurping loudly at the cold, dead dregs of his coffee.

'Target?'

'Play along, please!'

The waitress stopped at their table and cleared away the debris. 'Anything else?'

'We're okay, thanks,' said Paul.

'It's just you've been in here, what, most of the day, and–'

'We'll have two cartons of orange squash, please.' Richard smiled.

'You mean the kids' orange?'

'The very same.'

The waitress let out a sigh, rolled her eyes, and returned to the counter.

By five to five, with the waitress conspicuously plonking chairs on top of empty tables and glowering at them both ferociously, not a single person had approached number twenty-four.

'He's not coming,' Richard said. He grabbed his coat. 'Let's go.'

BANG! The door was slammed and bolted behind them before Paul and Richard had even stepped onto the street.

'One last walk up and down,' suggested Paul.

'Oh, Jesus,' said Richard. 'Really? Only if we go to the boozer after. And I mean *right* after.'

Paul didn't reply. He was already halfway towards the Tor-izon office. Richard had to run to catch up. Just then, turning a corner and heading straight towards them, appeared an elderly man in a grubby raincoat and tartan scarf.

'Keep walking,' whispered Paul.

The man passed, climbed the stairs to number twenty-four, fumbled with a set of keys, and let himself in.

'That's him,' said Paul.

'You think?'

'When he reappears, be ready.'

'I still don't know what it is I'm supposed to do.'

'Just do something,' said Paul. He set off down the street and ducking behind some bins.

Two minutes later, and the man still hadn't emerged. Richard shrugged at Paul, who jabbed his finger frantically at the door behind Richard. The elderly man had emerged at the top of the steps clutching a fistful of papers. Richard bounded up to him before he could close the door. Paul couldn't make out what was said, but both men laughed and stepped down onto the street, leaving the way clear for Paul.

Paul slipped past unseen and entered the building. A gloomy corridor led to a solitary door at the end. Paul looked for a handle, but the surface was smooth, offering no way in. He put his shoulder to it, but the reinforced steel was not for moving. He pressed his ear to the door. A loud hum came from the other side, like the dull whirring of a machine. A sudden laugh from outside had him turning and running back up the corridor. At the door, he peeked out. Richard was helping the man pick up some letters scattered across the pavement. Paul slipped out and was down the steps and away without anyone knowing.

Back at Waverley, they stopped at the station bar to catch their breath.

'So,' said Richard, picking up the pint Paul had just bought him, 'after all that, you didn't find anything?'

'No, but there's something odd going on in there.'

'Like what?'

'Like machinery, or a generator of some sort. I've never heard anything like it.'

'So you think we've uncovered an alien invasion,' said Richard sarcastically, 'is that it?'

'I'm just saying I don't know what it is. But it can't be anything good.' Paul took a sip of beer. 'It was bloody stressful in there. Well done for distracting the old bloke.'

'Piece o' piss. He just seemed happy to be chatting to somebody.'

'Did he tell you anything about Tor-izon?'

'No,' said Richard, 'but he did tell me about the two hernias he's had. Oh, and his ex-wife used to live in Glasgow, but she … sorry, *he,* since the op … is now living in Ealing with a hairdresser. Interesting guy.' He grinned. 'He was a wee bit clumsy with his mail, though. He dropped it everywhere.' He reached into his coat pocket. 'I kindly helped him retrieve most of it.' He pulled out a letter. 'Except this.'

'You stole it?'

'Don't be daft. I just forgot to hand it back.'

'You are a bad person.'

'I am that,' said Richard. He downed his pint.

'So …' said Paul. 'Should we open it?'

'Nah,' said Richard. 'I'll just run after him and hand it back. Course we're fucking opening it!'

Tentatively, Paul picked at the corner of the seal.

'Oh, give it here, for fuck's sake.' Richard snatched the envelope from Paul and tore it open.

'What is it?' Paul asked impatiently.

Richard opened up the letter and scanned its contents.

'Come on,' said Paul. 'Let me see.'

'It's an electricity bill,' said Richard.

Paul looked deflated.

'But look how much is due.'

Paul peered closer. £13,475.

'And that's for a month.'

'That's an awful lot of electricity for an unused office.'

Richard whistled the theme tune to *The Twilight Zone*.

'You have to admit it's strange, though,' said Paul. 'You think it's got something to do with that hum that I heard?'

'No idea, mate,' said Richard. 'Why don't you ask that lot next door?'

'Or …' said Paul. '… we could go back ourselves and find out.'

'Break in, you mean?'

'We could try round the back, see if there's an easy way in through the basement.'

'Since when did you become the gung-ho member of this franchise?'

'We'll wait until dark, then go have a recce. What do you think?'

'I think you've lost it, mate,' said Richard. 'I was happy to help you out with the mail guy, but this? This is breaking the law. And they're a multinational organisation, for fuck's sake! They're not just going to leave the back door open.'

'You've seen how run-down it is,' said Paul. 'Security might not be as tight as you think.'

Richard stood. 'Sorry. You're on your own on this one.'

'So you're not going to help me?'

Richard held Paul's gaze. 'I've done more than enough to appease your madness. Because that's what this is. Madness.' He picked up his bag. 'See you in Barlinnie.'

For a moment, Paul considered following him out. Instead, he crossed to the bar and ordered another pint, this time with a whisky chaser. He was going to need it.

It was dark by the time Paul left the pub. He crossed the road and slipped into the lane behind the terrace, counting the walled back entrances until he got to twenty-two. Tor-izon's. The door was locked, so he wheeled a bin over and climbed up onto it. There were no security cameras on the building, and the yard itself was empty. Paul waved an arm back and forth, but no light came on. *Perfect.* He was over the wall in seconds, careful not to slip on the grimy concrete. The back door had been bricked up, but there was a small window at ground level. He knelt in front of it and peered through the filth. A myriad of coloured lights flickered in the darkness: racks of electronic equipment, hard drives stacked to the ceiling. He turned at the sudden slamming of a car door. An engine purred and slowly faded away.

Did someone just get in, or did someone just get out?

Paul ran back to the wall and listened. Nothing. But the incident had him spooked. He clambered back over the wall but lost his footing on the bin and crashed to the ground.

A voice roared through the dark. 'Oi! Stop!'

Paul had no intention of stopping. He hauled himself up and limped back along the lane. When he got to the main road, he shot a look over his shoulder. Two men in dark suits were running after him.

Fuck!

He crossed the road and took a quick right and then a left. His ankle was killing him, and his lungs felt on fire. Hard-soled shoes pounded the pavement behind him, closing in. Jumping a low hedge, Paul cut through a front garden and up a lane, praying it wasn't a dead end. Halfway up, he tripped over a bin bag and fell flat, scraping and bloodying his palms in an effort to protect his face. Scrabbling to his feet, he stumbled on.

By the time he'd got to Waverley, Paul was sure he'd given his pursuers the slip. But he wasn't taking any chances. He leapt off the escalator and made a limping dash for the loos, kicking open a cubicle door and crawling up onto the seat. He sat like that for a full five minutes, a bloodied hand pressed against his mouth, stifling his fractured breathing. When the outer door suddenly burst open, he gasped and held his breath, his heart in overdrive.

A pair of polished black brogues appeared beneath the door of the cubicle.

THUMP-THUMP! THUMP-THUMP!

Paul was convinced his heart would give him away. Either that or explode. He backed up against the loo seat, trying to make himself smaller.

THUMP-THUMP-THUMP! THUMP-THUMP-THUMP!

The brogues retreated. Paul's relief was palpable, until … *PING!* A notification came through on his phone.

THUMP-THUMP-THUMP-THUMP! THUMP-THUMP-THUMP-THUMP!

The brogues ran back to the cubicle door. The handle rattled and shook and …

A couple of drunks stumbled into the loo, laughing and swearing. The brogues backed away, and a second later were gone. Paul waited until the drunks had left before sliding off the seat and easing the door open. All clear. *Jesus.* He stumbled to the sink and retched violently. He thought he was going to pass out but splashed water on his face, and that seemed to do the trick. He checked his phone. The ping had been a text from Alice. It read:

Hope you are okay. What did the police say? Missing you x

Whatever suspicions Paul had about Alice's motives, the kiss at the end of the text felt very comforting, and he had a sudden pang of longing for her bed. *No,* he thought. *Police first, bed later,* and pushed open the door.

18

The desk sergeant looked up from his *Racing Post*. 'You want to do what?'

'Report an attempted murder, an assault, stalking, death threats, and intent to cause physical and psychological torment,' said Paul.

The sergeant sighed. 'And your name, sir?'

'Paul Grant. We had a break-in a couple of weeks ago. I spoke to a PC Green.'

'Just a moment, sir.' The sergeant rolled off his seat and disappeared into the depths of the station. He returned moments later with three police officers, but no PC Green.

One of the officers walked up to Paul and held out his hand. 'Mr Grant?'

Paul reached out to shake it. 'Yes, that's right.'

'I'm arresting you–'

'What?'

The officer grabbed Paul's arm and twisted it behind his back.

The two other officers moved to the door, blocking it and making escape impossible.

'I'm arresting you,' the officer continued, 'on suspicion of stalking, harassment, intimidation, and intent to cause grievous bodily harm to a number of individuals.'

'But that's what's happening to me!' Paul protested, trying to pull his arm away. 'I've just come in to report it.'

'You do not have to say anything, but if you do so it may be used in evidence against you. Do you understand?'

'No, I don't fucking understand,' said Paul. 'I'm the victim here. Someone tried to run me down last night. I was attacked in my own home. You lot even came to the flat!'

The arresting officer pushed him towards a set of double doors leading to a stairwell.

'Please don't make things worse for yourself, Mr Grant,' he said. 'We wouldn't want you to get hurt.'

Paul took the hint and let himself be navigated to wherever it was he was being taken.

The cell door slammed shut behind him. Paul stood motionless in the centre of the bare room. *How could this happen? How is this justice?* He turned and battered on the door.

'Let me out! I need to speak to somebody!'

The slat in the door slid open, and a pair of eyes appeared. 'Calm down,' the disembodied voice said.

'Get Detective Quinn,' pleaded Paul. 'He knows what's going on. They've set me up!'

The slat snapped shut.

Paul banged on the door again. 'You can't just lock me up for nothing! I have rights! I want to make a phone call. Give me my one phone call!' He continued hammering at the door until his arms got tired. Giving up, he slumped onto the hard narrow bench and held his head in his hands. He felt as though his world was spiralling deeper into the darkest of sinkholes with no way out. Panic gripped his throat, and he choked.

No fucking way! he thought. *I'm not dying in a prison cell!*

He grabbed his coat, held it up to his nose and mouth, and breathed in hard. The world swam in shades of black and grey, stars winking in the corners of his vision. He lunged for the door but fell forward onto the floor and passed out.

When he came to he was no longer in the cell. He was seated at a table, in what appeared to be an interview room. The same burly officer from before was kneeling by Paul's side.

'Are you okay now, Mr Grant?' he asked. 'You had a panic attack and passed out.'

Paul's lips moved, but all he managed was an indecipherable slurring.

'Shh.' The officer held up a plastic cup of water. 'Drink this.'

Paul gulped the water down. It felt good. His surroundings were starting to make sense now.

'Your solicitor is here,' said the PC. 'We'd like to conduct a formal interview with you.'

'My solicitor?'

A figure to the right of Paul leaned over. 'Good afternoon, Mr Grant. I'm Brendan Cole, the duty solicitor.' Cole wore a moth-eaten suit, and the hand he offered resembled a rancid kipper.

Paul declined to shake it.

'I don't need a solicitor,' he said. 'I haven't done anything wrong.'

The PC stood. 'And yet you asked for one.' He crossed back to the table. 'I strongly recommend you have a solicitor present with you today, Mr Grant.'

'No, listen,' said Paul. 'I'm the one being stalked and harassed and threatened and assaulted. I need the police to help me, not arrest me.'

The PC sat. 'So you do not wish your solicitor to be present, is that correct?'

Paul's anger rose. 'Did you hear what I just said? I don't need a bloody solicitor!'

Cole leaned over. 'Mr Grant, I really–'

'Fuck off!' snapped Paul. 'Just ... fuck off!'

An aggrieved Cole grabbed his briefcase and left. The burly PC stared at Paul across the table for a second and then rose and followed Cole out.

A moment later, the PC was back, along with two men in matching dark suits, who sat opposite Paul. Registering the skeletal thinness of one of them and the borderline obesity of the other, Paul immediately dubbed them the Twin Peaks Laurel and Hardy.

Twin Peaks Hardy spoke first. 'This is Detective Inspector Marks,' he said, nodding to Twin Peaks Laurel, 'and I'm Detective Superintendent Burroughs.

Before we commence the interview, could we get you a tea or a coffee?'

'I just want to leave,' said Paul. 'I don't know what this is about, but I came in today to report an attempted murder.'

Twin Peaks Laurel bared his teeth. They looked like talons, barely held in place by sunken, emaciated skin.

'For your own protection,' said Twin Peaks Hardy, 'we'll be recording this interview.'

'Are you deaf?' asked Paul. 'I was almost killed. Go find the bastard.'

Hardy switched on the cassette recorder. 'Interview commencing at twelve thirty-four p.m.,' he said, 'conducted by detectives Burroughs and Marks, with PC Fields also in attendance.'

Paul shook his head in disbelief. *What a fucking farce.*

'For the purpose of the tape,' Hardy continued, 'can you please state your full name?'

'Paul Grant. Victim of stalking.'

'Okay, Mr Grant,' said Hardy, looking Paul in the eye. 'We've received a number of complaints recently, from various individuals, alleging harassment, intimidation, and death threats via text, email, and online social media. All from you.'

'Who are these individuals?' asked Paul sarcastically. 'The fucking seven dwarves?'

'The perpetrator goes by the name of Tor Fleck.'

'Oh, for fuck's sake,' exclaimed Paul.

Hardy shot Paul a look of disgust. 'May I remind you that this interview is being recorded?'

Paul rubbed at his chin. 'Tor Fleck is a completely fictitious name.'

'Go on.'

'What I mean is … my flatmate and I came up with a fictional author for a film script we were writing. We called him Tor Fleck.'

Hardy leaned in closer to Paul. 'Tor Fleck is a fictional character?'

Twin Peaks Laurel, his arms crossed, sneered at the thought.

'Can you explain, then,' Hardy continued, 'how these threatening messages, these physical messages, came to be signed off by a fictional character?'

'Look,' said Paul, 'we've been getting harassed for weeks. Our flat's been broken into, we've had death threats, and last night somebody tried to run me and my flatmate over. I can show you the texts, if you don't believe me.'

'It seems rather a wild coincidence,' said Hardy, 'that these messages would be coming from a man who you appear to have "invented"?'

Laurel nodded solemnly in agreement.

'Oh, come on,' said Paul. 'It's so obviously a setup. If I were a troll, I wouldn't be daft enough to use the name of a fictional character I'd just created, would I?'

'That's a good point,' agreed Laurel, speaking for the first time.

Hardy shot him a stern look.

'Speak to Detective Quinn,' said Paul. 'He'll back up what I'm saying.'

Hardy shrugged. 'Who the hell's Detective Quinn?'

'You know,' said Paul. 'Quinn. Big bloke. Bigger than you, even. American. Smells a bit.'

Hardy shook his head. 'From this station?'

'I don't know,' said Paul. 'Maybe.'

'I'll check it out,' said Hardy and wrote down Quinn's details. He looked back up. 'Why did you say you've been set up?'

'Well, it's the same lunatics who are stalking us, isn't it? They're trying to frame me.'

'An interesting theory,' said Hardy. He opened the folder in front of him. It was empty. He closed it gently and snatched Laurel's folder from him.

Laurel tried to wrestle it back.

'Could you confirm,' grunted Hardy, finally yanking the file free from Laurel's clutches, 'that your address is Top Flat, thirty-three Bale Street, Glasgow?'

Laurel sat back, exhausted from the tussle, and scratched his head.

Paul nodded.

'For the purpose of the tape,' said Hardy, 'the suspect has indicated that the address is correct.' He leaned across the table. 'How do you explain the fact that the emails were traced to various social media accounts set up in your name, and sent from a computer registered to you?'

'I thought you said they were sent by Tor Fleck?'

Hardy checked his papers.

'When were these messages sent?' asked Paul.

Hardy was flustered. He rustled through the folder looking for details.

'There,' said Laurel, reaching out and pointing to a page.

Hardy snapped the folder shut on his colleague's hand. Laurel winced and slowly withdrew his fingers.

'I've got this, thanks,' sniped Hardy and turned his attention back to Paul. 'Approximately thirty-six threatening texts, as well as a series of emails, all sent between sixth and eighth of October, to various individuals, from a source traced to your home computer,' he said triumphantly. 'How do you explain that?'

'Can you actually do that?' asked Paul. 'I mean, are you allowed?'

'We are allowed to do many things, Mr Grant,' replied Hardy.

'Really?'

'Yes, really.'

'What were those dates again?' asked Paul.

'The sixth to the eighth of October.'

'I didn't have my laptop then,' said Paul. 'It was at the repair shop.'

'How very convenient.'

'You can check if you like. I handed it in to Crash Test Computers, on Byers Road, last Friday. That was …' Paul counted back in his head. '… the seventh of October. Go ask Axel, the owner. He was going to do the repair.'

'We'll investigate that in due course,' muttered Hardy, 'but in the meantime–'

'He's right, though,' interrupted Laurel. 'He did have a break-in four weeks ago.'

Hardy frowned at his colleague. 'You want to swap places with him?'

'And PC Green attended.'

'That's right,' agreed Paul.

'Our PC Green?' asked Hardy. Suddenly, he was interviewing his colleague, not Paul.

Laurel nodded. 'His flatmate suffered an alleged assault. I had to sign off on the paperwork.'

'Then why didn't you–?' Hardy stopped himself and sighed.

'Fucking amateurs,' mumbled Paul.

Hardy slammed his fist on the table. 'I'd be very careful if I were you, Mr Grant. Very careful. Bad things happen to bad people all the time.'

'I didn't mean you,' said Paul. 'I meant the people trying to frame me.'

'The interview is suspended at twelve forty p.m.' Hardy switched off the tape recorder and stood. 'A word, Detective, please.'

Laurel followed Hardy out. Muffled shouting echoed in the corridor. *Idiots.* Even PC Fields was trying hard not to laugh.

Returned back to his cell, Paul didn't have the strength to bang on the door again. Fear and fury had exhausted him. Slumping onto the bare wooden bench, he resolved to wait it out until Quinn arrived and he got released. But as minutes turned into an hour, and beyond, Paul's paranoia escalated. Who was behind these attacks? Why had Alice feigned ignorance about Tor-izon? Was Quinn even a real detective? Christ, was Richard involved in any of this? Had his obsession with the script driven him beyond all reason? If so, why? For sole ownership of Agency O? As the questions continued to spiral, Paul's trust in those closest to him faded like morning mist.

'Stop!' he cried, his voice bouncing off the six-by-eight concrete walls. He stood and crossed to the door, thumping at it with what little strength he had left.

'Let me out!' he yelled. 'Let me out!'

To his surprise, the small hatch was pulled open.

'At last,' he said. 'Is Detective Quinn here?'

In response, a small tray was shoved at him. On it sat a plastic cup and a digestive biscuit.

'I don't fucking want tea!' Paul hollered. 'I want out of here!' But hunger and thirst sometimes get the better of protest, and this was one of those times. Reluctantly, he lifted the tray away and took it over to the bench. The over-brewed murky tea swirled in the polystyrene cup. He broke the biscuit in two and dunked it in, but it crumbled into the slurry.

Fuck's sake!

Holding his nose, he downed the lukewarm liquid in a single gulp, leaving a brown, biscuity sludge at the bottom. He yawned. He was knackered. He lay down on his side, the least uncomfortable position he could find, and pulled his coat over his shoulder. It wasn't long before he fell into a restless, semi-conscious state. It was a prod to the kidneys that eventually woke him.

'Mr Grant?'

Paul rolled over and squinted up through the glare of the strip-light. Twin Peaks Oliver Hardy hovered over him, flanked by two uniformed officers. *Uh-oh.*

'Some new evidence has come to light,' said Hardy. 'We're releasing you without charge. You're free to go.'

What?

'Well, well, well,' said Paul, hauling himself off the bench and gathering up his things. 'Common sense prevails at last. Did you speak to Quinn?'

'This is an on-going investigation,' said Hardy, 'so don't go booking any flights. We may need to speak with you again.'

Paul pushed past him to the door. Hardy grabbed his arm.

'Make sure you sign out on your way past the desk,' he said. Then, in a lower voice, 'This isn't over.'

The desk sergeant glowered at Paul and handed him the sign sheet.

'Do you still wish to report any other alleged crimes?' he asked with a smirk.

'Are you serious?' said Paul. 'You lot couldn't solve a *Scooby Doo* mystery.'

The sergeant shrugged and pushed the clipboard back under his *Racing Post*.

Paul needed to clear his head before facing Richard again so took the long way home through the park. As he emerged on the other side, he was suddenly grabbed from behind and wrestled to the ground, where he was gagged and blindfolded. His hands were bound, and he was bundled unceremoniously into the boot of a car. Soon he was being tossed from side to side, his head battering against the hard interior. He kicked out, but the car sped on regardless.

After fifteen minutes of claustrophobic torture, the car finally stopped, and then came the familiar crunch of feet on gravel. The boot hatch clicked open, and he was hauled out, legs flailing, and carried indoors. The stink of petrol and dust was everywhere. He was dropped onto a chair, ropes tightening around his chest, his waist, his ankles. A door slammed shut. Paul twisted his head round but couldn't see through the gag. He tried wriggling out of the ropes, but their tightness tore at his skin.

Minutes seemed to drag into hours before another door creaked open. Feet clicked across a concrete floor. Someone was breathing next to Paul's ear. He swung his head sideways and head-butted whoever was there. There was a yelp of pain, some shuffling and mumbling, and then the blindfold was removed. Paul screwed up his eyes against a piercing white light.

A shadowy figure was moving in and out of the glare. As Paul's eyes adjusted, he could just make out a large floor lamp being beamed into his face. Beyond the lamp, a bare concrete room slowly emerged. *A cell? A garage lock-up?* Someone pulled the gag from Paul's mouth, and he yelled as loud as he could.

'Save your breath,' growled a voice from beyond the lamp. 'Nobody can hear you.'

'Help!' Paul screamed. 'Help! Help!'

The figure moved in front of the lamp for a moment, and Paul caught brief glimpses of his captor: a large body, a long black coat, a mask.

'You're making things very difficult for us,' the figure hissed. His voice seemed to be artificially altered, as though filtered electronically.

'Oh, I'm so fucking sorry,' Paul barked back sarcastically.

'Indeed you will be.' The mask stepped closer.

Paul almost shat himself as a pouting Donald Trump emerged from the light, his loose rubber lips flopping and folding with every move.

'Fuck off!' Paul shouted, his body jerking and spasming against the straps, almost toppling his chair.

Trump Mask stepped back, waiting till Paul had exhausted himself.

'You continue to disappoint us, Mr Grant,' Trump Mask said. He was speaking into a small plastic mic, attached to what appeared to be a child's mini karaoke speaker.

'Oh, for fuck's sake,' said Paul, giving up on the ropes. 'What is this? A bad fucking Bond movie? What is it you want?'

'Two things,' said Trump Mask. He held the mic up to the wrinkled, ruby-red sphincter of a rubber mouth. 'Erase your script from all online sources, delete your files, and shred all hard copies.'

'That's three things.' Paul smirked.

'Shut your–' Feedback screeched through the karaoke speaker. Trump Mask smacked the side of the plastic box. It wailed again, and then stopped. 'Comply,' he said, his voice jumping a couple of octaves; he sounded like a toddler. He wrestled with the machine again, and it growled and barked as though it was fighting back.

'And if I don't?' asked Paul. 'Oh, let me guess. You'll get Odd Job to throw me to the sharks. Or will you just laser my bollocks in half?'

Trump Mask threw the karaoke machine across the room, where it smacked the wall with a fatal scream. He lunged at Paul, grabbing him by the throat, choking him. 'Comply!' he roared, tightening his grip.

Paul could barely breathe. He tried to wriggle free, but the ties were too tight. His lungs burned. He pleaded with his eyes for Trump Mask to stop. The man squeezed Paul's throat tighter still.

'Enough!' A roar from an unseen woman.

Trump Mask froze.

'Enough!' she repeated.

Trump Mask released his grip. Paul gasped in mouthfuls of air, coughing and spluttering as the oxygen raced down his windpipe. Trump Mask put his lips to Paul's ear.

'Comply,' he whispered.

'Okay, okay,' rasped Paul. 'I'll do as you say.'

'And the master file?'

'I'll give it to you.'

'Good boy,' Trump Mask sneered.

'Somewhere public.' Paul paused to catch his breath. 'St George's Square.'

Trump Mask grabbed Paul by the hair and shook him violently.

'Argh!' Paul yelled. A searing pain shot across his scalp.

'St George's Square,' Trump Mask hissed. 'Tomorrow. Ten a.m.'

Paul nodded in agreement.

'And let me be clear,' threatened Trump Mask, 'No-show or no stick, and it's goodbye Mr Grant and Mr Gann.'

'Okay, okay,' said Paul. 'I'll be–'

A blindfold was flung roughly over his eyes and a fresh gag stuffed into his mouth. He was dragged from the chair back out into the chilled air and squeezed into the back seat of a vehicle, sandwiched between two hulks. As the vehicle took off, the hulks grabbed his arms and pinned him back.

This journey was shorter than the last. The car pulled to a halt after only a couple of minutes, and Paul was thrown out onto cold tarmac. He spat out the gag and untied the blindfold to find himself outside Hillhead Tube station on Byres Road. It was rush hour, the street busy with commuters. He was bumped into by one of them and almost fell off the kerb. He searched for the departing car, but the road was already heaving with traffic. He stopped a passer-by.

'Did you see where that car went?' he asked.

The passer-by looked at Paul as though he'd just asked him to wipe his arse for him and hurried on past.

'Did nobody see that?' Paul asked the mass of passing bodies.

But everyone was too preoccupied: with their phones, their music, their getting home. They had no time for another student prank, or whatever this was. Paul straightened himself up and headed home. He'd only gone a couple of yards when he veered into a pub and ordered a pint and a double chaser, and when they were done, he ordered a couple more.

19

Paul threw up into the toilet as though in a sudden rush to rid himself of all the shit of the past few months. Nerves, stress, worry, and the remains of the previous night's chicken chasni all found themselves swimming together in a thick soup at the bottom of the bowl. *Better out than in,* he thought grimly as he pushed down on the button-flush and watched the gloop of his past swirl away. *If only it was that simple.*

He found some ibuprofen in the kitchen and made himself a coffee. He'd need both for what was to come, the dread of which had suddenly hit him like a runaway train. He squinted at the clock: eight-fifteen. Where the hell was Richard? He shouted for him, his temples pounding as the words reverberated around his skull, but the flat was empty. The one time he could really do with Richard's help, and he'd pulled his fucking Keyser Söze act. *Twat.*

Paul slumped down at the table and plotted out the handover in St George's Square. What was he thinking? He'd only said it to buy some time, but now he had to decide whether to actually go through with it or not. He could give them a blank USB stick, of course, or at least one with a bogus file on it. Maybe then he'd get a look at the perpetrators. Was he up to a citizen's arrest? Could he tackle his stalker, bring him down in the centre of St George's Square? He shook his head. *Bad idea.* No, he would hand over the stick and then attract the attention of the police. Maybe create a scene to make sure they 'engaged' with the situation. But then what? He rubbed his eyes. His head was still throbbing. *Fast-acting ibuprofen, my arse.*

On the way to the underground, Paul passed the computer repair shop. The shutters were down, and a small handwritten sign was taped to the door. *'Closed until further notice'.* Paul peered inside, but it was too dark to see anything clearly.

In the florist's next door, the elderly owner was busy arranging carnations on a large wreath.

'Excuse me,' said Paul, from the other side of the counter.

The florist glanced up. She seemed flushed and a little emotional.

'Oh, sorry, son,' she said. 'I didnae see ye there.' She gazed down at the floral display stretching from one end of the counter to the other. 'Poor man was only twenty-eight. Motorway pile up.' She placed a carnation strategically. 'This is for his wee daughter. She's only two.' She sniffed.

'You're doing a lovely job,' said Paul. He regretted coming in now.

'Thanks, son, though it'll be nae comfort to that poor mithir.'

Paul leaned over and placed his hands on the counter. 'I'm sorry, but do you know anything about the shop next door?'

The florist's eyes widened. 'No, that's very odd, isn't it? Axel usually tells me when he's planning on closing so I can keep a wee eye oot on his premises, ye ken? But he's never shut. I think the last time wiz when he went tae wan a they … sigh-figh … conventions.' She pronounced the word as though it was language from another planet. 'He's quite partial tae awe that guff. Dresses up in awe the gear, ken? Whit a sicht.'

'Thanks,' said Paul, feeling guilty for the intrusion. 'And please send my condolences to the family.' He nodded and left, leaving the florist to place the final white carnation at the end of the wreath, to complete the word *Daddy*.

Even at close to ten a.m. St George's Square was relatively busy. Tourists milled around, couples clinched on benches, and city workers puffed their way through one cancerous fag break after another. Paul checked his watch: nine-fifty. Christ, his heart was pumping. Weaving his way through a group of snap-happy Chinese and a troop of Chamber of Commerce dignitaries, he reached the fountain in the centre of the square and stopped. He slowly turned 360 degrees, checking the faces and body language of those around him. He clocked a shifty-looking male in dull blazer and scuffed shoes on the other side of the fountain. Was he one of them? The severe look on his face suggested he could be.

Paul took a breath and marched towards him, just as a woman appeared from the crowd and leapt into the man's arms. A lover. *Of course.* Paul bent down and pretended to tie his lace. He was sweating now. When he stood back up he was surrounded by a crescent of foreign tourists, all jostling for a perfect pose by the fountain. Above their heads, he spotted two men approach from the far side of the square, moving with purpose. Paul pushed his way towards them but tripped over a bag one of the tourists had placed on the ground and had to grab someone's shoulder to stop himself from falling. By the time he'd regained his balance, the two men had vanished.

Paul spun round. *There.* One of the men was about thirty feet away to his left. *Where's the other one?* Paul turned back the other way, but there was no sign of the accomplice. *Maybe they're just* – A sudden, thumping pain in Paul's side drew a sharp intake of breath from him and forced him to drop to his knees. His hand fumbled to his stomach. Something was sticking out of his abdomen. Something metal. Searing white heat shot across the front of Paul's body, and he slumped sideways. He tried to cry out, but no sound came. *DUNK!* His head hit the ground, a pool of blood quickly spreading across the tarmac from beneath his coat like melting raspberry ice cream. Screams echoed across the square as tourists and locals alike all fled. A pair of polished black brogues entered Paul's blurred eyeline, and he felt a hand grab at his clenched fist, twisting his fingers until his palm opened and he released the USB stick. Sirens sounded, growing louder and louder. The light faded, the world receded, and in a blink, he was consumed by darkness.

20

'Mr Grant … Paul … can you hear me?'

Paul opened his eyes. A woman in a white coat was leaning over him.

'It's good to have you back,' she said, sounding relieved.

'Wha–?'

'Don't try to speak. You've been through a long surgical procedure.' The doctor leaned in closer. 'You had us all a bit worried there for a while, but I think you're going to be all right now.'

The faint smell of her perfume had Paul wanting to throw up. 'What did they … the square?' he asked, incoherently.

The doctor looked Paul in the eye. 'You were shot by a crossbow, Mr Grant. The arrow penetrated your lower intestine and ruptured your bowel, causing quite a bit of internal bleeding. A nasty injury, but it could have been a lot worse.'

'Who?' Paul rasped.

'The police will give you more details when you're stronger. But for now,' the doctor smiled, 'you need to rest.'

'I saw–'

'All in good time, Mr Grant,' said the doctor. 'Rest first.'

When Paul next opened his eyes, Alice was sitting by his side.

'Hello, you.' She smiled and leant in, kissing him on the forehead. 'You are a worry, aren't you?'

'I was shot,' said Paul, his voice still weak.

'Shh,' said Alice, stroking his forehead. 'Don't speak.'

'Did they catch them?'

Alice stopped stroking. 'Who?'

'The two men in the square.'

'You need to let yourself recover.'

'They took the stick.'

'What stick?'

'There's nothing on it.' Paul shook his head.

'You're not making sense,' said Alice. 'You need to–'

'It's not over,' Paul interrupted. 'I still have the master.'

Alice put her hand back on Paul's forehead. 'Shh,' she soothed. 'Get some rest.'

Paul closed his eyes. Within seconds, he was gone again.

In the drug-induced blur beyond the bed, someone was moving. A figure in white. As his eyes adjusted, he saw it was a woman. A nurse. She was in the dresser at the back of the room, shifting his clothes from one side of the rack to the other. He thumped the bed, and she turned. She was wearing a surgical hat and mask, her eyes a glassy green. He pointed to the empty glass on the bedside table. She came over and grabbed his hand, forcing it beneath the sheet. He tried to resist, but his strength was shot. The nurse removed a syringe from her pocket and opened up the cannula on the back of his hand. He struggled, but she held him down and inserted the syringe into the socket. He wriggled in desperation, but her grip was too strong. Somehow, he managed to release his other arm from under hers and reached for the call button. The nurse snatched at his hand and pulled it free, but not before he'd squeezed out a silent call to arms. And then everything went black again.

'Are you sure it wasn't a dream?' the male nurse asked, refilling Paul's glass with water. 'Those painkillers are pretty powerful. They make you see all sorts of shit.'

You've got a tattoo of a fucking unicorn on your arm, thought Paul. *Why the fuck should I listen to you?* He grabbed the glass and gulped the water down.

'Steady,' said the nurse. 'You're going to burst that catheter.'

'It was real,' Paul croaked. 'She was here. She gave me something.'

The nurse took Paul's hand and inspected the cannula. 'Looks fine to me,' he said.

'She was trying to jab me with something. That's why I pressed the button.'

The nurse checked his watch. 'Look, man, I need to go,' he said. 'I'll be back later.'

'I don't feel safe,' said Paul.

'You're disorientated,' said the nurse. 'It's normal. You're doing fine.' And with that, he backed out of the room.

Paul could see him through the glass door talking with another nurse. They glanced back towards him, flashing fake smiles. *Who the fuck has a unicorn tattoo?*

Paul reached down and touched his side. A sharp pain shot down his leg. *Fuck.* He felt cornered and trapped, his injuries too painful to allow him to run. He might as well face it. He was going nowhere, at least for now.

'Did they do this to you?' Paul's dad hovered over the bed like a praying mantis.

'I don't know,' lied Paul, knowing the truth would send his dad into a tailspin.

'I tell ye whit,' said George. 'Those bastards huvnae half crossed the fuckin line here.'

'I don't know if it was them,' said Paul. 'It might have been some neds having a laugh, maybe aiming for the tourists, you know?'

George wasn't listening. 'Whoever it wis is as good as deed in ma book. An' ah've got friends who can help me find them.'

'Just leave it, Dad,' said Paul. 'I can fight my own battles.'

'You?' scoffed George. 'Ye couldnae fight yer wae oot ae a duvet.'

'All I'm saying is–' The sentence was never finished.

George flung a hand over his son's mouth as Paul's mum, Jean, swung through the door and approached the bed.

'The nurse said she'd get me a bowl for these grapes,' she said and placed them down on the bedside table.

'I'm sure they've got better things to do than hunt doon a bloody bowl, Jean,' huffed George, swiftly removing his hand from a gasping Paul's mouth.

Jean turned to Paul. 'Aw, son, we were really worried about you.' She leaned in to kiss him and accidentally brushed his side.

He winced.

'Oh, I'm sorry, son,' she said, quickly stepping back.

'Jesus Christ, Jean!' said George. 'Finish him aff, why don't ye!'

'Who told you I was here?' asked Paul.

'Oh, it was a nice young lady called … whit wis it, George?'

'Alice Lowe,' said George, looking increasingly uncomfortable in the sanitised surroundings of the ward. 'Never forget names. Part o' the trainin'.' He turned to Paul. 'Aboot time ye hud a click.' He winked. 'Ah wis beginnin' to think ye'd turned.'

'George, don't embarrass the laddie,' whispered Jean.

'She shouldn't have done that,' said Paul. 'How'd she get your number anyway?'

'I don't know,' said Jean, 'but she wiz awfa concerned about you. She's got a lovely soft voice, hasn't she?' She gave Paul one of her *'Shall I buy myself a new hat?'* smiles.

'She's from the film company,' said Paul. 'She's the one who likes our script.'

'Ah.' George grinned. 'Are ye sure that's aw she likes?'

George!' scolded Jean. She sat next to Paul and stroked his forehead. 'The doctor said you were very poorly but that you're out of danger now.'

'The bastards.'

'George!' Jean repeated.

'If I get my hands on them, they'll be in the fucking danger zone.'

'Oh, for God's sake, George. Not in the bloody hospital, please.'

Their squabble was interrupted by the arrival of a squeaky-trainered nurse. 'Sorry, but the police are here.' She looked at Paul. 'Are you ready to speak to them?'

'The polis?' sneered George. 'They're aboot as much use as a bag ae pork scratchins at a bar mitzvah.'

This time Jean's reprimand came in the form of a slap on the arm.

'Well,' said George, 'somebody needs tae tell them tae get thur trotters oot thur lazy arses an' catch the bastards who did this. Shower ae useless bloody morons.'

And so they proved. The two constables – only one of them old enough to remember dial-up Internet – took Paul's statement but offered no clues regarding the perpetrator of the attack. All they could confirm was that the investigation was ongoing and that they were going through CCTV footage from the scene. Their clearly rehearsed words were intended as reassurance but fell flatter than a peshwari naan. They were as disengaged and gormless as the pork scratchings George had compared them to. What was more pressing in Paul's mind, and what he couldn't let go of, was how Alice had gotten her hands on his parents' phone number. He needed to get closer to her; find a way through her bullet-proof armour and get to the truth about the mysterious Omni executive.

SCRIPT EDIT 14- HARVEY'S DISCOVERY SCENE

FADE IN:

INT: OPEN-PLAN OFFICE/SARAH'S OFFICE-NIGHT

In the middle of a large, empty office, a single desk is lit: Harvey's. He's at the PC, TYPING furiously.

SARAH (O.S.)

Your diligence is commendable.

Harvey jumps and swivels round.

HARVEY

Jesus. You scared me half to death.

SARAH

What are you doing, exactly?

HARVEY

Ballatine's asked me to come up with a new system to file archived accounts, but -

SARAH

Okay, so I need you to stop what you're doing and follow me.

HARVEY

I can't. He needs it by Thursday.

SARAH

I don't give a shit. Come.

Harvey rises reluctantly from his chair and follows Sarah to a minimalist space blocked off from the rest of the office by a glass wall. Inside, a nameplate with Sarah's name on it adorns a glass-topped desk.

Sarah PUNCHES a code into the tall, steel filing cabinet in the corner. The top drawer slides opens with a small CLICK. She takes out three large files and hands them to Harvey.

SARAH (CONT'D)

Take these.

HARVEY

What are they?

SARAH

Employee records.

Sarah sits at her desk.

SARAH (CONT'D)

I'd like you to look for any employees who have been fired or quit or … died.

HARVEY

There's a fuckload of records here.

SARAH

Ten years' worth. Make a note of personal details: name, address, employee number, et cetera. Also, the reason we 'let them go'.

HARVEY

Why?

SARAH

I'm not sure. Call it a hunch.

Harvey SIGHS.

HARVEY

What about Ballatine's accounts?

SARAH

I know you've been *very* busy oiling your way up the greasy pole, Harvey, but as far as I'm aware, I'm still your superior. Unless, of course, you've just been promoted again.

HARVEY

Fine.

INT. OPEN-PLAN OFFICE - NIGHT

A tower of files balance awkwardly on Harvey's desk. He glances back at Sarah's office.

Sarah is visible through the glass, writing at her desk.

Harvey SIGHS and opens the first file.

Viewed from the far end of the office, Harvey appears as a lonely, lighted island, surrounded by a sea of darkness.

FADE OUT

FADE IN:

INT. OPEN-PLAN OFFICE - NIGHT

Harvey flicks through page after page, until he sees …

… the name JAMESON. Harvey runs his finger down the page, stopping at the word DECEASED marked in red. He flicks back through the file. Other employee profiles have been marked the same way. A loud, dull SHOUT. Harvey looks up.

Sarah paces around her office. She's agitated, ARGUING with someone on the other end of the phone.

Harvey crosses to the water cooler, next to Sarah's office. He leans in close to her door, listening.

SARAH

I merely asked you why?

(pause)

Well, that's not a good enough reason.

(pause)

It looks to me like he's being groomed.

(pause)

I don't know what, you tell me!

(pause)

Oh, just be honest for once.

(pause)

Well, think what you like.

(pause)

Yeah, that's right. Fuck you!

Sarah SLAMS the phone down. Harvey returns to the water cooler and fills his cup. Then … a CRASH from inside. Harvey rushes back and KNOCKS on the glass screen.

SARAH (O.S.,CONT'D)

Go away!

INT. SARAH'S OFFICE - NIGHT

Harvey enters Sarah's office.

Sarah is on her knees, picking up shards of broken glass. On the floor is an upturned tray and a smashed water jug.

Harvey kneels beside Sarah.

SARAH (CONT'D)

It's okay. I have this.

Harvey turns the tray over. Picks up pieces of glass.

SARAH (CONT'D)

Leave it!

A shard of glass slices through Sarah's finger, and she recoils in pain. Blood oozes out.

SARAH (CONT'D)

Oh, great.

Sarah drops the shard and stands.

HARVEY

Let me see.

SARAH

It's nothing.

HARVEY

Give me your hand.

Sarah is reluctant but gives in. Harvey examines the wound.

HARVEY (CONT'D)

It's deep. Do you have any tissues?

SARAH

On my desk, there.

Harvey grabs the box, pulls out a tissue, and presses it against the wound. Sarah looks up at him.

HARVEY

Hold it and wait there.

Sarah silently does as Harvey says. He returns a moment later with a first-aid box. He takes out a surgical wipe and cleans the wound.

HARVEY (CONT'D)

You sounded upset. On the phone.

Sarah brusquely wipes a tear from her face.

SARAH

How many times have you been promoted since June?

HARVEY

What?

SARAH

It's a simple question. How many times?

HARVEY

Two.

SARAH

So what are you now?

HARVEY

My role? Assistant to the secretariat.

SARAH

So, in three months you have moved from office junior to assistant to the secretariat, one grade lower than me.

HARVEY

And?

SARAH

Have you ever stopped to think why you are being fast-tracked by our great leader?

HARVEY

I'd like to think it's because I'm good at what I do. Mr Ballatine seems happy with me.

SARAH

You honestly believe that?

HARVEY

Why wouldn't I?

Sarah shakes her head.

SARAH

You are so naïve. You have no qualifications, no experience, no life to speak of. Doesn't that strike you as a little … odd?

HARVEY

What is this? Are you feeling threatened?

SARAH

(LAUGHS)

By you? You're the one who should feel threatened.

HARVEY

What do you mean?

SARAH

Forget it.

HARVEY

You can't just say something like that and leave it.

SARAH

Mr Ballatine has plans for you. Big plans. But -

HARVEY

But what?

SARAH

Just … watch your back. Rewards round here come at a price.

HARVEY

What are you talking about?

SARAH

I like you, Harvey. But you need to know what you're getting into. All that glitters … might come with a nasty bite.

HARVEY

You're trying to scare me off.

You think I'm stupid?

Sarah grabs Harvey's arm.

SARAH

I mean it. Be very careful.

Sarah locks eyes with Harvey. She looks genuinely afraid. She slides her hand up his arm. He moves in closer and gently reaches around her waist. Their lips almost touch. They pause. Then they kiss. Passionately.

Sarah pushes Harvey up against the glass wall. He runs his hand up her leg and reaches for the zip of her skirt. She grabs his hand and pulls it away. Stepping back, she straightens her skirt and returns to her desk.

SARAH (CONT'D)

I suggest we call it a night … before we do something we regret.

Harvey is disorientated. What just happened?

HARVEY

I wouldn't regret it.

SARAH

Another life, maybe. Not this one. Not now.

HARVEY

Let's go for a drink.

SARAH

(smiling)

Goodnight, Harvey.

HARVEY

Just a drink, that's all. Colleague to colleague.

SARAH

Good. Night. Harvey.

HARVEY

You know I'm going to keep on asking you.

A bigger smile from Sarah this time.

SARAH

Idiot. See you tomorrow.

Harvey GRUNTS and leaves. He glances back …

… but Sarah's on the phone again.

Harvey's smile fades, his expression now one of worry.

FADE OUT

21

Paul slowly raised his left foot and placed it on the top stair.

'That's it, just one more push and we're there,' said Alice. She took a hold of his arm.

Paul swung his hips and, with Alice's help, made it onto the landing.

'There you go!' said Alice triumphantly. 'I told you you'd make it.'

Paul puffed his cheeks out and smiled. 'It's not that bad,' he said. 'As long as I take it slowly.'

'Exactly,' said Alice. 'And I'll remind you of that in a few days when you're climbing the walls. Metaphorically speaking, of course.'

Once inside the flat, Alice led Paul to the bedroom and carefully undressed him for bed.

'How's that?' she asked, tucking the duvet up around his shoulders.

Paul nodded tiredly in appreciation.

Alice sat next to him and rubbed his forehead. 'You want something to eat? Or drink?'

'Why are you doing this?' asked Paul.

'What?'

'Looking after me. We barely know each other.'

'We need to look after our future investment.'

'Is that all?'

'Of course,' said Alice. 'What other reason could there be?'

'Maybe that, I don't know, you might like me a little?'

Alice laughed and kissed him slowly on the lips. 'Of course I like you, you idiot.'

Paul leaned in for more.

'Right,' said Alice, standing, 'that's enough of that. You might split your stitches.'

'Thank you,' said Paul. 'I mean it.'

Alice shook her head. 'Shh.'

'No', said Paul, 'I'm serious. I couldn't face going back to mine. Not on my own.'

'You're better here,' said Alice. 'I can take care of you.''.

'I don't want to put you in any danger.'

'You won't. No one knows you're here.'

'Except Richard. I texted him.'

'He's your best friend,' said Alice. 'He's not going to put you in any more danger.'

'He's a blabbermou–'

Alice leaned over and pressed a finger against Paul's lips. 'Rest. Later on I'll bring you some soup.'

Paul nodded and smiled. Soup sounded good.

As the days passed, Paul grew stronger. At first, all he could manage was a slow shuffle to the kitchen for a coffee and then straight back to bed. But after a week or so, he felt well enough to explore the flat. With Alice at work, there was little else to do. Near the end of the second week of his confinement, he ventured into the living room and turned on the TV. The bland morning babble, the inane ads, the shock-and-awe blitz of the news, it was all too much for him. He wasn't ready for all that yet.

He switched it off and wandered back out into the hall, taking a left into Alice's office. Inside was as it had been before: a desk stacked high with folders and papers. The only thing missing was the Post-it Alice had stuck to the monitor. This time round, Paul noticed a large wooden unit in the corner. The top drawer was stiff, but after some gentle persuasion, it eased open. Papers glided to the floor in front of him. He tried to pick them up, but the pain in his side pulled him up short.

He closed the drawer and tried the second one. It was stuffed full of photograph frames. He took one out and studied the picture. Two men and a middle-aged, red-haired woman stood outside a building with a sign above the door: Omni Pictures. The same woman was also in the second frame he picked up, posing this time, alone, at a desk in a small, well-organised office. Paul looked around him. It was the office he was standing in. He dug a third photo out. This time the woman was linked arm in arm with an unknown man, posing in the sunshine beside a grand ornate fountain.

There were more photographs of the woman in the next drawer down. *Who the hell is this?* thought Paul. Beneath the photographs he found a large, framed certificate: a law degree from Cambridge University, the name Alice Lowe swirled across its middle. *Why would she hide this at the bottom of a drawer?* As he turned to lay the certificate on the desk, Paul's arm nudged the mouse, and the computer screen flashed on. He caught a brief snatch of a script – his script, with sections highlighted in red – before the screen went black and a login box appeared. Before he could guess the password, the downstairs buzzer sounded. He hastily stuffed the certificate and photographs back in their respective drawers. He gingerly bent for the stray papers on the floor, but the buzzer went off again. *Fuck!* Abandoning the loose sheets, he hobbled out to the hall.

'Who is it?' he asked. No reply. 'Hello? Is anybody there?' He was about to put the receiver back on the wall when Alice's voice came through.

'Paul, it's me. I've left my keys. Can you let me up?'

'Sure,' said Paul and pressed the buzzer. He dragged himself back to the office and pushed the loose papers beneath the cabinet with his foot. He then returned to the hall, just as Alice opened the door.

'I'm so sorry,' she said. 'I hope I didn't get you up.'

'I'd just put the kettle on,' said Paul, heading for the kitchen. 'You fancy a cuppa?'

'Sorry,' said Alice, 'I've got to dash. I'm late for a meeting. I'll just get my keys. They're in the office.'

By the time Paul had lifted a mug down from the kitchen cupboard and splashed a little milk into it, Alice had returned, her lips thin and accusing.

'Did you go in there?' she asked. 'Into my office?'

Paul shook his head convincingly. 'That's the only room I've yet to explore.'

'If you don't mind,' said Alice, 'I'd rather you didn't. It's just I've got confidential papers in there. You know, contracts and stuff.'

'Not a problem,' said Paul. 'I totally understand.' *Bit of an overreaction, surely?*

'I'll see you later,' she said sharply and swivelled on her heels.

No kiss, then.

From the front window, Paul watched Alice emerge out onto the street, her phone at her ear. She'd only gone a few yards when she was grabbed by the arm from behind and swung round. Paul strained to see her assailant clearly, but the man had his back to him. The pair shared a heated exchange before Alice slapped the man across the face. The man in turn shoved Alice angrily off the kerb.

'Fuckin hell!' shouted Paul and thumped hard on the window.

Both Alice and her assailant turned and looked up. Paul was shocked to see that the man who'd shoved Alice onto the road was Richard. Richard, too, seem shocked to see Paul and quickly ducked out of sight, disappearing below Paul's eyeline. As Alice used the interruption to take off around the corner, the downstairs buzzer went.

'What the fuck do you think you're doing?' yelled Paul, shoving Richard against the hallway wall.

'Paul …' spluttered Richard. 'Oh my God, you look terrible.'

'Never mind that,' said Paul. 'Why did you attack Alice?'

'Whoa,' Richard said. he slid sideways out of Paul's reach. 'Rest up with the fisticuffs, mate. I came round to see how you are. She's been keeping me away.'

'Do you blame her? After that fucking display?'

'She wouldn't let me near you,' said Richard, flustered. 'I begged and I begged. I just wanted to make sure you were okay. When she saw me downstairs, she just went off on one.' He shook his head. 'Man … what's her problem?' He wiped a hand across his forehead. 'Are you going out with her or what?'

Paul continued to stare menacingly back at him.

'I'd watch her if I were you,' said Richard. 'She's a control freak, you know? I mean, we could be talking boiled rabbits here.'

'Fuck off,' said Paul and hobbled back down the hallway.

Richard followed him. 'Paul,' he pleaded. 'I swear, I was just trying to be supportive. I was worried about you, bro. Why didn't you call me?'

'I was fucking shot, remember?' Paul reached for his phone. 'I need to make sure she's okay.'

'See? She's got her talons into you,' said Richard. 'You'll notice there's been nothing from her about the script. She's got the both of us dangling like puppets.'

'Shut up,' said Paul, waiting for Alice to pick up. Bu her phone went straight to voicemail. Paul hung up. *Was Richard right about her?*

'I just want to tell you …' Richard sank into a chair and put his head in his hands. '… I'm as fucking scared as you are,' he said, finally.

Paul couldn't tell if this sudden emotional outburst was genuine or just another of Richard's award-winning performances to smooth over his shite behaviour. He lowered himself onto the chair opposite, squirming around to find a comfortable position.

'I'm beginning to think you could be right,' Richard continued. 'That some evil bastard out there wants our script so badly, he or she will do anything to get it.' He sniffed.. 'Seriously, though, are you okay?'

'I'll live,' said Paul. 'For now.'

Richard sighed and rubbed the moisture from his eyes. 'It's a fucking nightmare. I should have listened to you from the start. That fucking script. I'm sorry. I've been a total cunt.'

'That's too polite a word for what you've been.'

'I'll take that.' Richard smiled. 'So, you and Alice. Are you or aren't you?'

'I'm here to recover,' said Paul, keeping it simple. 'That's all. It was too much to go back to the flat. And you were being ... well, you know what you were being.'

'But I just don't trust her. Why is she so bloody possessive?'

'She's just looking out for me. I said I didn't want to see anyone, especially you.'

'Oh, cheers.'

'I needed to get out. Get away from everything. I felt under siege.'

'But you're on the mend now, right?' Richard seemed genuinely concerned.

'I'm a bit slow on my feet,' said Paul, 'but I'm getting there.'

'So,' said Richard, 'can I tell you what I've found out, or will I just not bother?'

'No,' said Paul, unsure where this was leading, 'tell me.'

'Dr Evil himself, Tor Torrensen, will be in town tomorrow.'

'What?'

'Yep,' said Richard. 'Our favourite villain will be guest of honour at the opening of some energy firm he's just acquired over at the tech park in East Kilbride. While you've been enjoying bed baths in intensive care, Mr Fleck has been attracting quite a bit of press attention.'

'In what way?'

'It's just like you said. Tor-izon has been linked to all sorts of dodgy goings-on. Data theft mainly. There's a paper trail leading all the way to Blofeld's door.'

'We have to go.'

Richard held his hands up. 'No, no, no, that's not why I told you.'

There was a sudden look of the zealot about Paul.

'He could be responsible for all of this,' he said, licking his lips. 'We need to eyeball him. Ask him straight out.'

'But you're not well enough,' argued Richard. 'Jesus, I didn't mean to–'

'I'm fine,' said Paul. 'Anyway, I need to get out. I've been stuck in here for weeks.'

'With Glenn Close,' quipped Richard.

'She's been good to me.'

'Listen,' said Richard, 'why don't I just go and report back to you?'

Paul shook his head. 'I need to know for sure if he was the bastard who did this to me. And to us.'

'Okay,' said Richard, 'but we're in and out, that's it, and then we're straight back to *Fatal Attra–*' He stopped himself just in time.

'I don't want Alice to know,' said Paul. His suspicions about her were now running riot. 'She'll just worry and try to stop me,' he added, covering his tracks.

'Okay,' said Richard. 'I'll call round in the morning, after she's left for work. But how are we going to get in? Won't there be security and shit to get through?'

'We'll think of something,' said Paul. 'Or rather you will.'

'Me?' Richard laughed. 'You do know that ownership of the *Breaking Bad* box-set doesn't automatically make me a master criminal.'

'Doesn't matter,' said Paul. 'You owe me. Big time.'

'There's no way we'd get in there unless we were industry insiders, or–'

'Or what?' Paul could tell by Richard's grin that he'd just come up with a plan.

'Or journalists,' said Richard. 'Writing for an environmental magazine, supporting Mr Torrensen's efforts to save the planet. Yes! They'll welcome us with open arms! All we need are a couple of press badges and we're in.'

'Yeah, great.' Paul nodded. 'I've got three or four in my wallet.'

'Any old card on a piece of string'll do,' said Richard. 'Nobody ever looks at them anyway. It's all about making people believe what they want to believe.'

'Like acting?'

'Exactly.'

'Well, that's us fucked then,' said Paul, and for the first time in a long while, they both laughed together.

22

The energy company's HQ was in the heart of the Enterprise Technology Park, a near-abandoned, eighties-style industrial estate, more Chernobyl than Silicon Valley.

'Can't be much further,' said Richard. 'How you doing?' He'd noticed Paul's face contorting every couple of steps.

Paul just nodded, eager to keep going, less eager to share his pain. Up ahead were a bevy of TV vans parked at the end of a cul-de-sac. Beyond them stood a steel-and-glass multi-storey monstrosity.

'Follow me,' ordered Richard, slipping on his lanyard/old uni matriculation card.

Paul couldn't help sniggering at Richard's retro grunge mullet.

'So I loved Kurt Cobain.' Richard grinned. 'Shoot me.'

Paul pulled out his own lanyard from his pocket: an old Co-op loyalty card.

Richard shook his head. 'God help us.'

They joined a small group shuffling silently into the building. 'I hope they're serving booze,' Paul said to a pudgy, sweaty man fumbling with a briefcase.

'Champagne, no doubt,' the man replied. 'Can't stand the stuff myself. Not with these sinuses.'

Richard looked puzzled.

'The bubbles,' the man said, as though that explained everything.

'Do you work for Tor-izon?' Richard asked, forcing engagement with the man.

'God, no.' The man laughed. 'My working days are long gone. I'm a shareholder.'

'Ah, so *you're* paying for the champagne?' Richard rubbed his hands together.

'And a lot more besides in the coming months, by all accounts.'

'You don't have much faith in the new owners then?'

The man wiped his forehead with a handkerchief. 'In Tor-izon? Are you serious?' He glanced down at Richard's matriculation card. 'I'm sorry, who are you?'

Before Richard could put his story to the test, a large, uniformed guard instructed everyone to put their coats and bags through a scanner. As the group filed through, a second guard stopped Paul.

'Which organisation?'

Richard leaned across, smiling. '*Green Energy Magazine*.'

The security guard picked up a clipboard and ran a finger down the guest list.

'I can't see *Green Energy Magazine* on here,' he said, squinting at Paul's Co-op card.

'Strange,' said Richard. 'I spoke with Tor yesterday, and he was very keen for us to follow up on our interview with him last week. Didn't Mr Torrensen tell you?'

'Er …' The guard checked his clipboard again.

'I'll give him a call now, if you like.' Richard fished his phone out. 'You can explain to him why we're not on the list.'

The flustered guard waved them both through.

Once out of sight, Paul let out the breath he'd been holding. 'Jesus Christ, Richard,' he muttered. 'What if he'd said yes?'

'Then we'd be walking back to the station,' said Richard. 'No biggie.'

They continued on to a large glass-covered atrium where guests, journalists, and film crews were gathering. A bearded roadie on a makeshift stage was testing out a mic, his ONE-TWO! ONE-TWOs! reverberating around the cavernous space.

'Look!' yelled Richard, pointing to a waiter weaving towards them. 'Drink!'

'Richard, don't,' said Paul. 'We need our wits about us for once.'

'Oh, come on, a little Dutch courage won't hurt.'

'I'm on medication.'

'Even better!' Richard stopped the waiter as he passed and grabbed two glasses from the tray.

'Richard?' the waiter asked with a broad smile.

'Oh fuck,' Richard muttered. 'Calum. Wow. What a surprise.'

'What are you doing here?' asked Calum.

'Researching a part for a new play,' said Richard, squirming. 'This is my director.'

'Hi!' said Paul, playing along.

'Wow, you got a part!' Calum was impressed.

'Yep. I'm doing very well. Very well indeed. How about you?'

'Oh, you know,' said Calum. 'A few small walk-on roles, adverts, the odd radio commercial. But it's bloody tough. Hence this.'

'Bad luck,' said Richard. 'But listen. We're both here incognito, yeah? We don't want anyone to know who we are.' He leaned in, his nose almost touching Calum's. 'How the fuck can we get to the truth of our character if people know who we are? Am I right?'

'Absolutely,' agreed Calum. 'Game on.' After a quick fist-pump with a relieved Richard, he moved off, slaloming through the guests like a downhill skier.

Richard and Paul, meanwhile, pushed their way towards the podium, ending up next to a BBC film crew and interviewer, who were setting up.

'When's the great leader due to speak?' Richard asked the camera operator.

The man glanced at his watch. 'Should be any second.'

Just then, a group of bow-tied dignitaries appeared on the podium, headed by a young man seemingly out of place in t-shirt and tight jeans.

'Good afternoon, ladies and gentlemen,' Tight Jeans said. 'Thank you all for coming today, to this, the grand opening, and launch, of a new business partnership between OHM Energy and Tor-izon. It gives me great pleasure to introduce the Chair of OHM Energy, Dr Philip March, and the founder and Chief Executive of Tor-izon, Tor Torrensen!'

Dr March appeared from the wings to much applause. At the podium, he glanced back. Tor strode on next, to even greater applause. He had his signature flat cap on, pulled down at an angle.

'There he is, the bastard,' Paul muttered and received an elbow to the ribs from Richard by way of reward.

Dr March spoke first, his lengthy drone completely ignored by Tor, who stood gazing out at the audience like a rock star. After a short round of brittle applause, March handed Tor the mic. Tor stood waiting for the last clap to die away. When it did, he spoke low, his English near-perfect, with only a hint of a Scandinavian lilt. He thanked the audience, the press, and Dr March, and then walked off.

All hell broke loose.

'I'll take some questions now!' yelled March, but no one was listening.

The massed ranks of press had made a uniform dash for the door, all of them eager to catch up with the departing Tor. Paul and Richard found themselves caught up in the melee, careful not to trip over camera cables.

'This way!' Richard grabbed Paul's arm and dragged him across the auditorium to a half-opened door.

They pushed through it and slammed it shut behind them. They now stood in a deserted corridor, its bare stone walls silent and cold.

'Which way now?' asked Paul.

'Shh,' said Richard. 'Listen.'

Tor's voice sounded faintly at the far end of the corridor. Paul and Richard headed towards it by silent and mutual agreement.

Tor's voice grew louder. He was bellowing, in Swedish, seemingly from a room up ahead. As Paul and Richard drew nearer, there was a scrape and a roar, and a metal chair was flung out into the corridor, landing at their feet. Richard seized the moment and ran into the room. A more cautious Paul crept in after him.

'Mr Torrensen?' Richard addressed the now capless, flush-faced Tor-izon boss.

'Who the fuck are you?' barked Tor, his full head of greying blond hair slicked back with gel, a single stray quiff hanging down over his face.

His black-suited entourage moved as one towards the door.

Richard held up his hands. 'Sorry to interrupt, Mr Torrensen. We …' He looked back over his shoulder at Paul. '… represent *Green Energy Magazine*. We'd like to thank you for the sterling work you and your organisation are doing to preserve our fragile environment.'

'What?' Tor was confused.

'Your cutting-edge technologies,' continued Richard, 'have made it possible to change mindsets and human behaviour for the good of all mankind. In our view, this is Nobel-Prize-winning research.'

'Ah, fuck it,' said Paul, flopping down on an empty chair and gripping his side. 'How much money do you cunts actually need, eh?'

'I beg your pardon?' gasped Tor.

Richard looked aghast.

Paul rubbed at his wound. 'When will you stop? At ten billion? Fifty? Is it all about keeping up with the Saudis and buying a bigger island than Branson's?'

'Paul!' hissed Richard.

'Get the fuck out!' Tor growled.

'You people are fucking parasites,' said Paul. 'It's not enough to sell worthless tat to folks who can't afford it, is it? You need to brainwash them, too. So they comply and buy and fucking vote for whatever monster you install to prop up your Bilderberg bandwagon. Yeah, we're getting wise to your neo-liberal bullshit.'

'Are you finished?' sneered Tor.

'Oh, I'm just getting started, pal,' said Paul. 'There's a fucking revolution coming, my friend, and you all better watch your fucking necks. The truth is out, and we're coming for you, you totalitarian testicle.'

Tor pointed a wavering finger at Paul and spat out a string of Swedish obscenities, some directed at the interlopers, some at his own entourage. 'Do the job I overpay you to do,' he bellowed at his men, 'and get these two fucking trolls out of my face! With force, preferably! Now!'

As though poked with a cattle prod, his men rushed at Richard and Paul and hauled them out of the room.

'Whatever shit you throw at us,' hollered Paul as he was dragged from the room out into the corridor, 'you won't win! We'll make our film and show the world the monster you truly are! We will end *you*, you supercilious spunk stain!'

Catapulted onto the car park tarmac, one of Tor's mighty minions tossed Paul's Co-op badge at him.

'Don't forget your discount card!' the minion sneered and slammed the building's small side door shut behind him.

'That feral bastard tore the only decent jacket I have,' complained Richard. He dusted himself down, then suddenly started laughing..

'What's so funny?' asked Paul.

Richard laughed even more. 'Totalitarian testicle? Supercilious spunk stain?'

Paul cracked a smile. 'That's exactly what he is.'

Richard glanced over at the pack of journalists still milling around in the faint hope they'd land an exclusive last-minute interview with Tor.

'I'll be back in a sec,' he said.

He ran over and tapped one of them – a tall, thin-lipped woman in an ill-fitting pac-a-mac – on the shoulder.

She turned round.

'What paper do you work for?' he barked.

'The *Guardian*,' she snapped back, as though Richard should have recognised her.

'That figures,' he said. 'He's in there,' he added, pointing to the side door.

Thanking Richard with a crooked smile, she slipped furtively away from her colleagues and around the side of the building. Richard watched her go with a self-satisfied smirk. *I hope she breaks the story wide fucking open, you manipulative prick.*

Back on the train, Richard and Paul tried to unpick what had just happened.

'Well.' Richard smiled. 'That's what you call a man with anger management issues.'

Paul shifted in his seat. His side still ached like buggery. 'He's fucking unhinged. Did you see what he did to that fucking chair?'

'Not him, you!' Richard quipped. 'We clearly upset him.'

'Too right, we did,' said Paul. 'We called him out, the bastard. I just wish I could speak Swedish and understand what he was ranting about.'

'I suppose when you think about it, though …' said Richard, '… this is a guy under tremendous pressure. I mean, he's the subject of a major criminal investigation. He could be going down for a long, long time. Plus, he's got paparazzi all over him. He's not going to be too happy with us turning up and threatening him.'

'Well.' Paul grinned. 'Now he knows we know.'

Richard turned away to the window and stared out. 'That's what I'm worried about.'

As the train thundered on through the industrial dereliction of outer Glasgow, an ominous silence fell over the two friends; a silence that neither appeared willing, or able, to break.

SCRIPT EDIT 20 – THE BREAK-IN SCENE

FADE IN:

INT. HEAD OFFICE, LOBBY - NIGHT

An overweight SECURITY GUARD, his eyes closed, chews dreamily on a huge pastrami sandwich. A polite COUGH sounds, and he looks up.

Harvey, a lanyard around his neck, points to the lift.

HARVEY

Forgot my briefcase.

The guard, still chewing, nods impatiently. Harvey points to the man's face.

HARVEY (CONT'D)

You've got a bit of …

The guard wipes a large dollop of mayo from his cheek and keeps chewing.

Harvey walks to the lift. He glances back nervously at the guard - still engrossed in his sandwich - before pressing the button. The lift descends slowly.

HARVEY (CONT'D)

(looking up and whispering)

Come on.

PING! The lift doors open. Harvey steps in.

INT. ELEVATOR - NIGHT

The doors close on the starkly lit lift. Harvey leans against the back wall and EXHALES in relief.

INT. CORRIDOR - NIGHT

Harvey exits the lift and heads for the stairwell.

INT. STAIRWELL - NIGHT

Harvey leaps up two or three stairs at a time. He's in a hurry. After climbing a couple of flights, he stops at a stairwell door, out of breath. Cautiously, he pulls the door open and peers along the corridor.

INT. CORRIDOR - NIGHT

The corridor is empty, apart from two large, impressive Rothko paintings. Harvey walks briskly to the end, where he stops outside a door.

Ballatine's name and CEO post are announced in bold capitals on a gleaming gold nameplate fixed to the door.

Harvey glances over his shoulder, before pulling an ID card from his wallet.

The card reads:

Duncan Ballatine

Chief Executive Officer

NLightN Industries

Ballatine's profile pic and the company's eagle crest logo appear in each corner of the card.

Harvey swipes the lock with the card. *BLEEP!* A small red light flashes on the lock.

HARVEY

Shit!

Harvey tries again, slower this time. The light turns green, and the door CLICKS. Harvey checks the corridor again.

Still empty.

Harvey enters the room, the door closing quietly behind him.

INT. BALLATINE'S OFFICE - NIGHT

Harvey moves quickly to the rear of the office, past Ballatine's massive desk and outstanding, panoramic views over the city. He stops at a mahogany door, his fingers hovering over a small metal keypad.

Harvey struggles to remember the code. Eventually, he enters the letters A-B-A-C-U-S and then stops. His finger moves slowly to the letter O … then switches to the number zero. As soon as he hits it, the door swings open …

… revealing a safe room with wall-to-wall stainless-steel drawers and cabinets.

INT. SAFE ROOM - NIGHT

A stand-alone cabinet rests against the back wall. Harvey inserts his card into a slot in the front of the cabinet, and the drawer jumps open. From it, he removes a silver laptop.

Harvey places the laptop on an island table and opens the lid. He keys in a password, and a snatch of the *DR ZHIVAGO* THEME plays as the hard drive boots up.

Harvey glances nervously at his watch, then the door.

The desktop appears: a still of Omar Sharif from *Dr Zhivago*. Harvey removes a USB stick from his pocket. With shaking hands, he inserts it into the laptop's side.

Columns of files and folders scroll past on the screen and then stop. Harvey moves the cursor to a folder marked 'O' and CLICKS on it.

A box with 'Password protected' flashes up.

HARVEY

Fucking passwords!

Harvey slowly types in the word 'LANDFILL'. A folder opens, and a list of files cascade down the screen. Harvey slides the folder across to the USB stick.

The upload bar slowly edges its way across the screen as images of files and faces flash by.

Harvey TAPS his fingers impatiently on the table.

The transfer is eighty percent complete. The images now are of political leaders and celebrities.

HARVEY

Come on! Come on!

The transfer is ninety percent complete.

A NOISE from Ballatine's office has Harvey shooting a frantic look at the door. It's slightly ajar.

PING! The transfer is complete.

Harvey snatches the USB stick, shuts down the laptop, and shoves it back in the cabinet. At the door, he stops and peeks through the gap.

INT. BALLATINE'S OFFICE - NIGHT

An out-of-tune CLEANER in headphones runs a VACUUM HOSE over the floor, SINGING as he works. He sucks up a small, framed photo, and the vacuum SCREAMS in protest. The cleaner dislodges the frame and resumes hoovering and SINGING.

INT. SAFE ROOM - NIGHT

Harvey continues to stare, frozen to the spot.

INT. BALLATINE'S OFFICE - NIGHT

The cleaner moves closer to the safe room, checking messages on his phone. He glances up at the partially open door.

INT. SAFE ROOM - NIGHT

A startled Harvey holds his breath.

INT. BALLATINE'S OFFICE - NIGHT

The cleaner tilts his head, curious. He steps towards the door … but then his phone RINGS. He stops, switches off the vacuum, and takes the call.

CLEANER

Hi, baby. You know you shouldn't call me at work. You're such a bad girl. How bad are you?

(smiling)

Now that is very, very bad.

The cleaner slowly drags his vacuum back to the office door, turns out the light, and leaves.

INT. SAFE ROOM - NIGHT

Harvey closes his eyes. BREATHES OUT a huge sigh of relief.

INT. BALLATINE'S OFFICE - NIGHT

Harvey moves quickly and quietly to Ballatine's office door. Once again, he peers out into the corridor.

INT. CORRIDOR - NIGHT

The cleaner is at the far end, leaning on the wall, still talking into his phone. The lift door *PINGS* opens. The cleaner hauls his vacuum inside and disappears.

Harvey steps out into the corridor and closes the door silently behind him. A hand taps him on the shoulder.

DEREK BLAKE (O.S.)

What are you doing?

Harvey spins around in fear.

Vice President DEREK BLAKE leans into Harvey's face, too close for comfort. He's dishevelled and slightly inebriated. Stray wisps of his comb-over dangle down over his eyes.

Harvey steps back in shock.

HARVEY

Mr Blake … you surprised me there.

Blake tries to readjust his comb-over to hide his baldness.

BLAKE

What were you doing in there?

HARVEY

Oh no, I wasn't in there. I was just checking to see if Mr Ballatine was still here. I need to run a work problem past him.

BLAKE

But I saw you come out.

HARVEY

The cleaner … you see … had just left, and must have, you know, left the door open. I was just checking everything was okay and I pulled it shut.

BLAKE

You weren't snooping around in there, were you? You're not some kind of industrial spy.

HARVEY

Of course not.

BLAKE

Looking for some dirt to dish.

HARVEY

Mr Blake, I can assure you -

BLAKE

And get one over on me!

Blake lets out a coarse BELLY LAUGH, which Harvey pretends to join in with.

BLAKE (CONT'D)

I'm pulling your leg. You're a conscientious young ferret, aren't you?

HARVEY

Just trying to do my best for the organisation.

BLAKE

That's the spirit - you fool!

Blake LAUGHS again and THUMPS Harvey hard on the back, before heading off to the lift. He turns and shouts back.

BLAKE (CONT'D)

There's more to life than impressing the boss, you know!

Blake makes thrusting motions with his hips, LAUGHS a final time, and slopes off into the lift.

Harvey waits a moment, then runs for the stairs.

INT. HEAD OFFICE, LOBBY - NIGHT

Harvey crosses the lobby briskly, towards the exit. He walks past reception. The guard is engrossed in his mobile.

BRUCE WILLIS (O.S.)

Yippee ki-yay, motherfucker!

The guard GUFFAWS. When he glances up and sees Harvey, he fumbles with his mobile to try and stop the movie.

GUARD

Sorry, sir, I didn't see you there.

HARVEY

Goodnight.

GUARD

Goodnight, sir. Oh, did you get it?

Harvey smiles and pats his jacket pocket. As he leaves the building, he smiles and sets off across the vast futuristic concourse.

FADE OUT

23

By the time Paul finally made it back to Alice's flat, he was completely spent.

'Oh my God, Paul. Where have you been?' Alice asked, opening the door.

Paul hadn't expected her back this early and had hoped to sneak in under the wire. 'I needed to get out for a bit,' he said. He thought quickly on his exhausted feet.

'Where did you go? You've been out for hours.'

'How'd you know that?'

'I came back early to explain what happened,' said Alice. 'I saw you'd rung me. I'm so sorry. I was in a meeting and couldn't get out.'

'All day?'

'Pretty much. You look terrible,' she said. 'Let's get you to bed.' She reached a hand out to him.

'No.' he pushed away.

'What is it?'

'What was going on down there, between you and Richard?'

'Nothing,' said Alice. 'Seriously, it was nothing.'

'It didn't look like nothing. You were arguing about something.'

Alice sighed. 'He's just been pestering me to let him see you. I did as you said and tried to keep him away. Today he just turned up. What could I do?'

'He shoved you.'

'I annoyed him. I told him he needed to let you recover. I got angry.' She frowned. 'I didn't like it, you know. Him touching me like that.'

'How long has he been hassling you?'

'Forever, it seems. But hey, he's concerned about you, I suppose.'

'You should have told me.'

'I didn't want to worry you.'

She took his hand, and this time, Paul let her. He was too tired to think straight. He'd need all his strength to confront her about the red-haired woman.

'To be honest,' she said, 'I don't think he's good for you right now. You need to rest.' She stroked his face. 'You're done in.'

'I'm okay,' said Paul. 'I'm just angry with Richard.'

'I can deal with him,' said Alice, with a look Paul had never seen before. 'Come on,' she said, taking his arm and leading him to the bedroom. She helped him undress and got him into bed, gently slid the duvet over. 'Rest now,' she whispered. 'You need your beauty sleep.' She switched off the light and leant in, kissing him lightly on the lips, her fingers smoothing the lines on his brows.

As she sat back, Paul's tired eyes tried to focus. Something wasn't right. In the half-light, Alice's features seemed distorted. Her face folded in on itself, and she slowly morphed into the mystery redhead in the photographs, her long, thick curls brushing softly against his cheeks. *What the–?* But his eyes couldn't stay open, and within seconds, he was fast asleep.

24

He woke to Alice's cat cleaning itself on his chest. *Nice.* He sat up, and the cat slid off, landing at the bottom of the duvet where it resumed its morning bed bath. He checked the clock. 11:23 a.m. *Shit!* He'd slept in. He climbed gingerly out of bed, wincing as the pain in his side flared up again. In the kitchen, he found a note.

Working late tonight.
Dinner out? We can talk.
I'll book and text you.
X

'*We can talk?*' He read the line out loud. *What does that mean?* He'd no sooner put the note down when his phone pinged. It was Alice. Did she know he was up?

Morning, sleepyhead. Hope you're better.
Booked Celini's Italian, 7 p.m.
Rest today. See you tonight.

Alice x

He checked his watch. It hadn't gotten any earlier. *Rest, my arse.*

The script was on a USB stick tucked into the key pocket of Paul's jeans. He removed it out and inserted it into one of the library's free computers. When he'd opened up the document, he scrolled down to page seventy-four, the page Alice had had open on her laptop. He closed his eyes and visualised where the red highlights were.

HARVEY

Look at this.

Harvey hands Sarah his phone.

SARAH

What are these?

HARVEY

Copies of files from Ballatine's safe. Classified stuff.

Sarah scrolls through the files, stopping to read one or two, then carrying on.

SARAH

Where did you get them?

HARVEY

He's got a filing cabinet full of them. It's explosive stuff, every single document. They've collected incriminating data and filth on just about every political and business leader you can think of: celebs, movie stars, you name it, they're in there. Reams and reams of blackmail material. A simple click of a button, and they're ruined.

Sarah continues to scroll and scan, her mouth agape, the phone shaking in her hand.

SARAH

This is - But why are we … *they* doing this?

HARVEY

Their purpose is to create an environment of chaos and fear. To destabilise the economic, political, and social order.

SARAH

I don't understand.

HARVEY

Power and control. Bring the world to its knees, then step in with the silver bullet: a new order and command structure.

SARAH

You mean they're Nazis?

HARVEY

Too simplistic. They have no party allegiances. They operate way beyond that.

SARAH

So who are they?

HARVEY

Anyone with a vested interest in running the world: deposed presidents, fanatical religious leaders, business rivals, megalomaniac media moguls. Their tentacles slip and slide into every corner of our lives. Their fingerprints are everywhere, and every second of every day they spy on us …

Montage of rapid cuts:

TEENAGERS texting on their phones.

A YOUTH searching porn on his bedroom PC.

An open laptop filming a COUPLE watching TV.

A marching PROTESTOR taking a photo of waving banners.

Online shops. Total amounts. PAY NOW!

A YOUNG GIRL crying in her bedroom and typing: HELP ME!

A PASTOR preaching in church … then gambling online.

HARVEY (O.S.)

… through our phones, our search histories, our folders and files, our pictures and home movies. They spy on us in our homes, through our computers and cable TV. They know more about us than we know ourselves. What we buy, what we eat, how much we drink, who we like and love and hate, our political and religious beliefs, our sexual orientation, how much money we have, do we work or are we on welfare. They know our crimes and misdemeanours, our hypocrisies, our fears, anxieties, and weaknesses. They track and record it all.

Montage ends.

Sarah shakes her head.

SARAH

But I still don't get why?

HARVEY

Because we're just another cog in their shredding machine, and when finally all the chess pieces are aligned … checkmate. But it gets worse. Look.

Harvey takes the phone from Sarah, fiddles with a few buttons, and hands it back.

SARAH

What the fuck is this?

HARVEY

They have these files on dead presidents and corporate leaders. Assassinations and suicides, some still unexplained. All these documents point the finger right at them.

SARAH

Fuck. Are they killing people?

HARVEY

That's what it looks like. Maybe they bump off the ones who don't play ball or want more of the pie than they're willing to share.

SARAH

Murdering bastards!

HARVEY

And this.

Harvey takes the phone back, scrolls through it, and hands it over again.

CU - PHONE SCREEN

A group shot of world leaders fills the screen.

HARVEY (O.S.)

That was taken at the G20 meeting in Luxembourg, in March last year.

Sarah glances up.

SARAH

And?

HARVEY

Scroll down past the picture.

Sarah flicks the screen.

CU - PHONE SCREEN

A single, typed line underneath the photo reads: Termination - Approved.

SARAH (O.S.)

What does that mean?

Harvey's face shows no emotion.

HARVEY

I think they're planning an attack.

SARAH

On who?

HARVEY

On all of them.

SARAH

Oh no, no, no. This is too much.

HARVEY

I can't see any other explanation. Can you?

Sarah stares at the phone screen.

SARAH

When?

HARVEY

The next G20 meeting is in Switzerland next February. Check the date on the document.

Sarah peers closer at the screen.

CU - PHONE SCREEN

In a box in the top left-hand corner of the document is a date: 12/11/2023.

Sarah stares at Harvey, puzzled.

SARAH

But that was just last week …

Paul saved the section and googled 'G20 summit'. The date and location of the next meeting popped up on the screen: *18th – 21st February, Helsinki, Finland.*

Fuck. The coincidences were racking up. But this was overstretch, surely? It was too far beyond the realms of reality to make any kind of sense whatsoever. *That's the most ridiculous part of this whole ridiculous script,* thought Paul, clearing the search bar and typing in 'St George's Square attack'. He wanted to find out more about who'd shot him. He hit Enter. *What the fuck?* There was ... nothing. He changed key words. Still nothing. *What the* actual *fuck?* Somebody had shot him with a crossbow in broad daylight – in front of tourists, for fuck's sake! – so where was the coverage? Did Tor suppress it? Did Alice? He typed in 'Omni Productions'. There, again, was the pixilated area above Alice's profile pic. He squinted at it. Was that a hint of auburn? It triggered thoughts of the mystery redhead from Alice's office. *I wonder ...* He glanced around the library. A couple of teenagers in the study area sat hunched over a book.

'Excuse me.'

The teenagers glanced up in unison. The male – a Harry Styles lookalike, if Harry Styles had grown up on a diet of carrots and lived in a burrow – giggled through his enormous front teeth. The female – shyly demure, with a red spot on the tip of her nose that looked like it'd explode if she sneezed – kicked her partner under the table.

'Sorry to interrupt,' said Paul, looming over them. 'I wonder if you could help me.'

Harry Styles and Red Nose blinked back dumbly.

'I haven't got my glasses with me,' said Paul, 'and I need help to see something on my computer. It's over there.' He gestured across the room.

Harry giggled again and covered his mouth with one of the smallest hands Paul had ever seen in a human. Red Nose scraped her chair back and stood.

'Sure,' she said with a shrug. 'Why not.'

'I'm trying to work out what's in that blur,' said Paul, pointing at Alice's profile pic. 'Right there, behind the woman.'

Red Nose leaned over and squinted. 'It's a bit fuzzy. Actually, I think it might be a picture of somebody. Hang on.' She went and got Harry, dragging him reluctantly over to Paul's computer.

They squinted at the screen together.

'It's definitely two people,' said Harry.

'I'm not sure,' said Red Nose. 'It looks more like somebody on their own.' She glanced up. 'You know, there's software that can un-pixelate images.'

Paul scratched at his cheek. 'Yeah?'

'Oh yeah,' said Harry. 'There's apps for most things. You do know what an app is, don't you?'

'Ignore my little brother,' said Red Nose. 'It's past his bedtime.'

Harry punched his sister on the arm.

'Anyway,' she continued, 'I don't think you'll be able to download it on the library computer, but you could do it on your phone. You do have a smartpho–' She stopped when she saw Paul grinning at her. 'Sorry,' she said, turning red, and leant over the computer. She typed in 'depxlit.com' and clicked on the link. 'There you go. It's not perfect, but it should make it a bit clearer, hopefully enough to make out what it is.'

'That's brilliant,' said Paul. 'Thank you.'

'You're welcome,' said Red Nose. 'C'mon, you.' She hauled Harry to his feet and took him back to the study area. 'Algebra. Ten more minutes.'

Paul found the website on his phone and downloaded the app. While he waited on it installing, he changed his search to 'Tor-izon'. There were more articles than before. Their problems seemed to be escalating. They were now cited in more than ten insolvency cases, involving both financial and retail organisations, and one major tech company.

Paul followed the links to the tech story. It had recently gone bust, and Tor-izon had taken over the residual stock. Another article hinted at an imminent criminal investigation against Tor, with prosecutors in both the UK and US confident they had sufficient evidence to press charges. The noose was tightening, which would partly explain the chair and Tor's temper tantrum earlier.

Paul dug deeper. Buried away on the fourth page he found an article from 2009, written by the murdered journalist, Pedro Silvestre. Silvestre had claimed that Tor was responsible for a number of contract killings involving the top brass of a large financial conglomerate. Three executives had died mysteriously, and Silvestre had pointed the finger directly at Tor, claiming that not only was he a totalitarian testicle (Paul paraphrased as he read), he was also the Godfather of a Mafioso-style crime syndicate.

Paul's phone pinged, interrupting his search. The app had installed. He saved Alice's profile pic to his phone and uploaded it to the app. When he clicked the de-pixelate button, the image vanished and then reconfigured, line by line, from the top of the screen. When it reached the pixelated area, the upload paused.

Paul shook his phone. 'Come on!' The app resumed, and slowly the area re-emerged, clear and pixel-free. First the top of a picture frame, and then the detail of a photograph: a wall, a doorway, and then, finally, a figure. It was the redheaded woman, dressed in gown and mortar board, standing outside some university building. It was the same photograph he'd found buried away in Alice's office. *What the fuck?*

His phone pinged again. Alice.

Celini's Italian, Ashton Lane.
7 p.m.
See you there.
X

Paul closed down the computer. He needed to get back to Alice's office, right now. God knows what other secrets she might have hidden away.

25

Helsinki, 14th November, 5:23 a.m.

Hank Garfield shouldn't be sweating. The snow is up way past his ankles, and the wind chill is a teeth-chattering minus seven. In a previous life he'd carried out so many cool-headed missions for the CIA they've melted into one. And in this life – the one where he's head of logistics for ArmCor Security, the world's go-to firm for all high-profile, high-risk events – he'd be out on his arse if he crumbled under pressure. So no, Hank Garfield shouldn't be sweating. And yet he is. Big time.

Hank wipes his forehead and trudges through the pit-black arctic night. From the murk appear a couple of half-frozen security guards, loitering under the light of the command centre entrance. Hank's legs buckle beneath him. Shit. He stumbles slightly and recovers, but it's enough to alert the guards. Twenty-year-old Leo Blackman, aptly named, drops his cigarette and reaches for his holster. Coby Desmond, white, two years younger, and prematurely moustached, flashes a quivery torchlight in Hank's face.

'Halt!'

'At ease, gentlemen,' says Hank, his smile forced.

Coby drops the torch and nods.

'Early start this morning, sir?' asks the slender Leo, feigning alertness.

'Things to do.' Hank flashes his lanyard quickly before they spot his trembling hand.

Leo punches a code into the door, allowing Garfield through. When the door clicks behind him, he marches down the steel-lined corridor and takes a left into the gents loo. Inside the furthest cubicle from the door, he leans against the wall and tries to take control of his breathing. *I must be calm ... I must be calm* ... He repeats the mantra over and over in his head. Pressing two fingers to his wrist, he checks his heart rate. 235 bpm. Too fast. Far too fast. He closes his eyes and inhales. Twice. Three times. Four. *I must be calm ... I must be calm ...* 183 bpm. Better.

Hank opens his wallet and runs a thumb across a photo of his two kids, Alice and Mia, aged three and four. A tear wells in his eye. *No. I – must – be – calm.* He mouths the words out loud this time. Outside the cubicle, he runs his wrists under the cold tap, avoiding eye contact with his reflection in the mirror. The door swings open. It's David Truman, Hank's young and overenthusiastic assistant. *Fuck.* Hank turns off the tap.

'Oh – er – good morning, sir,' stammers Truman, embarrassed at bumping into his boss in the loo. 'I didn't expect–'

'Truman, it's five-thirty a.m.,' interrupts Hank. 'Why the fuck are you here?'

Truman blinks rapidly. 'I – er – thought I would familiarise myself with the layout of the auditorium. Yesterday you said you would quiz me.'

'Just keep out of my way,' snaps Hank, drying his hands on a paper towel.

'Of course, sir, no problem.' Truman is bobbing up and down like a child.

'For God's sake, go!' says Hank.

Truman scampers off to the urinals. Hank needs a concrete reason to keep Truman away. Something plausible. At the door, he stops and turns.

'Oh, and Truman?'

Truman swivels, caught mid-pee. 'Er – yes, sir?'

'One of the camera docks is misbehaving in the auditorium. See if you can find out where.'

'Will do, sir.' Truman nods.

'Okay,' says Hank, already out the door and marching towards the control room. 'See you at eleven a.m. for the daily briefing, and not before!'

I must be cal –

'Morning, sir!' The guard at the control room door snaps absurdly to attention. His colleagues must have tipped him off that Garfield was on his way.

Hank flashes his badge and nods, slipping through the opened door with nervous relief.

The control room is empty, the hot hum of the hard drives filling the stale air. Hank takes off his jacket, loosens his tie, and navigates his way past racks of state-of-the-art circuitry to his desk at the back of the room. He logs in to the system and works quickly through protocols and firewalls until he reaches the central security portal, the inner sanctum of the network. He throws a swift glance at the door and at the CCTV camera above it, its lens aimed straight at him. He lowers his head slightly, half obscured by the monitor, and reaches into his mouth. *Twist. Tug.* The molar comes out easily, a tiny USB embedded in its crown. Hank sits back up. Checks the door. Inserts the USB into the hard drive and waits for it to load. His head is screaming like a jet engine. *I must be calm … I must be calm ...*

Hank pulls the contents of a folder across to the hard drive. *Install.* Now for the security hub. The hack penetrates the security patch system, setting up temporary halt codes in each area of the network: cameras, trips, heat and light sensors, body scanners, noise detectors. Hank's heart thumps. The ports and junctions systematically flick from red to green. Done!

Next, the schedule box. Hank types quickly. *Sunday 4th February – 3:25 a.m. – 3:28 a.m.* He sets a three-minute system halt to minimise exposure risk and clicks *Go*. The hardware buzzes and whirrs as the halt point races back through the network, registering the date and time in each patch. Hank glances up again. Sweat runs down the inside of his shirt. All he needs is –

The control room door swings open, and Garfield's right-hand man, Ed Harker, appears, sharing a laugh with the guard on the door.

'Fuck,' mutters Hank, stealing a look at the status bar. *C'mon.*

Harker steps down into the heart of the room. 'Well, good morning.' He smiles. He seems surprised to see Hank. 'In to catch the worm?'

'What?' Another check of the status bar. Eighty percent complete.

'You're an early bird,' says Harker. 'What are you worrying about now?'

'I'm worrying about an empty coffee cup,' says Garfield. *Please … turn around.*

Harker turns and heads over to the coffee station. 'You took the words right out of my parched mouth. Black, no sugar, isn't it?'

Hank's attention remains glued to the screen. Ninety-two percent. 'Could you put a couple of sugars in that?' he says, not looking up. *I need to find a way to stall him.*

'Your funeral,' says Harker.

Ninety-eight percent.

Harker rummages in the cabinet for sugar. 'So, three weeks to D–Day.'

Ninety-nine percent. *Come on!*

'Is this your third or fourth G20?' *Clink clink.* Harker stirs the coffee.

PING! 100 percent task complete. Hank closes down the USB and whips his tooth out of the port.

'Here,' says Harker and places the mug of coffee on Hank's desk. 'So … what are you doing?' He squints at the security network flashing on the screen.

'I think there's a problem with one of the cameras in the main auditorium,' says Hank. 'I'm just running a system check to try and locate the issue.'

'You really don't have a life, do you?' Harker smiles and sips his coffee.

'I sent Truman down there to check.'

'Oh God, is Truman in? That boy is after our jobs.'

'Don't worry,' says Hank, 'he'll be in there for hours. I've set him an impossible task.'

'Ha!' Harker barks. 'You seem worried, my friend. Is here anything I should know about?'

'Like?'

'Like with the system. The clock's ticking, and I've worked with you long enough to recognise that face.' He points at Hank's creased and sweaty brow.

Hank can't bring himself to meet Harker's gaze. 'I just like to keep on top of things.'

'Don't I know it.' Harker grins. 'You're the company's secret weapon.'

'So why are you in so early?' asks Hank, wiping his forehead with the back of his hand.

'Oh, you know…'

'Your wife?'

'Yeah. She's – well, let's just say it's easier for me to deal with fifty thousand rampaging anti-capitalist anarchists than deal with her.'

'Sorry to hear that.'

'C'est la vie.' Harker spins on his heels and heads over to his desk, far enough away for Hank to start covering his virtual tracks without being seen.

As Harker mumbles on about his domestic woes, Hank erases his digital footprint, deleting all trace of the hack from the system, until the temporary halt is completely cloaked and undetectable. He closes the network and stands. A sudden pressure in his temples has him reeling.

'You okay?' asks Harker from across the room.

'I've just been sitting too long,' says Hank. 'I need to get some air.' He climbs the stairs and leaves the room, avoiding eye contact with the guard on the way out. In the open space of the central compound, he makes a bee-line for the power substation, over by the perimeter fence. The panic and nausea returns, and he has to hold a hand to his mouth to quell his rapid breathing. It helps, but not much.

There's a blind spot – forty seconds' worth – between the rear of the substation and the fence, out of eyeshot of the guards and the CCTV camera mounted on the gate. There, Hank scrabbles with his phone, pushing buttons. He holds the handset to his ear. He's chosen his location well. The electrically charged drone surging through the substation is enough to scramble the call. He's safe. For now.

The number connects and is answered before the first ring.

'Done,' manages Hank, his voice all but gone. 'Three minutes.' He waits. White noise hisses in his ear. 'Hello?' No response. Just more hiss and the click of static. 'My kids,' says Hank. 'Are they safe?' There's a desperation to his voice that no amount of time in the CIA can mask.

The line is unbearably silent. And then...

'Of course,' says a female voice sharply. The call disconnects.

Hank's eyes are watering again. Whatever chaotic hell he's brought upon the world, his kids are safe at last. Nothing else matters. He did what any father would do. And in three weeks' time he'll be with them again, with new names and new lives, far away from the madness about to come.

Pretending to check the locks on the substation unit door, he waves at the guards and makes his way slowly back to the control centre, muttering to himself as he crosses the compound.

I must be calm ... I must be calm ...

26

Celini's Bistro was a cosy, family-run Italian restaurant occupying a tiny space above one of the chain pubs that had taken over Ashton Lane. Paul had walked past it twice before he'd noticed the entrance at the top of an external staircase. As it was, he was still early. So early that his table wasn't ready yet. He ordered a brandy from the bar as he waited and eyed the scattered clientele: an elderly couple in tweed, a businessman on his laptop, and a trio of Asian students. In contrast to how he felt inside, the ambience was relaxed. He downed the brandy in one, just as the waiter beckoned him to a table at the rear. Paul sat.

'Would you like another drink, sir?' the waiter asked.

'Another double brandy, please,' said Paul, handing over his empty glass. 'Oh, and a pint of 80 Shilling.' When the waiter left, Paul checked his watch, then nervously rearranged the cutlery in front of him. *Relax.* He fixed his eyes on the door. *Come on, come on.*

The waiter came back with his drink, and Paul gulped it down. He checked his watch again, then spotted her. *Finally!* Alice stood by the door, shaking a damp umbrella. She saw Paul and waved, but he didn't wave back.

'Sorry I'm late,' she said. 'It's been meeting after meeting all day.'

'May I take your coat, madam?' asked the returning waiter with faked politeness.

Alice slipped it off and handed it to him, along with her wet umbrella. 'Sorry,' she said, with one of her disarming smiles, 'it's coming down in sheets out there.'

Paul had to turn away. He couldn't bear to look at her.

'Would you like a drink?' the waiter asked, grappling with the dripping garments.

'White wine spritzer, please,' said Alice, flashing her gleaming white teeth.

At least her drinking habits are consistent, thought Paul. As she sat, she reached for his hand, but he pulled it away.

'How are you feeling today?' she asked. 'How's the pain?'

She seemed concerned, but Paul wasn't buying it.

'Fine and dandy,' he replied sarcastically.

They sat in silence for a few moments. Alice glanced over to the bar, as though mentally willing her drink to hurry up. When the waiter finally returned, she thanked him and took a long, slow sip of her spritzer.

'Oh,' she said, closing her eyes, 'I needed that.'

'So, did you do your degree in London?' asked Paul.

Alice's eyes flicked opened. She seemed surprised. 'Er … yes,' she replied. ''What made you think of that?'

'I was reminiscing about my own degree today,' said Paul, 'and how much I enjoyed it. Did you enjoy yours?'

'I suppose so,' said Alice. 'It was just a stepping stone really. What did you study?'

'Creative writing and literature.'

'Course you did. I should have known that.' She rolled her eyes. 'Sounds a lot more fun than what I did.'

'What was that again?'

'Media and Politics. It seems like a lifetime ago.'

'I thought you said you studied Law.'

'Law?' Alice's eyebrows shot up a little higher than normal.

Gotcha.

'Isn't that what the certificate says in your office?' Paul's paranoia was building.

'You've been in my office again?'

Feigned anger. To mask the guilt.

'Your phone rang,' lied Paul. 'I went in to answer it.'

'I've told you there's confidential stuff in there.' *Real anger now.* 'You can't just–'

'Who's the redhead in all those photographs you've got hidden away?'

Alice sat back. Her eyes narrowed. 'I can't believe you've been going through my personal stuff. For fuck's sake, Paul, what is this?'

'Call it curiosity.'

'I told you my office was out of bounds.'

Was that a tear? God, she's good.

'Who is she?' Paul persisted.

'She's none of your fucking business.' Alice wiped her cheek, leaned forward, and took a long drink. 'It's personal,' she said quietly. 'It's got nothing to do with you.'

'You don't have a law degree, do you?'

'So I'm a suspect now, is that it?' Alice raged. 'Oh yes, that's right, did I not tell you? I'm a crack-shot with a fucking crossbow. I'm beginning to regret missing your fucking heart now. Or maybe you don't have one to hit.' She stood and accidentally knocked her chair over.

The elderly tweed couple peered up from their shared Stornoway black pudding panini and then when they saw Paul glaring at them, they quickly averted their gaze.

'Sit down,' hissed Paul, grabbing Alice's arm. 'Please.'

She hesitated, briefly, then lifted her chair off the floor.

'I just don't understand why you'd lie about something so innocuous,' said Paul. 'I don't care what degree you did.'

Alice sat back down, her eyes ablaze. 'But my employers might,' she snapped. 'I lied to you for the same reason I lied to them: to get the job. They were looking for an experienced journalist, and I bullshitted. It's not something I'm proud of.'

'So all that stuff in your company profile is … bullshit?'

'Of course not. Apart from that one thing, everything else is true.'

'So who's the woman?'

'What woman?'

'The redhead at the bottom of your filing cabinet.'

'Leave it, Paul. Please.' Alice's hand shook as she raised her glass to her lips.

'And why is she on the wall of your office at work. Are you gay?'

'She's my fucking sister!' Alice yelled.

Across the room, a Stornoway black pudding panini was demolished in record time.

'My little sister,' said Alice, taking a deep breath. 'Lucy. She died.'

'What? When?' Paul was confused.

'Last year. I put the photos away because I couldn't bear seeing her so alive like that.'

Paul studied her face, hoping for a flicker of deception. There was nothing. Just genuine grief.

'I'm so sorry,' he said.

'Are you?'

'Of course I am. Something like that … it's awful. How did she–?'

'She killed herself.'

'Oh God,' said Paul. 'God, that's tough.'

'One minute she's talking about working abroad, the next she's gone. We never – *I* never thought for a second that she was depressed or worried about anything. She was always so up and full of life.' Her lip trembled as the words fell out.

Paul reached for her hand, and this time, it was her pulling away.

'I'm sorry,' said Paul. 'I shouldn't have taken my anger over the attacks out on you. I've been an idiot. I can only imagine what you've had to go through.'

'You can't,' said Alice. 'No one can.' She broke down then, the tears flooding her face.

It had been inevitable, but it still took Paul by surprise.

'Fuck,' he said. 'I really didn't mean to dredge all this up. Fuck, fuck, fuck!'

Alice shook her head. 'It's not that,' she mumbled. 'It's Richard.'

'Richard?'

'I was just starting to come out the other side of Lucy's death, but he's knocked me right back down again.'

'What's he been doing?'

Alice wiped at her smudged mascara with the corner of a napkin. 'Texting … emailing … he's been doing it ever since we met.'

'What?

'At first he just asked how things were going with the board, but then he wanted me to help him scare you off. He said we could own the script outright, together.'

'What the fuck did you say?' Paul sat back.

'I told him that was illegal and that I couldn't believe he'd betray you like that.'

'No,' Paul exclaimed.

'I swear it's the truth. But confronting him like that just made him angry.' She rubbed her eyes.

'What a bastard,' Paul muttered.

'His messages started to get more personal, you know?' She held Paul's gaze.

'In what way?'

'What do you think?

'Sexual?'

'It was disgusting.'

'The fucking nasty …' Paul was furious. 'What was he saying? Wait, don't tell me. I don't want to know.'

'But then,' said Alice, 'about three weeks ago, around the time you went into hospital, he started following me.'

Paul ran a hand through his hair. He was struggling to keep up.

'I'd see him everywhere I went,' said Alice. 'Loitering near the flat or waiting for me to leave work. Once, when I'd had enough of it, I confronted him, but he just denied it. Said I was mad.'

'Jesus Christ. He's been stalking you.'

'He's fixated,' said Alice. 'And then, the day before he came round to the flat, things got a lot worse.' She dropped her head into her hands.

Paul leaned over the table. 'What happened?'

'He was following me again,' whispered Alice, the tears thickening. 'But this time he grabbed me. He was so full of rage. He pushed me into an alley and … tried to force himself on me.' Her breathing quickened with panic. 'He's a monster, Paul.'

'He didn't, though, did he? Force himself, I mean.' Paul felt sick at the thought.

Alice shook her head. 'I kicked him in the balls and ran off.' She let out an anxious laugh and wiped a thin line of snot from her nose.

'I can't believe he's stalking you.'

Alice snatched up her phone and fiddled with the buttons before thrusting it in Paul's face. 'If you need proof …' And there it was, in black and white: reams of threat-filled texts, all from Richard.

'He's lost his mind,' said Paul. *She's telling the truth. Jesus fucking Christ.*

'Good evening.'

They both spun round at the booming voice.

Looming over their table was the obese hulk of Detective Frank Quinn. 'What a pleasant surprise,' he said, offering Paul his hand.

Paul was still reeling from Alice's revelations. Quinn's sudden appearance before them dizzied him even more. He couldn't ley Alice know he was a detective.

'Professor Quinn,' he finally managed, standing and shaking the man's hand vigorously. 'Indeed, this is a surprise.'

Quinn turned to Alice who tried desperately to clear away the last of her tears.

'I'm sorry,' he said. 'Obviously my timing could have been better.'

Alice shook her head and offered up a weak smile.

'Alice,' said Paul, 'this is Professor Quinn, my … old English supervisor from Glasgow uni.'

Alice took Quinn's hand and shook it gently. 'I'm sorry. I had some bother at work, and Paul was counselling me.'

That's a very convincing lie, considering your emotional state, thought Paul.

'Oh, the pleasure is all mine,' said Quinn, rather creepily.

The moment stretched out into an uncomfortable silence. Paul felt an obligation to break it.

'So … er, Professor,' he stammered. 'Were you just passing, or …?'

'That's exactly what I was doing,' said Quinn. 'I was on my way to a talk at the Art School and just popped in for a drink. I have a thirst like you wouldn't believe.'

'Are you an American, Professor Quinn?' asked Alice, her composure seemingly fully recovered now.

'For my sins,' replied Quinn with a slight bow. 'Even though I taught at the university for–' He stopped and looked at Paul.

'Forever,' Paul cut in quickly.

Quinn laughed. 'Very good,' he said, and winked. He swivelled back round to Alice. 'I take it you are burdened with the challenging role of Paul's girlfriend?' he quipped.

'Alice is a friend, yes,' Paul interrupted. *Where's he going with this?*

Quinn shifted his bulk further towards Alice. 'And how did you come to meet this talented young writer?' he asked, laying on the home-school charm with a lard spoon.

'I work for a film company that's interested in one of Paul's scripts,' said Alice.

'Oh, now that sounds exciting,' said Quinn. 'Paul was an excellent student with a very imaginative and creative mind. He was always able to take on advice and follow it. Many of our current students actually seem incapable of listening and end up in all sorts of trouble.' He glanced over at a nervous-looking Paul. 'But Paul was always smarter than that. Oh dear,' he said, grinning, 'I seem to be embarrassing him. But what Paul had was an uncanny ability to dig out the truth and capture it in his writing. He has such a keen eye for detail.' Quinn took a handkerchief from his pocket and mopped a sheet of sweat from his brow. 'I'm so glad his talents are finally being recognised. Which company is it you work for, Alice?'

'Omni Pictures,' said Alice.

Quinn stared at her for a second, his features completely frozen. 'That is marvellous,' he said finally. 'I'm thrilled for you. For both of you.' He took a step back. 'Well, I'll stop pestering you now and let you get on with your … er … counselling and your meal.' He turned to Paul. 'It's always a delight seeing you, Paul, and hearing how well your life is going.' He held his hand out for Paul to shake and passed him a piece of card tucked into his palm.

Paul slipped it into his pocket without Alice seeing it.

'Goodbye, Alice.' Quinn smiled, a little nauseatingly. 'It was very interesting to meet you.'

Alice smiled back, but Paul sensed the insincerity behind it.

They watched Quinn negotiate, not entirely successfully, the closely placed tables and hobble his way out of the restaurant. Alice took a long drink of her spritzer.

'God, he was creepy,' she said.' I'm so up to here with sleazy men.'

'Strangely, he was a very good lecturer.' Another lie convincingly told.

'The way he looked at me …' Alice shivered. 'And he's so overweight. Revolting. Has he always been that size?'

'As long as I've known him.'

'He creeps me out.'

Does he? And why's that? It wasn't just his size, was it?

'Excuse me,' said Alice, standing. 'I suddenly have an urge to wash my hands.'

While Alice was in the loo, Paul examined the card Quinn had slipped him. One side was blank, but a phone number had been scribbled on the other, alongside three words: WATCH YOUR BACK. Keeping an eye on the loo door, Paul rang the number. *Come on, come on.* The line clicked. 'Quinn?' No reply. 'Quinn!'

'Sensible boy.' Quinn's self-satisfied reply had a hint of Southern drawl to it.

'What the fuck are you doing following me, you freak?'

'Paul, listen to me. This is important.'

'How did you even know I was here?'

'Listen!' Quinn roared.

Paul shut up.

'You are in grave danger.' He lowered his voice. 'You need to get out of there. Right now.'

'What are you talking about?'

The line garbled and popped, and Quinn's voice disappeared.

'Quinn?' rasped Paul. 'Quinn? Are you there?' The line went dead. *Shit.* Paul slipped the phone back into his pocket just as Alice returned to the table.

'Who was that?' She pushed a strand of hair back behind her ear.

'What?' Paul's voice slid a tad higher than normal.

'On your phone. Just now.'

'Oh that,' said Paul. 'It was Richard. He'd left a message, checking how I was. As if he fucking cares.'

'Promise me you won't reply,' said Alice. 'He scares me.'

'He's fucking dead as far as I'm concerned,' replied Paul. He thought he caught the hint of a smile in the corners of Alice's mouth. 'Listen, I'm not feeling too great. I'm going to go back to the flat.'

Alice gathered up her bag. 'I'll come with you.'

Paul put a hand on Alice's arm. 'I'll be fine. You get yourself something to eat. You must be starving.' He felt bad leaving her on her own, but he needed to find out what Quinn meant. He also needed to confront Richard, look him in the eye, and find out if he was telling the truth or not.

'I don't want to be alone.' Alice said with a look of fear in her eyes.

Fuck, thought Paul. *What kind of shit leaves a woman on her own?* He sighed. 'Okay. We'll get a taxi.'

They collected their coats, made their apologies to the waiter, and left.

The journey home allowed Paul time to think. Alice's story about her sister was one thing, but Richard, a stalker? It was hard to believe. He was so self-obsessed, the only person he was likely to stalk was himself. But then how could Alice fake the texts he'd seen? They definitely came from Richard's phone. Had something inside him snapped? Had the script triggered some long-gestating, and inevitable, downward spiral in his brain?

Alice leaned over and kissed him passionately, stopping all rational thought.

'I need you to hold me tonight,' she whispered. She kissed him again and ran her hand along his thigh.

He pulled back. 'I'm not sure I'm up to anything energetic,' he said weakly, glancing up at the taxi driver.

Alice leaned back, took his hand, and kissed it seductively. 'We'll see.' She smiled.

Paul's phone was in his jacket, hanging on the back of the bedroom door. He waited until Alice's breathing had steadied to a slow, gentle rhythm before slipping out of bed and retrieving it. He took it into the bathroom with him and was about to punch in Quinn's number when Alice appeared at the door, yawning.

'What are you doing?' she asked sleepily.

Paul grabbed a towel and covered the phone with it. 'I was looking for my painkillers,' he said, wincing.

'I put them up there,' said Alice, pointing to the mirrored cupboard on the wall.

'Thanks.' Paul smiled. 'I'll be out in a minute. You go back to sleep.'

Alice about-turned, still yawning. When he heard her climbing back into bed, Paul flushed the loo. He'd call Quinn tomorrow.

In the bedroom, he returned the phone to his jacket pocket and slid under the duvet. Alice snuggled into his back.

'You okay?' she asked, but before he could reply, she'd begun to snore quietly.

Alice took forever to leave for work in the morning, but the second she'd gone, Paul grabbed his phone and found Quinn's number. He was about to call it again when a text pinged. It was from Quinn. *What the fuck?* He fumbled open the message.

You are not safe
You need to get out now

We can protect you
Go to 12 Ballhill Rise
Today at 12:00
I will meet you there and explain
Bring the master USB

Ballhill Rise was the bloody beating heart of Castlebank, Glasgow's most notorious housing estate. *Why the fuck does Quinn want to meet there? Does he think it's safe because what surrounds it is so unsafe?* Paul sat at the table and considered his options. Could Quinn be trusted? Richard didn't think so, but Paul couldn't give a fuck what Richard thought. Saying that, Richard had been right about one thing: Alice was a control freak. Paul could see that now. And for some reason, she wanted him kept captive at the flat: the trophy boyfriend, evidence of her victory over him. Well, no more. He returned to the bedroom and emptied everything he owned into a holdall. He was getting the fuck out of there.

SCRIPT EDIT 22 - ROOFTOP FIGHT SCENE

FADE IN:

EXT. SKYSCRAPER ROOFTOP - NIGHT

Crane shot of panoramic views across the city. We zoom to …

… Harvey running across the rooftop, pursued by GRIFFIN ZANE, a remorseless intern. Griffin tackles him to the ground, fists, arms, and legs flying. Harvey wrestles free and runs to the railing at the edge of the roof. He's cornered.

Griffin catches Harvey again, grabs him by the throat, and forces him over the edge of the railing. Harvey glances down past the seemingly endless storeys.

The view to the ground below is nauseatingly vertiginous.

Harvey swivels and punches Griffin in the head. Dazed, Griffin lets Harvey go, allowing Harvey to punch him, hard, in the gut. Griffin crumples. Harvey kicks him in the face, knocking him onto his back. He stands over Griffin, PANTING.

HARVEY

Just stop, Griffin.

Griffin lands a kick to Harvey's groin, leaps to his feet, and punches Harvey in the face. Harvey returns with a head-butt. Griffin's nose explodes in a hail of red.

HARVEY (CONT'D)

For fuck's sake, stop.

Griffin looks up, holding his broken nose.

HARVEY (CONT'D)

You don't have to do this.

GRIFFIN

It’s too late.

HARVEY

We can stop this.

GRIFFIN

It’s gone too far.

HARVEY

What have they told you?

GRIFFIN

They want you gone. You fucked them over.

HARVEY

They’re fucking *us* over. They’re using you, Griffin. You’re their errand boy. They’ve promised you riches beyond your wildest dreams, am I right?

Griffin wipes away the blood pouring down his face.

HARVEY (CONT’D)

And all you've got to do is this one little favour. Get rid of me and you get my job.

GRIFFIN

They've got me by the balls. They said if I didn't do this, they'd kill my girlfriend and my parents. I don't have a choice.

Griffin pulls out a revolver and points it at Harvey's head. Harvey backs away, towards the building's edge.

HARVEY

Wait! We can stop them, together.

GRIFFIN

It's too late. I'm sorry.

Griffin's hand is shaking. Harvey is now at the railing.

HARVEY

Listen. I have files, documents, incriminating - fucking devastating - information that'll blow their whole fucking organisation wide apart.

GRIFFIN

The likes of us can't stop them. They'll roll right over us.

HARVEY

But can't you see? That's what they want you to believe. But we're more powerful. We have the means to destroy them. We can put an end to this madness, once and for all.

GRIFFIN

I don't want to die.

HARVEY

You kill me, they'll kill you. That's how it works. You honestly think these are the sort of people to honour a promise? They get rid of one liability and create another. And so it goes.

You're a dead man walking, Griffin. Wake up! They've brainwashed you. All that psychometric shit they poured into our heads. We were selected for a reason.

Griffin shakes his head and presses down on the trigger.

HARVEY (CONT'D)

Look.

Harvey rolls up his sleeve, exposing his forearm. He points to a small red scar.

HARVEY (CONT'D)

They put a fucking implant in there. Check your arm. You'll have one, too.

Griffin glances at his own arm.

HARVEY (CONT'D)

We're their little puppets, and when they pull our strings, we dance. They've made us believe they're unstoppable. Invincible. But if we say no … if we block them and cut them out … then they're weakened. We're their Achilles heel.

Griffin hesitates. His hand wavers. The pistol drops.

HARVEY (CONT'D)

We do this together, okay? Put the gun down. We're strong. We can beat them.

Griffin lowers the gun further. Harvey holds out his hand.

HARVEY (CONT'D)

That's it. You're doing the right thing.

A sudden change of heart. Griffin lifts the gun back up again, aimed straight at Harvey's head.

GRIFFIN

I can't risk it.

Griffin FIRES.

The bullet narrowly misses Harvey, and he leaps over the railing, landing on a narrow ledge.

Griffin leans over the railing and FIRES again.

Harvey stumbles along the ledge. Another shot RINGS OUT. He ducks and slips but doesn't fall. He reaches a ladder and climbs it.

Griffin FIRES a fourth shot from the top of the ladder.

Harvey dodges to the side and keeps climbing. He reaches the top before Griffin can fire again and knocks the gun away.

The gun FIRES and topples over the edge of the building.

Harvey and Griffin fight on the ladder. Griffin pushes Harvey off, but Harvey grabs Griffin's coat and takes him with him. As they fall, Harvey latches on to the last rung of the ladder. Griffin misses it and tumbles into the dark.

Harvey hauls himself up onto the ledge and peers over.

Griffin dangles precariously from the narrow walkway below.

GRIFFIN (CONT'D)

Help me, please!

Harvey reaches down.

HARVEY

Take my hand.

Griffin shakes his head. His fingers slip.

HARVEY (CONT'D)

Come on!

Griffin lifts his hand, and Harvey catches it just in time.

HARVEY (CONT'D)

Now the other one. Quickly! I don't think I can hold -

Griffin throws his other hand up, but the cross-wind swings him to the side, and he misses.

Harvey struggles to keep hold of Griffin. The effort is too much, and Griffin's hand slips free. He falls backwards, arms flailing, mouth wide, and disappears into the blackness.

Harvey GASPS in shock. He can't move. It takes SCREAMS and SIRENS from below to galvanise him into action. He clambers back onto the roof and sprints towards the exit.

INT. HARVEY'S OFFICE - NIGHT

Harvey holds the base unit of his computer above his head and throws it onto the marble floor.

DUMPF!

Sarah appears in the doorway. She runs to Harvey.

SARAH

What are you doing?

Harvey picks the base unit up and throws it down again. Sarah steps back in alarm.

DUMPF!

The outer casing buckles but doesn't break open. Harvey picks it up again.

SARAH

Harvey, stop!

Harvey pushes past Sarah, carrying the base unit outside to the terrace. Sarah follows him. When he reaches the sliding door, she grabs his arm. Harvey shrugs her off and steps outside.

EXT. HARVEY'S OFFICE, TERRACE - NIGHT

A dark rippled river is visible dozens of floors below.

Harvey lobs the base unit over the edge of the terrace and watches its descent.

Partway down, the base unit clips the side of the building, and sections fly off. It eventually impacts the water with a silent, and underwhelming, SPLASH.

INT. HARVEY'S OFFICE - NIGHT

Harvey empties drawers. Stuffs a briefcase with papers.

HARVEY

I tried to reason with him, but he wouldn't stop. It was an accident.

SARAH

I believe you.

Harvey thrusts more documents into his now bulging briefcase. Sarah takes Harvey's hand. He stops.

SARAH (CONT'D)

I believe you.

Harvey flashes a nervous smile.

HARVEY

They'll be coming for me. I need to go.

SARAH

I'm coming with you.

HARVEY

No!

Harvey lifts the briefcase. Sarah tries for his arm again.

SARAH

I'm coming!

HARVEY

They'll kill you, too. They won't stop.

SARAH

Let them fucking try.

INT. OFFICE CORRIDOR - NIGHT

Harvey and Sarah run down the corridor. *PING!* Up ahead, a lift door opens. Harvey and Sarah barge through a stairwell door just as two MEN IN BLACK - complete with sunglasses and immaculate suits - exit the lift.

INT. STAIRWELL - NIGHT

Harvey and Sarah CLANK NOISILY down the stairs. Sarah trips and CRIES OUT.

INT. OFFICE CORRIDOR - NIGHT

The men in black hear Sarah's cry and BURST through the stairwell door.

INT. STAIRWELL

Harvey and Sarah take the stairs two at a time. HEAVY FOOTSTEPS can be heard above them.

Harvey glances up.

The men in black are closing fast.

Harvey and Sarah, both sweating now, speed up. Suddenly, Sarah pulls to a halt outside a door marked …

… STAFF ONLY.

Sarah shoves Harvey through the door.

INT. SERVICE CORRIDOR - NIGHT

Harvey and Sarah flee along a dank corridor. Above them, exposed pipes and flickering strip-lights. Behind them, the CLANK of their pursuers' feet. They reach a set of metal steps and climb down rapidly.

At the bottom of the steps is a door. Harvey tries the handle. It's locked. He RAMS it with his shoulder and winces in pain, but it doesn't budge. ECHOING FOOTSTEPS behind them are getting closer.

Sarah pushes Harvey aside and KICKS the door hard. It flies open. Harvey stares at Sarah in astonishment.

Sarah shrugs.

INT. UNDERGROUND CAR PARK - NIGHT

Sarah runs through the door into a car park and stops.

SARAH

My car!

Sarah's car is visible between two other parked cars.

Sarah takes off. Harvey follows, weaving between vehicles. A shot RINGS OUT, and a bullet RICOCHETS off a fender. Harvey and Sarah duck lower and run faster.

One of the men in black, his arm extended, FIRES again.

The bullet SMASHES a car windscreen beside Harvey. He pulls Sarah down behind a four-by-four. FOOTSTEPS grow louder. Harvey and Sarah hold their breath.

Two sets of black shoes appear either side of the four-by-four, moving towards the rear. Harvey pushes Sarah out, and they make a run for it.

The men in black give chase.

Harvey and Sarah reach Sarah's car. She unlocks it, and they jump in.

INT. SARAH'S CAR - NIGHT

Sarah fumbles with the ignition.

INT. UNDERGROUND CAR PARK - NIGHT

The men in black race towards Sarah's car.

INT. SARAH'S CAR - NIGHT

Sarah's key won't fit in the lock.

SARAH (CONT'D)

Come on!

The key turns, and the car STARTS.

INT. UNDERGROUND CAR PARK - NIGHT

The men in black raise their guns in unison and FIRE.

INT. SARAH'S CAR - NIGHT

Both bullets RICOCHET off the bonnet. Harvey and Sarah instinctively duck.

Suddenly, the engine ROARS, and Sarah ACCELERATES towards the men in black. She HITS one of them. He bounces off the bonnet and onto the ground. The second man in black dives out of the way.

INT. UNDERGROUND CAR PARK - NIGHT

The car SCREAMS past. The second man in black swivels on his back and FIRES at the fleeing vehicle.

INT. SARAH'S CAR - NIGHT

The rear windscreen SHATTERS, and Harvey YELLS. Sarah puts her foot to the floor.

INT. UNDERGROUND CAR PARK - NIGHT

Sarah's car careers out of the car park. Sparks and wood fly as it CRASHES through the exit barrier.

EXT. ALLEYWAY - NIGHT

Sarah ROARS along a narrow alleyway, CLIPPING bins and SCRAPNG the side of the car against a wall.

INT. SARAH'S CAR - NIGHT

Harvey glances behind him. Sarah changes gear.

EXT. ALLEYWAY - NIGHT

The car makes a sharp right turn, SCREECHING onto the main road.

INT. SARAH'S CAR - NIGHT

Sarah's eyes are fixed dead ahead.

SARAH

Can you see them?

Harvey looks back over his shoulder again.

HARVEY

I think we lost them.

EXT. STREET - NIGHT

A neon-lit, rain-drenched street. Sarah approaches a red light and slows down.

INT. SARAH'S CAR - NIGHT

Harvey glances back over his shoulder.

HARVEY

Uh-oh.

Through the broken rear window, a car can be seen approaching at speed.

HARVEY

We've got company.

SARAH

Hold on.

Sarah CRUNCHES GEARS.

EXT. STREET - NIGHT

Sarah ROARS through the red light and takes a hard left, then a right. The car rolls onto two wheels.

INT. SARAH'S CAR - NIGHT

Harvey lets out a YELL.

SARAH

Are they still there?

The car from earlier is closing in.

HARVEY

(quietly)

Oh Jesus.

Sarah SLAMS on the brakes.

EXT. STREET - NIGHT

Sarah makes a 180 degree handbrake turn. The tyres SQUEAL, smoke billows.

INT. SARAH'S CAR - NIGHT

The car spins wildly.

HARVEY

Fuuuck!

EXT. STREET - NIGHT

Sarah's car is now facing the oncoming car.

INT. SARAH'S CAR - NIGHT

Sarah REVS the engine.

HARVEY

What are you doing? Fuck.

Harvey grabs his seatbelt.

EXT. STREET - NIGHT

Sarah ACCELERATES straight at the oncoming car. Closer and closer, faster and faster.

INT. SARAH'S CAR - NIGHT

Harvey closes his eyes.

HARVEY

Fuuuckk!!

EXT. STREET - NIGHT

At the last moment, the oncoming car veers off to the left, SMASHING into a lamppost. A body flies through the windscreen and onto the crumpled bonnet.

Sarah SPEEDS away. Takes another hard left. Drives on.

INT. SARAH'S CAR - NIGHT

Silence. Harvey is in shock. He can't speak. Sarah, changing gears fluently and weaving through slow-moving traffic, looks as cool as a cucumber.

HARVEY

Where'd you learn to drive like that?

SARAH

I'm a farm girl, that's how we drive.

HARVEY

Where are we going?

SARAH

I know a place.

HARVEY

Where?

SARAH

Don't worry, we'll be safe there.

Harvey stares out the window. When he glances back, he catches Sarah grinning.

EXT. STREET - NIGHT

The shiny wet street is deserted. There's only Sarah's car, ACCELERATING into the neon blur of the metropolis.

27

The bus pulled up in the middle of a vast waste ground, a graveyard of forgotten tenements and factories.

'Last stop, mate,' the driver said, sucking on the end of his dying cigarette and gazing up through the smudged glass of the windscreen as though expecting a sniper bullet any second.

Paul was sitting at the front of the bus, the only passenger left. He held his phone up. 'Do you know this address?'

'I don't know Castlebank, son,' said the driver. 'Only that ah wouldnae be flashin' that hing aboot if ah wis you.'

Paul tucked the phone back into his pocket. 'Thanks,' he said and stepped off the bus.

The driver kicked the bus back into gear and took off down the road as fast as the ancient diesel motor could propel him.

Old folks love to mump and moan about how this place or that place was far better 'back in the day' – that seemingly mythical time when front doors could be left open without fear of being robbed, and a penny bought you a three-piece suit, a night at the pictures, four cans of Tennants, and a bunk-up with a prossie – but Castlebank had never had its 'day'. Every day in Castlebank, from its inception in 1963 as a 'model town' to its current incarnation as 'a fucking horrible place to live', had been a purgatorial hellhole of utter misery and casual, shit-faced violence. Poverty wound itself around the town like a snake strangling its young. It was a prison, from which the only escape was a swan-dive off a high-rise roof or a chilled cell in Barlinnie.

And now, it was all about the gangs. Gangs were family, and you only belonged to one. You fought for it, and you died for it. You grew to accept that territoriality was sacrosanct. You could no more wander onto someone else's turf than you could invade North Korea. The one was as outlandish an idea as the other. You carved your own niche, or someone carved a new one for you, on your face. Incidents would occasionally flare up – as incidents do – but if you kept to your own, if you didn't stray, and if you knew your place, then maybe – just maybe – the only blood you would ever see would be from a nosebleed.

Paul found himself alone amongst the rotting weeds, the empty beer cans, and the broken shopping trollies of a pestilent, present and correct Castlebank. The landscape was alien and jagged, yet familiar. Beirut, *sans* sunshine. In the distance hovered a row of houses, loomed over by a vertiginous block of flats.

Paul took off towards them. When he reached the first house, he stopped. A gaggle of gangly youths were huddled around a burnt-out car. One of them – a glassy-eyed, skinheaded scally – was jumping up and down on the blackened bonnet, his heels denting it a little more each time.

Can't afford a trampoline, huh?

Paul crossed the road and hurried on past. A shout went up, and the gang roused themselves in his direction. He picked up the pace, his breathing heavy. At the next corner, he turned back. The gang had stopped, distracted by the rusted skeleton of a pushbike. One of them glanced up and flicked Paul the Vs. *Wee bastards.*

Finding a signal in this wilderness was an exercise in futility. Paul gave up on his GPS and decided to go old-school. 'Excuse me,' he said, running after an elderly man in a tartan bunnet. 'Could you tell me where–?'

Tartan Bunnet spun round. He had a bread knife in his hand. 'Fuck off,' he snarled. 'Or ye'll get this.'

Paul stepped back. 'I'm sorry, sir,' he said, holding his hands out. 'I didn't mean to startle you.'

'Whit dae ye want?'

'I'm looking for Ballhill Rise.'

Tartan Bunnet glanced Paul up and down and grinned. 'Ballhill Rise, ye say?'

'That's right.'

'Ye sure about that?'

'That's the address I have.'

'Are ye polis?'

Paul shook his head. 'I'm just visiting a mate.'

'A mate.' Tartan Bunnet nodded. 'I see. Well, Ballhill is about three streets up that way. Keep goin' and ye'll come tae it. I take it yer no fae roon here?'

Paul scratched his nose. It was pretty obvious he wasn't.

'Well,' said Tartan Bunnet, 'I suggest ye watch yersel, son. This place hus gone tae pot since they shut yon youth club. But whit dae ye expect when the toon hall's fu o' arseholes?'

Paul nodded. 'Thanks. I'll watch my back.'

'Afore ye git a knife in it.' Tartan Bunnet grunted. He winked at Paul. 'Guid luck tae ye, son.' As he shuffled off, Paul heard him laugh and mutter '… and it's goodnight from him. Goodnight.'

Paul followed Tartan Bunnet's directions. As he wound deeper into the estate, the environment grew more hostile. The houses were either burnt out or boarded up. Household rubbish lay piled up on pavements or scattered across roads. There was also a disconcerting absence of … people. There was nobody around at all. No hoodies, no teenage mums with prams, no Saturday Sannies, and, most surprisingly, no kids. It was as though the zombie apocalypse had kicked off and the zombies were still to arrive.

Eventually, he reached Ballhill Road, leading to Ballhill Rise, which turned out to be a great concrete carbuncle of a building reaching up more than thirty storeys into the grim Glasgow skyline.

Paul gazed skywards, every bone in his body telling him to just turn around and run. *Fuck it.* He shoved open the decrepit front door, almost taking it off its hinges, and walked in. The entrance lobby was filthy. Mini-pyramids of dog shit formed a faecal assault course to be carefully navigated, whilst a larger pyramid of ripped garbage bags all but obscured the out-of-order lift. The stench of urine was so overpowering Paul had to grip his nose. Beneath the stairwell lay the ruins of a recent fire: charcoaled chair legs, cigarette butts, and a melted doll. Paul gave it a wide berth and cautiously made his way up the paint-peeled stairs.

The second floor corridor ceiling light flickered like a prop from a bad B-movie. The pungent aroma of piss was now accompanied by the rancorous reek of drains. Through the intermittent flashes, Paul could just make out the door numbers. *Where the fuck is nineteen?* He had to hold on to the wall for support as he made his way through the intermittent dark. Sixteen ... Seventeen ... Eighteen ... When he reached the last door, there was no number. *You've got to be shitting me.* He looked back at the previous door. *A one and an eight. Eighteen. Which makes this one ...*

RAP! RAP! RAP! He didn't care how loud he was knocking. His head was already thumping from the flashing ceiling light. *Might as well spread the joy.* There was no reply. He rapped again, and suddenly the door flew open. A hollow-cheeked skinhead in stained white vest and boxers stood in the doorway brandishing a bright-orange baseball bat.

Oh Christ, it's a junkie John McClane. Paul raised his hands and cowered at the same time.

'Who the fuck are you?' roared Junkie John.

'Sorry, mate. Is this number nineteen?' Paul anticipated an imminent blow to the skull.

'Who. The. Fuck. Are. You?' This time the bat was shoved right in Paul's face.

'I'm trying to find a friend,' said Paul. 'She lives at nineteen Ballhill Rise.'

'He's efter a burd!' Junkie John shouted back into the flat.

Muffled laughter came from inside. The bat was raised again, and Paul recoiled again.

'Nineteen's oor there,' said Junkie John, indicating opposite. 'Ya manky wee bastard.' He grinned a broken-toothed grin and slammed the door in Paul's face.

Paul fell back against the wall. *What the fuck am I doing?* Just then, the flickering light lit up the door opposite. It was slightly ajar. Curious, Paul pushed himself off the wall and, with a single finger, eased the door open.

'Hello?' There was no reply, so he stepped inside. 'Detective Quinn?' Paul poked his head into a room off the hallway. It was completely empty, bare wires dangling ominously from the walls and ceiling, a black hole like a decaying tooth cavity the only evidence that a fireplace had once heated the room. Further along the hall was the remains of a kitchen, the remains in question being a mouldy fridge with a missing door. *What kind of safe house is this?* thought Paul.

'Awright, wee man.'

Three stereotypical neds – in crispy shell-suits and with even crispier zits – had formed a silent triangle behind Paul.

'How's it gawn?' one of them sneered through a pubic-hair moustache.

'Fine, thanks,' said Paul, in a voice he thought – hoped – masked his nervousness.

'Ye lookin' fur anything in particular?' asked Pubic Moustache, his noticeable squint aimed somewhere over Paul's left shoulder.

'Just a friend.'

'Oh, a friend?' Pubic Moustache stepped forward, as did his compadres. 'Who's that, then?'

'A mate …' said Paul, '… and his mates. They should be back any minute from … the judo club.'

All three neds laughed.

'Hear that, boys?' said Pubic Moustache. 'Bruce Lee and his pals are on their way.' He moved his gaze even further over Paul's shoulder. 'Are yeez efter ony skank tae take back tae yer posh mates at the judo club then?'

'Thanks,' said Paul, edging around towards the door, 'but we're fine. We're just, you know … visiting.'

'Visiting, eh?' Pubic Moustache spread out his arms and grinned. 'Well … welcome to the fuckin Hotel California!' He suddenly ran straight at Paul and grabbed him by the collar, ramming him up against the wall.

He's got a fucking squint! thought Paul randomly as air rapidly escaped his chest. *He shouldn't have that level of visual accuracy!* He instinctively kicked out at Pubic Moustache, but only succeeded in getting an elbow to the throat for his trouble. The pain was hot, immediate, and massive. He screamed. Loudly.

'Shh,' hissed Pubic Moustache. 'Ye'll wake the wean.'

'Fuck off!' wheezed Paul. He continued to valiantly to resist.

'Watch him, bawbag,' Pubic Moustache told the plookiest of his two accomplices. 'He'll get his mates tae karate chop ye.'

Bawbag and Least Plookiest Ned roared with laughter. Paul kicked out again, and this time connected with Pubic Moustache's shin.

'The wee man's a bit feisty,' said Pubic Moustache, biting his lip and forcing Paul back against the wall. 'We like feisty, don't we, boys?'

His accomplices nodded. In a quick one-two motion, Public Moustache thumped Paul on the side of the head and followed it up with a punch to the gut, inches away from Paul's scar. Paul fell to the floor in pain. Pubic Moustache grabbed the back of Paul's head and slammed his face against the wooden floorboards.

'Behave!' he yelled and shoved Paul's face down a second time.

Paul held up his hand in defeat and was bundled back to his feet.

'Oh, that's a nasty bruise you've got there.' Pubic Moustache grinned and head-butted Paul.

Blood spurted everywhere.

'I tell you what, lads,' he said, 'that judo's fuckin dangerous, innit?'

Bawbag and Least Plookiest Ned nodded in sycophantic unison.

'What do you want?' Paul coughed through the blood and pain.

'Ah, there we are.' Pubic Moustache smiled. 'That's better. Now,' he said, cocking his head like a yearning puppy, 'tell me. Did you bring it?'

'I've no cash, but take my phone,' said Paul, trying to reach into his pocket.

Pubic Moustache turned to his mates. 'He thinks we're common thieves, gentlemen.'

Bawbag shook his head sadly.

Pubic Moustache forced Pual's his head back by his hair. 'Stop wasting my time, uni boy. Did you bring it?'

'Bring what?'

'Oh, come, come, Mr Bond,' Pubic Moustache quipped. 'The wee sticky wicky.'

Paul blinked in surprise. 'The USB stick?'

Pubic Moustache cupped his ear. 'Echo … echo …' From behind his back, he suddenly whipped out a long carving knife. 'Shall I carve the turkey, dear?' he sneered.

Bawbag and Least Plookiest Ned nodded enthusiastically. Pubic Moustache turned the blade and slid the tip into Paul's left nostril.

'Don't move,' he said and twisted it a little further.

'Stop! Stop!' cried Paul.

'Really?' asked Pubic Moustache. 'But I'm having such good fun. I thought you were, too.' In a single swift move, he sliced through the tip of Paul's nose.

Paul screamed in agony as blood gushed from the wound. 'Jesus Christ, stop! Please!'

Pubic Moustache pressed the blade against Paul's windpipe. 'I'm going to ask you one … more … time,' he said, picking at the skin with the razor-sharp tip. 'Where. Is. The. Stick?'

'I don't have–'

Suddenly, the door flew open, and a second group of stereotypical neds stormed in, complete with baseball bats, knives, and, in one case, a large machete.

'Jez McQueen!' roared Machete, pointing his blade at him. 'You're on ma turf.'

'Just a wee bit o' extra-curricular activity, Gordo, man,' managed Pubic Moustache, unable to hide his fear.

Machete Gordo pointed to Paul. 'The fuck's this?'

'Just a mark, Gordo, man. Nae cunt special. Sincerely sorry for the intrusion, man. We're oota here.' Pubic Moustache's pubic moustache was sweating now.

'Too late for that, Jez. You have breached protocol.' Machete Gordo grinned horribly at his waiting gang. 'FUCKIN AT THEM!'

A baseball bat to the head forced Pubic Moustache to let his captive go, and Paul ducked his way to the door to escape the flying limbs and weapons. Agonised shrieks followed him along the corridor and all the way down the stairs. At the bottom, a single gunshot echoed around the upper floors. Paul raced on through the estate and across the waste ground to the bus stop, where a young mother with a pram sat waiting in the burnt-out shelter.

'Jesus Christ,' she said through a haze of vape smoke. 'Whit the fuck happened tae you?'

'I fell over a shopping trolley.' Paul wiped the blood from his face.

'Ye need tae get that seen tae.' The woman dug around in the pram and produced a packet of wet wipes. 'Here,' she said, handing him the box.

'Thanks,' said Paul and padded gently at the flap of skin across his nose.

The woman blew out a lungful of smoke. 'This fuckin' place,' she muttered.

'Is there a bus due?' Paul asked. He glanced anxiously up the road.

'Should be. As long as the driver husnae bricked it and turnt roon.'

Paul's face fell. *Oh, fuck.* Pubic Moustache had exited the high-rise, clutching his face, and was now heading towards them, Bawbag and Least Plookiest Ned close behind. Paul only realised he was holding his breath when the approaching bus overtook them and he visibly relaxed. But not for long.

'What's he doing?' he asked the woman as the driver stopped the bus about twenty feet away from the stop.

'This is whit they dae,' she said. 'Can you run an tell him tae wait fur me?'

The driver took one look at Paul's bloodied face and refused to open the doors. Paul banged on them until they hissed apart.

'See that woman up there?' he shouted in. 'She's got cancer and needs to get to her chemo appointment!' Glancing back along the road, he could see the neds closing.

The driver tutted, put down his paper, and started up the engine.

'She's fucking terminal!' yelled Paul. 'Have a heart, for God's sake.'

'Awright!' said the driver impatiently.

Paul jumped on, and with great reluctance, the driver rolled up to the stop. Paul checked the rear mirror. The neds were only yards away.

'That's her husband chasing after her,' he said. 'He's a fucking animal. He wants to kill her. And the wean!'

The driver shook his head. 'This fucking place.'

The doors hissed open, and Paul leapt out and grabbed the pram. 'Get in!' he yelled at the mother. 'Now!'

She got on just as the neds reached the bus, the door closing practically in their faces. All three immediately ran to the front of the bus and banged on the bonnet. The driver never said a word, just revved the engine and took off, knocking the three of them over like skittles.

'Wee cunts,' he growled, not even looking back to see if he'd injured any of them. When the mother tried to pay, he waved her away. 'You've been through enough, hen,' he said, 'wi that arsehole husband ae yours.'

'Ah dinnae hay ah–' the woman started but then thought better of telling the driver she'd chucked her last boyfriend four years ago. But she'd just saved herself three quid, so she kept shtum and pushed the pram to the back of the bus.

Paul, meanwhile, slumped back in a seat near the front and called Richard. It went straight to answerphone.

'Richard, if you get this, call me now! It's really fucking urgent. We're being played. The whole thing is a scam to get our script. Torrensen, Alice, Quinn – they're all in it together. We've got to get out. Now! Pack your bags, I'm on my way over. I'll explain when I get there.'

Suddenly, it all made sense. Alice and Quinn had poisoned Paul's and Richard's minds with paranoia, suspicions, and lies, and turned them against one another. Paul kicked the seat in front of him. *How could we be so fucking stupid? Maybe the whole G20 thing wasn't so far-fetched after all. Maybe that was the smoking gun, the coincidence too far. Fuck!* He tilted his head back and pushed a fresh wipe into the gash in his nose. The last train to Oban was under an hour away. *If I can find Richard before those bastards get to him,* he thought, *we might just make it out of this thing alive.*

28

As the bus pulled into the terminal, Paul leapt off and raced across the station concourse. He needed something to dress the wound and stem the blood still flowing from his nose. The station was unusually busy, the exit blocked by a large crowd gazing up at a plasma screen. *C'mon, c'mon.* Refusing to wait, Paul elbowed his way through the throng and out onto the street. There was a corner shop opposite, and he made a bee-line for it. Inside, the turbaned shopkeeper was busy serving a customer, yet his eyes never wavered from the portable TV perched precariously on top of the cigarette cabinet.

''s awful that, int it?' the customer commented, digging into her joggies for a pound to pay for her single swiss roll.

'Aye,' said the shopkeeper. He tugged on his silver beard, his gaze still on the TV, 'the whole flat's totally gone. That aw ye want? Just the swiss roll?'

'Hurry up!' Paul muttered.

'Aye,' said Joggies Woman, 'thur's a tin a custard in the hoose.'

Paul couldn't take it any longer and barged to the front. 'Do you have something to cover this?' he said, pointing to his nose.

'I'm serving a customer, sir,' the shopkeeper said politely.

'It's fine, Jahinder,' said Joggies Woman. 'I need tae git up the road onyway.' She held up the swiss roll. 'Ma man'll hink ah've gone aw the way tae Zurich fur this!' She laughed and left the shop.

'Do you have any plasters?' asked Paul.

'It's A and E yer needin,' said Jahinder. 'Afore ye bleed oot on the flair. Ah'm no insured fur blood.'

'I'm in a hurry,' said Paul. 'Please. A packet of plasters. That's all I need.'

'Suit yersel,' said Jahinder and rummaged under the counter.

Paul glanced up at the screen. An explosion at a block of flats had left a gaping hole in the building's side, exposing the devastated interior. Shredded clothes and burnt-out furniture covered what little floor remained.

Jahinder dropped a box of plasters onto the counter. 'Yer really gonna need stitches, pal.'

'Where's this?' asked Paul, nodding at the screen.

'That new yuppie apartment block they built up the west end. Bloody death trap.'

'Gartfield Terrace?'

'Aye, that's the wan.'

'That's Alice's block.'

'Who?'

'Turn it up!' urged Paul.

Jahinder stabbed at a ragged remote.

The scene cut to a reporter standing at the end of the street behind a police cordon, the decimated building visible over her left shoulder.

'Neighbours say they heard a loud explosion in an upper flat around three-thirty this afternoon, which blew out a number of nearby windows. The flat is believed to be owned by a Ms Alice Lowe, a film production manager. Firefighters say the blaze is now under control and the building safely evacuated. No one is willing yet to say what caused the explosion, but police have confirmed one fatality, as yet unnamed, who was found dead at the scene. Police are appealing for eyewitnesses and urge Ms Lowe's boyfriend, a Mr Paul Grant, to contact them as soon as possible.'

Paul's passport mug shot flashed up on the screen.

Jahinder spun round 'Isn't that …?'

'Jesus Christ!' cried Paul and ran out the shop.

'Hey!' yelled Jahinder. 'Ye huvnae paid fur yer plasters!'

But Paul was already out of sight. He'd disappeared into the subway station next door and was racing towards the platform.

A crowd gathered around the police cordon, staring, open-mouthed, at the decimated building. Fire trucks, ambulances, and police cars were lined up along Gartfield Terrace as TV crews jostled for the best views of the carnage. Paul pushed his way to the front of the cordon, his face crumbling when he saw what the explosion had done. The crater in the side of the building was enormous, far more shocking than the images on TV. He pushed in further and ducked beneath the tape.

'Where do you think you're going?' A police officer grabbed Paul by the arm.

'I need to get in there,' said Paul. He tried to pull away.

The police officer's grip tightened. 'Sorry, sir, no one's permitted near the building until fire crews complete their safety inspections.'

'But my wife and kids are in there,' lied Paul.

'What's your name, sir?' The officer peered closer at Paul.

Shit, he knows who I am. Panicking, Paul yanked his arm away and spun around, pushing back into the crowd.

'Stop!' the officer hollered and gave chase.

Paul rounded a TV van and leapt over cables and equipment, ducking down a side street and hiding in a doorway. The officer ran past, allowing Paul to double back along Gartfield Terrace and on towards Byers Road.

A second police officer appeared, seemingly from nowhere. 'Hoy!' he yelled.

Shit! Despite his wound, Paul tore along Byres Road, swerving past shoppers and early-evening drinkers. At the lights, he clipped a couple of young lads and almost tumbled onto the road. A volley of abuse was hurled at him, but he ran on. He sensed the officer over his shoulder getting ever closer. He took a sharp right and disappeared down a narrow alleyway, stumbling over bins and boxes and emerging onto University Road. Breathing hard now, he made it through the gates of the old university building and cut across the green. When he reached the Gothic arches of the quads, he staggered to a halt and dropped to his knees. The wound in his side roared with pain, and his lungs were on fire, his laboured gasps for air reverberating around the ancient domes. The officer was nowhere to be seen. Paul had lost him, either to boredom or exhaustion.

When he was sure the coast was clear, Paul left the quads and hobbled out front, taking the path that led down to the river. He spied a place he could hide: a thicket of bushes close to the water's edge, separated from the riverbank by a wire fence. As he climbed over, his foot slipped, and he fell onto his backside, the slippery muck taking him down towards the water. Snatching frantically at roots and branches, he found a handhold just in time. A second more, and he would have been caught up in the fast-flowing, murky River Kelvin.

Paul climbed back up the bank and crawled into a shallow dip beneath a bush. Sirens wailed in the distance, and somewhere nearby a helicopter *whup-whupped* across the city, its searchlight scanning streets and houses on the far side of the park. Were they looking for him, or was it just another joyrider trying to fuck over the traffic cops?

Paul tucked his legs in further to avoid being seen from the path or from above. He found his phone and dialled Richard's number. He needed to warn him before Torrensen's men got to him. The number rang out and then went dead. He tried again. No response. Hopefully, Richard had made his escape, or maybe he was too late. Maybe it was all too late. Paul suddenly felt scared. He was bewildered and exhausted, like a cornered rat waiting for the dogs to come and tear him to pieces.

He zipped up his coat, tucked his hands under his arms, and mentally counted down the minutes till morning.

29

At first light, Paul dragged his shivering and broken body back up the riverbank. Two students hurrying to their first lecture of the day spotted him navigating the fence.

'Rough night, pal?' One of them laughed as they passed.

But then they saw the state of Paul's face and scurried off in fright.

Paul had tried Richard's number three more times in the night, but still he hadn't answered. Paul needed to be sure his friend was safe. He decided to take the river path to Kelvinbridge, a roundabout, but safer, route for a wanted man. It enabled him to avoid the main drag. He could stick to side streets and lanes until he got home. At the junction near his flat, he stopped and scanned the road. It was clear of police cars and uniforms, but he couldn't take any chances. Not at this late stage. He doubled back and headed up an adjacent street, entering his own block from the opposite side. He managed to sneak across the drying green between the tenements unseen and slid in through the back door of the close. There, he stopped and squinted up the stairwell to his floor. It was deserted. A wave of relief washed over him. It didn't last long. At the top of the stairs, he found the door to his flat wide open.

'Richard!' Paul ran down the hall and into the living room, then checked Richard's bedroom. There was no sign of him, but his bed had been stripped, and his wardrobe was empty. The drawers, too, had been cleared. *Shit, shit, shit!* The dishes in the kitchen sink looked as though they'd been there for days, yet when Paul touched the side of the kettle it was still warm. *Where the fuck is he?* He tried Richard's number again, but the line was dead. *'Fuck!'*

THUMP! THUMP! THUMP!

Maybe Mrs McGilvray knew where Richard was.

THUMP! THUMP! THUMP!

Her front door flew open, only it wasn't the Mrs McGilvray of now, it was the Mrs McGilvray of thirty years ago: the same skeletal features and morose expression, her hair tied up in a bun like a foetal beehive. 'Yes?' barked the 'young' Mrs McGilvray, waving a sink plunger in Paul's face.

'Excuse me,' said Paul, taking a step back. 'Is Mrs McGilvray there?'

'Who wants to know?' 'Young' Mrs M rasped through her sphincter-like mouth.

'I'm from next door,' said Paul.

'My mother passed away last Tuesday,' said Mrs McGilvray's daughter, barely a ripple of emotion registering on her face. 'We're clearing her flat for the sale.'

'I'm so sorry to hear that,' said Paul, genuinely surprised.

Mrs McGilvray's daughter didn't flinch.

'My condolences to your family,' Paul added. 'Sorry, it all seems so sudden. May I ask how she passed away?'

'Electrocution.' The word was said with prosaic precision. 'Her hot water bottle leaked onto the electric blanket switch.'

'A hot water bottle *and* an electric blanket?'

'We're a cold-blooded family,' replied Mrs McGilvray's daughter, in a manner that fully supported her words. 'My father would have told you that, if he hadn't … accidentally died.' She sniffed. 'The funeral is at the crematorium on Friday at two. No flowers.'

'I understand,' said Paul. 'I just wondered if–'

He never got to finish. With a curt nod, the 'Cocoon' version of Mrs McGilvray slammed the door shut and double-locked it.

Back at the flat, Paul rechecked Richard's room. Maybe he'd left a note. Around the other side of the bed, he found a bulging holdall, half hidden beneath the frame. He yanked it out and unzipped it. It was crammed full of hastily packed clothes. A flash of tweed caught Paul's eye. He pushed his hand in deeper and pulled it out. It was rolled up, but he recognised it immediately: the Peaky Blinders flat cap.

Paul's entire body shivered as the truth became obvious: it was Richard all along. *Evil bastard! He double bluffed me. And he fucking killed Alice!* Paul's rage boiled over. He threw the cap across the room and snatched up his phone, intending to have it out with Richard once and for all. But he stopped himself. *No,* he thought. *That's too easy. There's a better way.* He opened up his messages and carefully composed a text. It was time to end this.

Alice is dead. I'm going to the caravan to get the master USB and destroy it. I can't take any more.

When he was sure the message had landed, Paul stuck the cap back in the holdall, zipped it up, and returned it to its original position beneath the bed. The trap was set, but would Richard take the bait?

30

It was already dark when Paul arrived in the village. The snow that had started as a flurry at the bus station in Oban was rapidly approaching blizzard strength. To add to the fun and games, the wind was whipping it into four- or five-foot drifts, making progress even more treacherous. Battling through the storm, Paul bypassed the hotel's front door and slipped around the back, navigating his way along the lane that ran behind the caravan park. He'd managed to evade the transport police at the station and wasn't going to blow his cover now.

At a bend in the road, he stopped and peered through a thick line of pine trees, shielding his eyes from the snowstorm peppering his face with bullets of ice. He could just make out the dim lights of the caravan park's entrance, but the rest was blurred by a billowing cloud of white.

By the time he reached the park's boundary, he was almost completely submerged under a thick layer of snow and ice. He may have resembled the abominable snowman, but he couldn't have wished for better camouflage. The caravan was now only twenty feet in front of him. He crouched behind a wall, folded his body into the snow that had built up behind it, and waited. Twenty minutes later, the storm blew a final farewell, and the clouds parted. A luminescent moon emerged from the pit-black sky and bathed the snow-smothered caravan park in a cool grey light.

Paul scanned the park's entrance. There was still no sign of Richard, or anyone else for that matter. He stood, stretched, and shook the accumulated snowdrift from off his head. *Jesus,* he shivered, *it's cold.* He rubbed his hands together furiously to try and get his circulation going. *Fuck it.* He'd had enough of waiting. He climbed over the wall and crept up on the caravan, the blanket of snow helping to deaden the sound of his approach. When he reached the door, he found it slung wide open. There was a window along the side wall. He snuck over and peered through. Nothing. He crossed back to the door and stepped inside.

Silence. It was as though the whole world had stopped breathing.

Paul peered into the gloom, his arms raised in defence, just in case. His heart tripping, he slowly worked his way through the caravan: hallway, bathroom, bedroom. He jumped at a noise at the rear of the bedroom and threw open the wardrobe.

'Come out, you fucking bas–!'

It was the electric meter, clicking through another cycle.

And … breathe. Paul waited until his lungs had calmed down and carefully retraced his steps back outside. The park was still deserted. At the rear of the caravan, he dropped to his knees. From behind one of the props holding up the frame, he removed a small plastic bag. Inside was a USB stick, which he removed and dropped into his coat pocket. As he pulled himself up, he caught sight of a figure silhouetted by the open gate. His heart rate doubling, Paul pushed back into the caravan's shadows. *Softly-softly catchee Richard.* The figure moved closer, the outline of a Peaky Blinders cap all too visible.

otcha, ya bastard! Paul retreated further behind the caravan.

The figure reached the caravan door. Richard's profile emerged from the shadows, silhouetted by the light of the moon. Paul lunged at him, and they tumbled to the ground.

'You fucker! Paul yelled, throwing punches wildly, until a fist connected with Richard's jaw.

'Wait!' shouted Richard.

But Paul was too far gone with rage to stop now. He continued punching Richard's face until his friend's nose exploded and blood sprayed out over his cheeks, spattering Paul's knuckles.

'Fuck's sake, stop!' Richard pleaded. In defence, he grabbed Paul's wrist and bent it back as far as it would go.

Paul screamed in pain.

'Just fucking stop! Richard repeated, maintaining the pressure on Paul's wrist.

'Let me fucking go,' cried Paul, pain searing up his arm like an executioner's electric bolt.

'I'll let you go when you promise you won't fucking attack me again,' said Richard, blood streaming down his face.

'Fuck you, you fucking traitor!'

It wasn't the answer Richard was looking for. He applied more pressure and elicited more screams. 'Promise me!' roared Richard.

'Okay, okay,' said Paul. He held up his free hand in submission.

Richard released the pressure a little, but for insurance, didn't let go completely.

'I said I promise,' said Paul. 'Just let my fucking wrist go.'

Richard considered it briefly, then pushed him away.

Paul rubbed at his throbbing wrist. 'How could you do this to me, you cunt?' he moaned.

'How could you do this to *me*?' Richard retorted. He pushed the ball of his fist against his nose to try and stem the flow of blood.

'I'm going to do a lot more than that, believe me,' Paul spat back.

'You're a bloody idiot.'

'What?'

'I'm trying to fucking save you,' said Richard. 'Save us both.' He ran a finger up the bridge of his nose. 'I think you've bloody broken it, by the way.'

Paul didn't say anything. He was glad he'd hurt him. The bastard deserved it.

'I came to warn you,' said Richard. 'We need to get out of here, as in right now.'

Paul snorted. 'What … is Tor Fleck coming for us?'

'I'm not the bad guy, Paul,' said Richard. 'Alice and Omni, they're the bad guys. And we need to get the fuck out of here now before they find us.'

'I'm supposed to trust you now, is that it?'

Richard sighed. 'I know you think I'm a cunt, but that's because I needed you to think that. I needed you to believe I'd sold you up the swanny and that I was with her, and them, so she'd let her guard down.'

'Who, Alice?'

'Something about her just didn't add up. I was working on a way to trap her.'

'Fucking crap. I fucking told you that over and over, but you said nothing. That's because you were fucking me over.'

'I knew that if I told you what I was doing, you'd blow it. You're useless at lying.'

'Unlike you.'

'I'm the actor, remember?' said Richard. 'I'm a trained liar.'

'Bullshit,' said Paul. 'You just thought you'd come all this way in a fucking blizzard to save me? I'm the one who set a trap … for you, you fuckwitted cock-wipe.'

Richard shook his head frantically. 'You've got to believe me, Paul. I was getting closer to the truth, but when you got shot, I realised that Alice and the people she works for are capable of anything and we were in real trouble. But then she took you in and blocked me from getting to you.'

'So why didn't you reveal all then, if you were so fucking worried about me?'

'I was scared. I *am* scared. It was too dangerous. I was way out of my depth, and you were in no fit state to do a runner. All I could do was sit tight, play along, and wait till you were stronger.'

Paul glanced away. 'Yeah, well, she's dead now,' he said quietly, 'so you don't have to worry about her anymore.'

'What?'

'Forensics are probably trying to scoop up what's left of her right now.'

'Oh, Jesus Christ,' said Richard. 'What the hell happened?'

'Come on,' scoffed Paul. 'You're telling me you know nothing about it?'

Richard looked genuinely frightened. 'It's worse than I thought,' he said in a low voice. 'I should have–' Something whizzed past Richard's head, and he glanced up, just in time to see one of the caravan windows explode. 'Fuck!' he yelled as shards of glass shot outwards towards them. He grabbed Paul's arm and dived round the side of the caravan.

The two of them made a haphazard scramble for the park entrance, skidding and stumbling to find the path in the blank white void of the snowfall. *TWANG!* A crossbow quivered in a tree trunk directly in front of them.

'Shit!' cried Paul, stumbling to his knees.

Richard hauled him back to his feet, and they ploughed on up the path, heading for the safety of the hotel. A third arrow ripped through Richard's coat sleeve and screamed past. It hurt like hell, and he wanted to roar in anger and pain, but the adrenaline forced his body onwards, dragging Paul behind him towards the beckoning lights of the village.

The icy slush on the road outside the hotel almost claimed the two of them, but they clung to one another like drunken skaters and all but fell through the front door of the saloon bar.

The sudden commotion, and the sheer state of the pair who had caused it, surprised Duncan who seemed to forget he was pouring a pint of beer until it spilled over and splattered onto his shoes. *Shit and bugger!* He quickly snapped back the pump and tipped half the contents of the overflowing pint down the sink before any more of it escaped. 'What the hell's all this?' he growled. He returned to the bar, wiped his hands on his trousers, acting as though nothing had happened. 'Have you two been having a barney?'

'You could say that,' mumbled Paul.

'And what in God's name have you done to your nose?' Duncan stared at Paul's makeshift dressing that was now dangling from his cheek.

'Shaving accident,' huffed Paul. He peeled the plaster off and slapped it back on again.

Duncan stepped out from behind the bar. 'Jesus Christ, Richard, is that you? I haven't seen you in years. Yer looking well.' He winked at one of the ageing barflies nearby, who coughed into his pint. 'So whit's aw this aboot then? I thought you two were mates.'

'So did I,' said Paul.

'We're still mates,' said Richard. 'Don't listen to him.'

'Now we don't want any trouble,' warned Duncan. 'And believe me, you don't want any trouble from me. There's many a deid Argie'll tell ye that.'

'Hypothetically speaking,' asked Richard, 'how long would it take the police to get here?'

'Why exactly?' asked Duncan warily.

'Cos there's a maniac out there who thinks it's fun to fire crossbow bolts at folk, that's why exactly.' He glanced over at Paul. 'And since I've been hit, that maniac can't be me.' He braved a look at his damaged sleeve, but the sight of blood on the torn fabric had him wincing. Paul screwed up his face. He still wanted Richard to be the enemy, but his mind was turning.

'Whoa, whoa, whoa,' said Duncan. 'I'm the only one with a licence to threaten folks round here. One of the many perks of my training with the SAS.'

Richard wasn't sure even the beast of a man towering over him was capable of stopping the threat lurking outside. 'The police?' he asked again.

'Well ...' said Duncan, rubbing his chin, '... oor local bobby, Frank the Tank – well-named, by the way – can be up here in less than fifteen minutes, snow or no snow, dependin' on the urgency o' the matter.' He peered out the bay window opposite. 'An' if someone's wandering around shootin' at folks, then …'

'It's fucking urgent,' Paul butted in. he glanced up at Richard with the slight hint of a forgiving smile. 'Ring them now. Please.'

But before the landlord could even get his phone out, a set of headlights lit up the bar from outside. A split-second later, the bay window exploded as a four-by-four came crashing into the lounge, narrowly missing Paul, who had to leap out the way.

'Jesus Christ!' yelled Duncan Everyone ducked for cover.

'Seems pretty bloody urgent right enough!' one of the barflies whispered to his mate as they cowered on the floor.

The car's engine roared, and the vehicle reversed out of the gaping hole. Paul pulled himself to his feet and checked for Richard, but he'd gone.

'Call the police!' he shouted again to the shell-shocked Duncan and ran out of the bar and into the street.

The car was still screaming up the road in reverse, its spinning tyres spraying up slush and snow. But then it screeched to a halt, revved its engine, and took off again, heading straight for Paul. It would have hit him if Richard hadn't rammed into him and knocked him over. The car tore past, missing them by millimetres. It drove to the end of the street and then swung round for a second run.

From nowhere, four men stepped into the middle of the road. George Grant and his neighbourhood watch crew raised a variety of antique weaponry to their chests and fired at the vehicle as it thundered towards them, shattering its windscreen and exploding its tyres. It spun off the road, smashed through a fence, and disappeared down a steep bank to the lochside below.

'This time,' said George. He emptied the smoking barrels of his shotgun, 'ah didnae miss.'

But as George lowered his gun and walked back to his son, sitting on the tarmac, an arrow fizzled through the cold air and dug deep into his shoulder. His knees buckled, and he dropped to the ground.

'Dad!' Paul scrambled to his feet and ran over.

'I'm all right, son,' snarled George through clenched teeth. 'Just you go get the bastard.'

Richard grabbed Paul by the shoulder.

'Give me the stick,' he said. 'I'll draw them away.'

Paul hesitated, but he knew it was the only plan they had. He ferreted out a tiny USB stick from his jeans pocket and handed it to Richard. Richard stepped away to the other side of the road and raised his arm.

'I've got what you want!' he shouted.. 'Come and get it!' He spun round and ran up the road towards the edge of the village.

Paul turned back to his dad, who was clutching his chest.

'I'll be okay, son,' said George. 'It's yer pal who needs yer help.'

'I can't leave you,' said Paul, his voice choked with emotion.

'Fucking go!' shouted George. 'Don't make me have to tell you twice!'

Paul nodded. He knew better not to cross his dad. He took off up the road with the echoes of 'Gie the bastard a kick in the baws fae me!' ringing in his ears.

The snow was more treacherous the further out of the village Paul went. That, coupled with his aching wound, meant that the going was slow. A single misstep, and he'd end up in A&E. Up ahead, Richard wasn't having it any easier. He'd only just kept his footing when a patch of black ice took his legs from under him and he slid across the road and into a wall of hard-packed snow, knocking himself out. Paul skittered his way over to him and was about to call out when a tree shook to his left and a shadow in the woods flitted past. *No, no, no!* Paul leapt at Richard and managed to push him to the ground just as a crossbow bolt flew millimetres above them.

The impact brought Richard around, and he stared into Paul's face. 'I wish you'd stop fucking doing that.'

Paul grinned. 'What … saving your life? Come on, this way's safer.'

He pulled Richard to his feet, and they headed towards a stile that led to the mountain path.

As they climbed the slope, the snow got deeper, slowing their progress even more.

'Why are we going this way?' wheezed Richard.

Paul ignored him, and they carried on, battling through thick snowdrifts and using the high-line scrub to stay out of the moonlight. At the top of the ridge, Paul stopped and checked for anyone behind them. There was no one there. They were safe.

Ahead of them, the path finally opened out, and the headland appeared, bright moonlight glistening across the vast expanse of loch far beneath them.

'What the fuck?' cried Richard.

'Trust me,' said Paul, continuing on towards the point.

When they got to within a few feet of the cliff top, Paul slowed. He had to navigate carefully around the cairn to avoid slipping and falling.

'What are you doing?' Richard asked fearfully.

Paul inched closer to the edge. 'Come on.'

'I'm not going over there.'

'Come on!' Paul urged.

Richard was reluctant but shuffled forward anyway, his gaze fixed to the ground. When he got to the edge, he peered over the side and down to the dark loch below.

'I hope you believe me now and you're not planning on tipping me over,' Richard wheezed.

'I believe you,' whispered Paul. 'Now give me the stick.'

Richard handed it over, and Paul dangled it over the side.

'Is this what you want?' he roared into the dark.

They waited and listened, but there was no response, just the crash of waves against the rocks fifty feet below.

'I don't think this is a good idea,' said Richard, his voice trembling.

'I'm going to let it go!' shouted Paul. He feigned a fumble. 'Oops! Nearly.'

'Please don't do that.'

Paul and Richard turned at the sound of the voice, as onto the path stepped a black-clad figure. 'Surprise!' said Alice. She flashedthe same warm smile that had first seduced them both. She was holding a crossbow, aimed directly at Paul's head. It was attached to a leather harness, strapped around her shoulders and waist. She looked like she was about to play a psychotic round of golf. She approached them slowly. There was a large gash on her forehead, and blood streaked her cheek.

'You're … dead!' exclaimed Paul.

Alice smiled. 'Not anymore, apparently.' She raised the crossbow higher and squinted down its length. 'Now why don't you just hand that to me?'

She spoke with a menacing Scandinavian accent that had Paul confused.

'Who the fuck are you?' he asked.

'I work for Agency O', said Alice, then laughed. 'Or is it the CIA? Or am I …? Oh, I'm not sure who I am these days at all!'

'You fucking shot me!' thundered Paul, his voice reverberating across the loch.

'I'm quite proud of that shot,' said Alice. 'A millimetre or so in either direction, and it would have been bye-bye baby.'

'My dad is lying back there. He could be fucking dead!'

Alice's voice hardened. 'He killed my car.'

'You're a fucking bitch!'

Alice pulled a face. 'Aww, don't be like that. I thought you had feelings for me. You were such a gentle and considerate lover.' She glanced over at Richard. 'Kind of boring, really.' She grinned and shrugged playfully.

'You fucked him?' Richard raged. 'You told me you wouldn't do that.'

Paul spun round, incredulous. 'You two are in on this?'

'We were going to be partners,' seethed Richard. 'See the deal through, she said. Split the profits, she said. Bitch.'

Alice ignored the slur and turned back to Paul. 'He was so easy, your best friend. He was like a little plasticine toy in my supple hands. Such a soppy little bubble, weren't you?'

'Shut your fucking face!' shouted Richard. 'She played us both, Paul. And we fucking fell for it.'

'You think I feel sympathy for you, you prick?' said Paul. He was enjoying this, knowing that Alice hadn't a clue what they were up to. 'You both fucking lied.'

'Oh, I do so love your simple tiny brain,' said Alice, tilting her head condescendingly at Paul. 'It's one of your more attractive features. You'll break someone's heart one day.' She moved closer, the crossbow still aimed at Paul's head. 'Did you really think a major film company would set up its head office in Glasgow? Create a Scottish Hollywood?' She laughed.

'But the company is on the internet,' said Paul. 'And your profile.'

'Can I let you in on a trade secret?' Alice whispered. 'We let you see that.'

'It's fake?' Paul was quite impressed by his own acting. 'But it's everywhere. On public computers … everywhere. You can't do that.'

'Oh, we can do anything.'

Paul thought about what Alice was admitting to. 'So, Alice Lowe …'

'Ah, poor Alice,' said the fake Alice. 'Such a beautiful young thing. Funny how those gorgeous ginger locks of hers didn't seem to hold her back.' She sniggered. 'Loved her flat, though, didn't you? I bet her London pad is only half the size.'

'So you stole her identity?'

'Borrowed sounds more polite.'

'What did you do to her?'

'Poor Alice is currently on long-term leave. Or is it permanent leave? Not sure.'

'They found a body in the flat, after the explosion. Whose was it?'

'The thing about diets,' said Alice, randomly, 'is that quite often you're tempted by something you shouldn't have. Something that isn't good for you. Say, for example, you suddenly give in to the temptation of a big fat steak, but in all the excitement of cooking it you forget to switch off the gas …'

'What are you talking about?' Paul had no idea where Alice was going with this.

'I'm surprised they didn't think it was more than one person they were scooping up,' continued Alice.

'But then Operative Quinn *did* have a lot of weight to lose.'

'Quinn?' Paul was mentally putting two and two together. 'It all makes sense now. And here you are,' he added, 'sent by Tor to do his dirty work.'

'Nice,' said Alice. She jabbed the crossbow at Paul like a cheeky finger. 'I see what you did there. It's the accent, isn't it? You're not such a stupid face after all.'

'And Mrs McGilvray. Was that you, too?'

Richard jumped in. 'She's not dead as well, is she? Christ, I liked her.'

Paul's brows narrowed. 'Really?'

'Lovely woman,' said Alice. 'Interesting hair. We had a really sweet chat on her landing – riveting – Feisty, though, I'll give her that. And pretty handy with a bread knife.'

'Is there anyone left you haven't fucking killed?' snapped Richard.

'Give me a chance.' Alice rolled her eyes theatrically and stepped closer. Paul noticed the shoes she was wearing. They were men's brogues, the moonlight glinting off the polished black leather.

Alice glanced down at them. 'I'm into shoes, so shoot me!' She laughed. 'They're Doc Martens, though, so not entirely impractical.'

'But I still love you,' Richard said suddenly as Paul inched to within arm's-length of Alice.

'That's so sweet of you. And I so wish I could love you back, but you see I have a problem with actors and the way they tend to blur the lines between truth and fiction.'

'Grab her, Paul!' Richard cried.

But before Paul could make his move …

ZING! The crossbow sang, and an arrow shot into Richard's thigh. He screamed in agony and dropped onto one knee.

'Oops,' said Alice. 'Butterfingers.'

'Stop, for fuck's sake!' pleaded Paul. He dangled the USB stick out over the cliff edge again.

'I really wouldn't do that if I were you,' snarled Alice.

'Why the fuck did you shoot me, you fucking psychopath?' moaned Richard, clutching at his leg.

'Don't call me a psychopath,' said Alice. 'It's not polite.' She reloaded the crossbow. 'You honestly think I'd be so stupid as to fall for your sixth form drama club performance?' She giggled and turned to Paul 'He's such a ham, isn't he? I was onto him the minute he tried on that stupid hat.' But then her mood suddenly switched 'Give me the fucking stick!' she bellowed, her finger twitching on the trigger.

Paul looked at her, then at the crossbow. 'So what's next?' he asked. 'The G20?'

The comment took Alice by surprise. 'Oh, you are a proper little Nostradamus, aren't you?' she said with a sneer. 'Hand it over, now!'

'No!' Paul yelled defiantly and dropped the stick over the edge.

Alice fired, and the two friends ducked, but Richard's leg gave way, and he tumbled over the side, taking Paul with him. On the way down, Paul's coat caught on a branch, and he hung there, dangling in mid-air, high above the loch, with Richard beneath him, clinging on for dear life to Paul's waistband.

The black brogues appeared at the cliff edge, just above Paul's head.

'Oh, how sweet,' said Alice, peering over the side. 'Like two peas in a pod. Don't you make a lovely couple?'

'Help!' gasped Paul. 'Help me, please!'

'Just you?' asked Alice. 'Or would your duplicitous friend like to be saved, too?' Richard's face was rammed tight against Paul's arse, and when he spoke, his voice was muffled.

Alice laughed. 'He does talk shit, that man.'

'Please!' Paul pleaded.

'I'm afraid you've upset me now,' said Alice. 'You've upset my people, and my people don't like to be upset.'

Paul shook his head. 'Sorry!'

'– seems to be the hardest word,' sang Alice.

The branch creaked, and the roots became dislodged from the cliff face.

'Oh, that's interesting,' said Alice. She prodded it intently.

'No, please,' begged Paul. 'That wasn't the master. I swear to you.'

'Oh, now,' said Alice, 'is that a teeny-weeny porky to save your tinky-winky bacon?' She kicked at the branch.

It loosened and sagged. Dangerously so.

'I hid it back at the caravan!' shouted Paul. 'Under the gas tank!'

Alice knelt and stared into Paul's straining, terrified face. 'What have you done to your nose?' she asked, concerned. 'That's going to need stitches.' She reached down and brushed his cheek with the back of her hand. 'I could have loved you. You might have been the one.'

'We could still–'

It was too late. Alice raised her foot, and with one swift martial arts kick, snapped the branch in two. Paul and Richard tumbled out into the darkness and hit the freezing black water below like two sacks of potatoes smashing into solid concrete. Alice leaned over the edge to check they were gone, and then, whistling the *Dr Zhivago* theme, headed back to the caravan park.

31

What follows next is based on a combination of eyewitness testimony, speculation, and the limited DNA evidence recovered from the crime scene.

Alice lay on her belly and scanned the approach to the caravan park, checking all exits and possible attack points. Even when she was convinced the coast was clear, she still exercised extreme caution, keeping low to the ground as she ran, zig-zagging, across to the caravan. The gas tanks were tucked under the frame, easily located. She lifted the first tank and then the second. There was nothing under either of them.

That fucking little –

The sudden crunch of feet on gravel. Alice stopped and turned.

Paul's dad stood in the driveway, flanked by the neighbourhood watch crew, his trusted shotgun resting on his forearm.

'Gies a wee smile, hen,' he sneered. 'Ya son of a bitch!'

Before Alice had time to raise her weapon, George fired off two shots. The pellets struck the gas tanks and engulfed the caravan in a massive fireball, the shockwave blowing George and his mates clean off their feet, taking them almost as far as the loch. It was a good five minutes before George could raise himself from the dirt, his face like a coalminer's, the arrow from earlier still sticking out from his shoulder.

One of the neighbourhood watch crew – the octogenarian, Erchie Todd, looking like he'd lost a fight with a blow torch – staggered over to where George was sitting up.

'You okay there, George?' he asked, a liver-spotted hand fluttering up around his own face, as though testing its solidity.

George looked up at him and grinned. 'Ah'm Jim dandy, Erchie,' he said. 'Ye ken why?'

'Ah think ah dae, George, aye.' Erchie nodded. 'Cos–'

'Cos nae cunt messes wae a Grant!' finished George.

EPILOGUE

In a deserted side street just off Byers Road, Glasgow, Axel Rhodes, former computer repair shop owner, choked on his words.

'Everyone still thinks you're—' he stuttered. The earpiece clicked. 'Dead—hello, are you there?' The line hissed. He replaced the receiver, checked the slot for change, and left the phone box. Keeping his head down and his hands in his pockets, he dodged a barrage of rain-soaked shoppers and pedestrians until he reached Hillhead Library. Inside, as instructed, he made his way to a computer desk at the back, near the large-print section. The desk was currently occupied by an elderly, rain-coated individual with thick glasses, staring at a giant letter G.

'Excuse me,' said Axel. 'Are you planning on reading that letter or can someone else have a go?'

Raincoat Man glanced up at Axel, then swept his gaze around the near-deserted library. 'Thur's plenty tae choose fae, son. Awa' an' no bother me.'

Axel stood his ground, tapping his foot impatiently. Eventually, accompanied by a great deal of huffing and puffing, Raincoat Man picked up his Tesco carrier bag and shuffled over to a desk in the large-print section, farting loudly as he went.

Axel slid into the empty seat and glanced over at the librarian. She looked up and smiled. Axel smiled back. Once she'd gone back to her book-stamping, Axel reached beneath the desk and searched the underside with his palm. Nothing. He switched hands and tried the other side. *Gotcha!* The item was hard, and he picked at it with his nail. *Fuck. Chewing gum.* He tried further back. *Voila!* Whatever it was had been securely taped. Slowly, he picked and peeled until, finally, he released the object from its gluey cage. He tucked it into his fist and sat for a moment, letting his heart rate slow, trying hard not to think about what was on the USB stick he'd just stolen.

Fuck it. He reached over and wiggled the mouse. The giant G reappeared. Raincoat Man had forgotten to log off. Readjusting the font size from one thousand percent to normal, Axel inserted the stick. It contained a single folder: 01001111. He smiled, recognising the binary code for the letter 'O', and double-clicked. When the document within the folder appeared, Axel couldn't help but grin. With shaking hands, he shut the entire system down and slipped the stick into the coin pocket of his jeans.

If he was quick, he might still make the last train to Oban.

ALSO BY TG REID

THE DCI BONE SCOTTISH CRIME SERIES.

Dark is the Grave

Blood Water Falls

Dead Man's Stone

The Killing Parade

Isle of the Dead

Night Comes Falling

Burn it all Down

The Devil's Share

The DCI Bone Collection Vol 1 (Books 1-3 Box Set)

The DCI Bone Collection Vol 2 (Books 4-6 Box Set)

ABOUT THE AUTHOR

TG Reid is a bestselling British crime novelist. His DCI Bone Scottish detective series has topped the Amazon charts in the UK, USA, Canada and Australia. Since publication of Book 1 in the series, Dark is the Grave, in 2021, he has sold over 800,000 books and surpassed 90 million page reads on Kindle Unlimited.

This bestselling series continues to grow from strength to strength, with many more books still to come, and plans to adapt DCI Bone for TV. Sign up to the author's mailing list to keep informed about future release dates, giveaways, and exclusives.

TG Reid grew up in his native Scotland and the DCI Bone series is set in and around his hometown, among the brooding hills and glens of Scotland's Campsie Fells. After working as a musician and English lecturer, TG turned to full-time writing and has never looked back. He now lives in Bath with his wife, daughter and hyper-neurotic cat.

TG Reid's books will appeal to readers who enjoy dark, atmospheric, edge-of-you-seat mysteries with added touches of Scottish humour.

Readers can reach him via his website at ***www.tgreid.com*** or find him on Facebook, Instagram and Twitter.

ACKNOWLEDGEMENTS

I would like to thank the following people for helping me make all this nonsense happen:

Gordon Robertson – You saw it… You saved it… You nailed it.

Dave Busby – I told you we shouldn't have had that extra cup of coffee!

Annette Thomson – My bloody brilliant, beta book-reading bandita!

Emmy Ellis – The Word Bouffant Queen!

Printed in Great Britain
by Amazon

50677244R00243